CONFEDERATE LIKE ME

S. K. LONG

WingSpan Press

This book is a work of fiction. Names, characters, settings and incidents are either the product of the author's imagination or used fictitiously. Any resemblance to actual events, settings or persons, living or dead, is entirely coincidental.

Published in the United States and the United Kingdom
by WingSpan Press, Livermore, CA

The WingSpan name, logo and colophon are the trademarks
of WingSpan Publishing.

Publisher's Cataloging-in-Publication Data
Long, S. K.
Confederate like me / S. K. Long.
pages cm
ISBN: 978-1-59594-686-7 (hardcover)
ISBN: 978-1-59594-540-2 (pbk.)
ISBN: 978-1-59594-876-2 (e-book)
1. Race relations—Fiction. 2. Interracial marriage—Fiction. 3. Man-woman relationships—Fiction. 4. Virginia—Fiction. I. Title.
PS3612.O525 C66 2014
813`.6—dc23

2014948132

First edition 2014

Printed in the United States of America

www.wingspanpress.com

1 2 3 4 5 6 7 8 9 10

Acknowledgments

Thank you Lord for revealing the truth of my existence and sustaining my faith. With sincere gratefulness, I would like to acknowledge the following:

My parents, Arnetta and Arthur Kidd, your priceless unconditional love allowed me to be a free spirit;

My loving and devoted husband, George Long, Jr., your undaunted commitment allows me to be creative, thank you for being my soul mate, best friend, editor, supporter, financier, and protector;

My supportive sons, George Long, III and David Long, thank you for your assistance in editing, character development, and historical continuity;

My sister and brother, Sharon Perrin and Arthur Kidd, Jr., thank you for building my confidence in the early years and your continued support;

My aunt, Nancy Denny, thank you for your encouragement and homemade cakes and pies;

My esteemed friend and colleague, Katrina Richardson, thank you for sharing your family heritage from Thomas Jefferson and encouraging me to culminate my research into a manuscript;

Brenda Rogers, thank you for your impartial feedback;

Thelma Richards, thank you for directing me to Winifred's family in Occupacia;

Phi Kappa Tau Nation, thank you for your unconditional love, laughter, music, and support;

My focus group and editors, Barbara Harrick, Jennifer Meeks, and Barbara McDonald, thank you for your crucial editing;

My literary hosts, Stephen Clark, Susan Clark, Patrick Clark, thank you for providing a meeting place;

My professional advisors, Paul Whitcover and Leslie Eckard, thank you for your invaluable advice;

College of William and Mary, Swem Library, Special Collections;

The King and Queen County, Virginia Historical Society;

The Essex County, Virginia Historical Society;

Library of Virginia;

Central Rappahannock Regional Library, Virginia Room;

R. Hayden Smith Funeral Home, Hampton, Virginia, Lori;

Ancestry.com

Dedicated to my father

Arthur H. Kidd, Sr.

Prologue

From my earliest childhood memories, the identity of my great grandfather has been a mystery. My father and his siblings had no knowledge about who their grandfather was or what he looked like. My grandmother did not discuss her father–in-law's identity. When she was asked about his identity, she told everyone that she didn't know who he was. I asked my father if he had ever heard other members of the community talking about who his grandfather may have been. He told me that he liked listening to the conversations of my grandmother's friends and church officials who came to visit. He also told me that he liked to listen to his father's friends and coworkers when they came to visit his father on his boat. My father did not recall any of these individuals discussing his grandfather or his identity.

I remember listening to my father and his older sister Mary discussing various incomplete details about who their grandfather may have been. Shortly after reaching my fifty-first birthday, I decided to search for the true identity of my great grandfather. I wanted to definitively identify my ancestors and bring closure to my own identity.

My grandfather was born in 1895. The state of Virginia did not require counties to record birth certificates until June 1912. Trying to locate accurate information about my grandfather's birth was difficult to find on the state level. At the Federal level, the United States Census was constitutionally mandated and its records provided much greater detail. On August 2, 1790, the Secretary of State, Thomas Jefferson, initiated the first United States Census. Between 1790 and 1840, the head of households/families were listed by name and all others in the household were simply counted. The 1850 United States Census was the first census that provided detailed information (name, age, and relationship to head of household) about each household member.

I was able to locate my grandfather in the 1940 United States Census. He was listed as the head of household, 45 years old, male, and Negro. In the 1930 United States Census, my grandfather was listed as the head of household, 35 years old, male, and White. Upon visual observation, the 1930 census taker decided that my grandfather's physical appearance was that of a Caucasian male. The census taker (who most likely had no knowledge of my grandfather's parents or family history) concluded that my grandfather was White. These official contradictions of my grandfather's race inspired me to continue searching for the hidden history of my paternal family tree.

I had read billboard, internet, and magazine advertisements about researching one's family tree for several decades. I did not bother to act upon the invitations because my ancestors on my maternal side of my family were well documented. I knew that the ancestors of my mother had purchased the land and founded First Baptist Church Harmony Village in 1886. These facts were a part of the family oral history and were documented in the church records and the Middlesex County Courthouse records.

On the other hand, I did not bother to act upon my curiosity about my ancestors on my paternal side of the family, but the reasons were totally different. History had proven that the subject of my grandfather's paternal lineage was mute. My grandmother, aunts, uncles, and father acknowledged limited facts about my grandfather's mother and still fewer facts about his father. By sharing and comparing information with family members, I compiled several important facts about my grandfather's mother.

My grandfather's mother was not born in Middlesex County Virginia. She was born in King and Queen County Virginia about 1854. I decided to go to the King and Queen Courthouse to locate birth records and/or other vital statistics. I asked my father for directions to the King and Queen Courthouse and on a hot sunny day in August 2012, I journeyed to the King and Queen Courthouse.

When I arrived at the courthouse, I went directly to the County Clerk's Office. I told the lady behind the counter that I was doing research on my family history in King and Queen County. As I was about to proudly share that I had my great grandmother's birth name. She quickly and politely interrupted me and directed me to the Old Courthouse Building across the courtyard. I collected my papers and started walking to Old Courthouse Building. The bricks on the building were worn and the small windows and doors clearly indicated that the building was constructed well over one hundred years ago.

I opened the small white wooden door and entered a room with several file cabinets and an exit to adjacent rooms on the left and the right. Two ladies were working in the office; one White lady at the front desk and an African American lady at the rear desk. I greeted both ladies and told them that I was looking for birth certificates and census information from the Nineteenth Century. As I began to give the approximate year of birth for my great grandmother, the African American lady at the rear of the office began to smile and shake her head slowly from side to side. The White lady politely interrupted me and told me that all of the records from the Civil War Period were burned in the fire. I stepped back from the counter and raised both eyebrows in surprise. The lady went on to explain that many of the courthouses in the south were set on fire as the Union soldiers claimed the area. I dropped my shoulders in disappointment and began to turn my head slowly from side to side.

I began to share my disappointment about what was developing into a failed research mission with the ladies. I began to think that some force greater than I did not want me to locate any information about my paternal ancestors. The lady began to further explain that I may be able to find some information at the Virginia State Library. She told me that King and Queen County had moved all of their records to the Virginia State Library Collection. I looked at my watch and realized that I would not be able to drive to the Virginia State Library in Richmond, Virginia and drive to Fredericksburg, Virginia in time to pick my husband up at the train station. As I began to think of the unproductive day of research, the lady at the front desk told me that she had a copy of a book that the King and Queen Historical Society sold for twenty-five dollars. The book, *Land And Heritage In The Virginia Tidewater: A History of King And Queen County*, was very helpful in painting the historical setting for my great grandmother's youth. The book explained why the King and Queen records were burned.

Apparently, in 1864, the Union Army decided to take Richmond, Virginia. General Kilpatrick was supposed to attack Richmond from the north. He had about 3,500 soldiers under his command. Meanwhile in a coordinated effort, Union Colonel Ulric Dahlgren was supposed to attack Richmond from the south. He had approximately 550 soldiers under his command.

At this time, a bad storm with heavy rains prevented Colonel Dahlgren from reaching the city of Richmond. He was also counter-attacked by Confederate troops. Colonel Dahlgren decided to retreat to the southeast to Gloucester Point, Virginia. He would travel through King and Queen County on his way to Gloucester Point. Colonel Dahlgren was ambushed by Captain James Pollard of the Ninth Virginia Cavalry Company H. Colonel Dahlgren was killed in the ambush near Stevensville in King and Queen County.

Colonel Dahlgren was carrying papers that detailed his orders to take

Richmond and free any Union soldiers. The papers stated that he was supposed to destroy the city of Richmond and kill Jefferson Davis and all of his Cabinet. Once the news of Dahlgren's death near Stevensville reached General Kilpatrick in Gloucester Point, he retaliated by sending Union troops to burn the King and Queen Courthouse. The Union soldiers burned homes, stores, the jail, the clerk's office and the King and Queen Courthouse.

The fire of 1864 destroyed most county records. Oral history claimed that some papers were saved from the fire, but the water damage from dousing the fire, eventually destroyed the documents. The county clerk had some papers at his house and they were saved from the fire. This information moved my research base from my great grandmother and King and Queen County to the Virginia State Library in Richmond. I had no choice; I would have to search the records, microfilm, and Journals at the Virginia State Library.

At the Virginia State Library, I was able to locate Winifred Tate in the 1870 United States Census. Her birth date was listed as about 1847. All vital statistics for King and Queen County were most likely destroyed in the fire of 1864, so the exact year was difficult to match. I asked the librarian for clarification and he informed me that all of the birth dates for the early United States Census data are listed with the word, "about" in front of the birth year. Many of the records were copied from other state and local sources. Some information was copied from family Bibles. He suggested that I use other pertinent information about the individual in order to eliminate questions about identity.

I decided to research the history of the community in order to gain more insight about the social and/or economic factors that may have affected my great grandmother's family (Winifred Tate's family). Upon my return home, I decided to explore the online requirements of Ancestry.com. I decided to try the one month free trial. I was able to search immediately.

After finding my great grandmother, Winifred Tate, in the 1870 United States Census, I was not able to locate her in the 1880, 1890, or the 1900 United States Census in King and Queen County. I was unable to find Winifred Tate as a head of household or as a member of my great-great grandfather's household. I had to find a reason for the family's disappearance from the 1880, 1890, and 1900 Census.

In the latter half of the 19th century, during a fourteen year period, the Northern Neck agricultural community endured three devastating droughts. In the drought of 1872, there was no rain for approximately two months in King and Queen County, Virginia. Tobacco crops, oat, corn, and vegetables died in the fields. The drought was crippling for the entire county and much of the southeastern United States. This crisis was so severe that the farmers could not use their water mills. Many farmers and citizens ordered meal from a steam mill in Middlesex County. The steam mill did not have to depend on water from surrounding rivers, creeks, and streams in order to operate.

The third drought hit King and Queen County in 1883. In order to improve economic conditions, Virginians needed to change their way of thinking. Virginians and Southerners in particular were not open to change, especially after losing the Civil War. The quality of the soil and crop production had deteriorated in King and Queen County and much of Virginia. Disease also increased in the latter half of the Nineteenth Century. In 1872, equine influenza was identified. In 1876, anthrax bacillus was identified. The agricultural community was suffering.

The Federal Government provided assistance to many communities. The beginning of 1867 through the year 1878 was identified as the Reconstruction period for many people of color. It is during the Reconstruction period that my great grandmother, Winifred Tate, decided to prepare herself for the future.

In December 1867, Judge John C. Underwood presided over the Virginia Constitutional Convention. Judge Underwood was a Unionist who proposed that Virginia should have free public schools for Whites and Blacks. His proposal was ratified in 1869. This provided free public schools for the first time in Virginia history. In 1872, King and Queen County had three schools for Blacks in the Stevensville District. In 1885, the Stevensville Academy became the first graded school in King and Queen County. During the Reconstruction period, the freedman's education societies continued to educate Black citizens. Many of these societies relinquished land ownership of properties to the local authorities. The main goal of the academies and colleges was to train Black clergymen, teachers, and other professionals within the Black community. Winifred Tate attended school in Stevensville. She was able to read and write. Winifred Tate was educated, but her physical appearance may have caused social consequences. The 1870 United States Census listed Winifred Tate as female, 23 years old, and White.

On March 15, 1861, an Act was passed in King and Queen County that required county citizens to complete and file the "Certificate to obtain a Marriage License" with the county clerk. This document was annexed to the Marriage License. Winifred Tate completed the Certificate to marry Carpenter Cain on June 14, 1873 in King and Queen County. The Certificate listed the place of wife's birth as King and Queen County. The names of the wife's parents were listed as Thornton Tate and Sarah. The age of the wife was listed as 20 years old. Winifred Tate's name was written as Mary Tate (which was actually an alias). The clerk of the county wrote the ethnicity of the husband and wife on the Certificate to obtain a Marriage License. For Carpenter Cain, the clerk wrote "colored". For Mary Tate, the clerk wrote "colored". Three years earlier, the United States Census taker listed Winifred Tate as White.

In 1691, The Commonwealth of Virginia had a law banning marriage between Whites and other races. That law stated:

> For prevention of that abominable mixture and spurious [children] which hereafter may increase in this dominion, as well as by negroes, mulattos, and Indians intermarrying with English, or other white women, as by their unlawful accompanying with one another, "Be it enacted … that … whatsoever English or other white man or woman being free, shall intermarry with a negro, mulatto or Indian man or woman bond or free shall within three months after such marriage be banished and removed from this dominion forever …
>
> And be it further enacted … that if any English woman being free shall have a bastard child by any negro or mulatto, she pay the sum of fifteen pounds sterling, within one month after such bastard child shall be born, to the Church wardens of the parish … and in default of such payment she shall be taken into the possession of the said Church wardens and disposed of for five years, and the said fine of fifteen pounds, or whatever the woman shall be disposed of for, shall be paid, one third to their majesties … and one other third part to the use of the parish … and the other third part to the informer, and that such bastard child be bound out as a servant by the said Church wardens until he or she shall attain the age of thirty years, and in case such English woman that shall have such bastard child be a servant, she shall be sold by the said Church wardens (after her time is expired that she ought by law serve her master), for five years, and the money she shall be sold for divided as if before appointed, and the child to serve as aforesaid."

Virginia expanded the fines for the law in 1705. The law included large fines on ministers who performed marriage ceremonies between a white person and any person of color. Half of the fine (5,000 pounds) was awarded to the informant. Many politicians and lawmakers felt that the ban on interracial marriages was unconstitutional and violated the Fourteenth Amendment. The Fourteenth Amendment states:

> Section 1
> All persons born or naturalized in the United States, and subject to the jurisdiction thereof, are citizens of the United States and of the state wherein they reside. No state shall make or enforce any law which shall abridge the privileges or immunities of citizens of the United States; nor shall any state deprive any person of life, liberty, or property, without due process of law; nor deny to any person within its jurisdiction the equal protection of the laws."

In 1883, a case from the state of Alabama (Pace v. Alabama) was tried at the United States Supreme Court. The court ruled that the state-level laws prohibiting interracial marriage did not violate citizens' rights as outlined in the Fourteenth Amendment. The Court's unanimous ruling held for 80 years. The clerk of King and Queen County had to issue the Certificate to obtain a Marriage License" to Mary Tate (colored) because it was against the law for Winifred Tate (listed as White on the 1870 United States Census) to marry Carpenter Cain (colored). By completing the paperwork in this manner (a colored man marrying a colored woman), the clerk of King and Queen County and the minister did not violate any laws of the county or state. Maneuvering around the county and state ban on interracial marriage was not the only significant issue that Winifred Tate Cain and Carpenter Cain faced as newlyweds.

Three years earlier, 1870 marked the beginning of major post Civil War changes for King and Queen County as well as the rest of the Country. The Fifteenth Amendment was passed on February 26, 1869. This Amendment prevented states from denying its citizens the privilege to vote based on grounds of color, race, or condition of servitude (previous condition included). Virginia ratified the Amendment in 1870 and was restored to the Union.

Most citizens were wage earners rather than self-employed. The end of the Civil War ignited a labor movement that was inclusive of all Americans. This movement created a free-labor working environment. All laborers were free to offer their services to whomever they wished to work. They did not have to work in a group. They could work land and accumulate wealth individually. The southern tax rates in 1870 were about three and a half times the rate of taxes in 1860. Small farm owners had difficulty paying their taxes. The freed slaves would work the land and offer a portion of the crop harvest as payment for the land use.

In 1873, economic conditions deteriorated. The United States plummeted into a Depression that lasted from 1873 until 1878. President Ulysses S. Grant, Civil War Union commanding General, was reelected as

President, but political upheaval within the Republican Party exacerbated the Country's partisan divisions. Washington, D.C. newspapers frequently wrote articles describing the northern Republican fatigue with the southern Republican complaints about equal rights for Negroes. These articles described the concerns about equal rights for Negroes as an unwanted and unnecessary distraction from economic concerns (unemployment, high farm prices, lower crop prices, and high taxes). It was during this time period that my great grandmother, Winifred Tate, married Carpenter Cain.

Chapter 1

On Saturday, June 14, 1873 in King and Queen County Virginia, Winifred Tate awakened with a sense of fear and excitement twirling in her mind. She was nineteen years old and it was her wedding day. Her father, Thornton Tate, had arranged the marriage with the Plantation owner. The Plantation owner's name was Tate. Winifred could never get her father to talk about how the Plantation owner's name was the same as their last name. Thornton Tate was born and raised on the Tate Plantation. He was very light complexioned. One could say he looked like the almond color of tapioca pudding. Thornton never knew his parents.

All babies born on Plantations took the name of the Plantation owner, but Thornton's life began under a cloud of secrecy. Winifred's mother shared the story of Thornton being brought to slave row as an infant. None of the slaves knew who his parents were. Many of the women whispered that one of the house keepers became pregnant, gave birth, and shortly thereafter left the Plantation without saying farewell to anyone. At the same time, a very pale baby was delivered to slave row and the women were told to take care of the baby. Many of the slave women thought the baby was White. The women fed and clothed the baby, but no one claimed the baby as their child. As Thornton grew older, Mr. Tate requested that Thornton work in the stable. As a young man, Thornton worked the fields and when Mr. Tate travelled to town or wanted to visit neighboring Plantations, Thornton drove the wagon. In the 1870 United States Census, Thornton Tate was listed as head of household, male, 58 years old, and Mulatto. Thornton Tate also learned to read and write. Whether by choice or coercion, he agreed to the marriage between Winifred Tate and Carpenter Cain.

Carpenter Cain was born in August about 1840 in Middlesex County, Virginia. Oral history conveyed that Carpenter Cain was a very dark complexioned man. It was often said that his skin looked like the dark porous surface of a piece of coal. He was born in Middlesex County, Virginia.

After the wedding ceremony was completed, Winifred and Carpenter ate the food that had been prepared by Winifred's mother and the other Negroes on the Plantation. Winifred and her mother packed some food in a picnic basket for the long wagon ride to her new home. The wedding was conducted during the morning hours so that the young couple would have time to reach their home before dark. The farm was located about fifteen miles south of Stevensville in Middlesex County. As Carpenter drove the two horse wagon, Winifred numbly waved to her solemn father and weeping mother and siblings. She and her mother knew that family visits would be few and far between, if at all.

1873 was the beginning of a Depression that lasted until 1878. Carpenter was a farmer and Winifred was a housewife. The "Historical Statistics of the United States Colonial Times to 1957 reported that 53% of Industrial Distribution of Gainful Workers in 1870 were agricultural workers. Crop prices dropped, profit margins dropped, and citizens could not afford to purchase staples. Carpenter had to work long hours in order to maintain the household. There were few alternative jobs available. These harsh living conditions did not affect Winifred and Carpenter's relationship.

On Winifred's wedding day, she arrived at the two story farm house and unpacked her belongings. The house was somewhat clean with some food in the pantry. There were two bedrooms on the first floor and a kitchen. The larger bedroom had a double bed and the smaller bedroom had a single bed. The home generally looked as if someone had lived in the house on a regular basis. As Winifred toured the house, located cleaning supplies, located linen, and cooked, Carpenter worked around the property.

As Winifred worked, she felt more and more anxious about her new husband's expectations on their wedding night. After the meal was completed, Carpenter came through the back kitchen door. He had washed his face and hands in the back yard near the surface well. Carpenter came in politely and sat down at the kitchen table. Winifred served a bowl of vegetable pork stew, cornbread, and buttermilk. She sat at the opposite end of the table carefully, slowly, and quietly as Carpenter began to eat. Winifred waited for him to comment on the taste of the meal.

Carpenter ate the entire meal without saying a word. He ate steadily and never looked at Winifred. Winifred ate in silence and did not speak to Carpenter. After drinking his buttermilk, Carpenter said, "Thank you". He turned without looking at Winifred and went to the barn. Winifred cleaned the kitchen table of dishes and nervously washed the dishes as she anticipated the marital demands of her new husband when he returned to the house.

While Winifred was returning the plain white dishes to the cupboard, Carpenter entered the room through the back kitchen door. He came into the kitchen and placed an arm load of wood in the wood box. Carpenter picked up the round sharpening stone that was leaning against the left side of the wood box and placed the stone at his end of the kitchen table. He politely stepped around Winifred and gathered all of the cutting knives from the kitchen drawer. He examined each knife and sharpened each as needed. Winifred nervously untied her off white cotton apron, neatly folded it length wise and draped the apron over her chair. As she turned from the chair, Carpenter asked Winifred if she needed anything for the house. She told him everything was fine and thanked him for the wood. Carpenter nodded and continued sharpening the knives.

Winifred turned from the chair and softly told Carpenter good night. Carpenter continued sharpening the knives and politely answered, "Good night". As Winifred slowly walked toward the larger bedroom with the double bed, she hastened her pace as she neared the dark cherry solid wooden door. She carefully turned the dark brown round metal knob to the right and slowly pushed the wooden door open. She stepped to the right of the door frame and fell back against the wall as she closed the door with her left hand. Winifred felt the weight of the first day of married life pressing against her five foot two inch frame. She knew that in a few moments the five foot ten inch dark muscular man would walk through the very same door and demand privileges with her body that no other man had taken. As Winifred's stomach fluttered as if butterflies were taking off into flight, she walked toward the double bed and began to unbutton the collar of the light green plaid cotton dress.

Winifred placed the cotton dress on the tan wooden frame wicker chair at the left of the mirrored dresser. She walked in front of the mirrored dresser and reached for the tan hair brush at the center of the dresser. Winifred stared at her pale breasts and torso as she clutched the tan brush in her right hand. As she slowly reached for the black hair pin that held her vibrant red hair in the bun, she realized that soon the petite body in the mirror would no longer belong to her alone. As her straight bright red hair fell over her breasts, she was startled out of her thoughts by the abrupt sliding of Carpenter's chair across the bare wooden floor on the other side of the solid wooden door. Winifred began to brush her hair, holding the ends and gently brushing across the open palm of her sweaty hand. As she continued to brush her hair in a methodical manner, she could hear the sound of Carpenter's large feet scraping and pounding the bare wooden boards. She could not bring herself to rush and open the second drawer on the left and find the white cotton nightgown that would cover her untanned body. Carpenter continued walking and secured the back kitchen door. Winifred placed her head through the larger opening in the gown and released the folds of the gown that she held in both hands. As the fabric of the gown brushed down the tips of her hardened nipples, Winifred tied the satin ribbon at the collar of the gown. She turned from the mirror and walked toward the double bed that was covered with a white cotton spread and sheet. Winifred pulled the sheet and spread back and sat on the bed facing the mirrored dresser. The window on the other side of the bed filled the room with the last bit of daylight before nightfall. Winifred took the small cotton shoes from her tired tender feet. As Winifred laid her head on the soft white pillow, she could hear Carpenter's footsteps approaching the door. Her stomach muscles tensed as she listened to the metal latch clink against the door frame. Winifred closed her eyes and decided to wait in darkness for the inevitable surrender of her innocence. Again, she heard Carpenter's large feet scraping the wooden floor. This time, the sounds of the footsteps sounded farther away and then they suddenly stopped. Winifred dared not open her eyes. She feared seeing the towering muscular frame of her new husband shadowing her face. On that night, Winifred fell asleep in the large soft double bed alone. She was awakened by the crows of the roosters and the soft caress of the morning sun beaming through the window on the other side of the large double bed. Winifred awakened and realized that her new husband had chosen not to enter her bedroom and consummate their marriage. She was somewhat relieved and at the same time, Winifred felt rejected and undesirable. Winifred wondered why her new husband didn't want to claim her as his woman on their wedding night.

Winifred jerked her head up from the pillow and looked around the bedroom. She needed to assure herself that she was still resting in the soft white double bed in which she began her wedding night. After clearing her head, Winifred quickly placed her feet on the cool bare wooden floor. She quickly and clumsily placed her feet in the cloth white shoes and tied the cotton strings. Winifred twisted her flowing red hair into a bun on top of her head and rushed to the mirrored dresser and picked up the black hair pin. She pinned her hair and quickly turned to pick up the cotton white house coat from the hook on the outside of the closet door. As Winifred hurriedly unbuttoned the front of the house coat, she smelled the faint smell of coffee. She rushed to the door, turned the door knob and quickly pulled the door open. As Winifred stepped into the kitchen, it was obvious that Carpenter had awakened, made coffee, and journeyed to the fields to tend the crops. His coffee cup was at his end of the kitchen table.

She poured herself a cup of coffee and began making breakfast. Next she cut the slab bacon that Carpenter left on the counter and placed it in the frying pan. Winifred opened the silver tin and scooped one cup of flour for the biscuits. She made biscuits, scrambled eggs, bacon, and a fresh pot of coffee.

Somehow, Carpenter knew when the meal was completed. As Winifred placed the food on Carpenter's plate, he opened the back screen door of the kitchen and placed an arm load of wood in the wood box.

Winifred thought that perhaps she should be more polite to Carpenter and then he would fully accept her as his wife. As he turned from the wood box and hung his hat beside the door, Winifred greeted Carpenter with a smile and he greeted her without making eye contact. He sat down at his place setting on the kitchen table and began to eat the hot breakfast. Winifred served her plate, poured the coffee and sat at the opposite end of the table from Carpenter. She thanked him for making a pot of coffee and bringing in the bacon. He nodded and continued to eat. At the end of the meal, he asked Winifred if she needed anything. She told him she didn't need anything and Carpenter slid his chair back, walked to the door, removed his hat from the hook beside the door and turned to face Winifred. He told her that he would see her at lunch, placed his hat on his head, and pushed the screen door open with his right hand. As he stepped out of the kitchen, Winifred felt a sense of accomplishment and relief. Carpenter was not upset that she did not make the coffee. As she cleared the breakfast dishes from the kitchen table, she realized that she could handle married life. She looked for the small white metal basin as she prepared to take a bath before gathering the eggs from the chicken coop. Winifred remembered the routine that her mother followed each day. She also remembered the verbal reminder that her mother told her as she departed after her wedding. Her mother told her to set a routine for each day and follow it.

Winifred had made it through one night of marriage. She anticipated that her wifely demands would increase, but the second day of marriage was uneventful like the first. Winifred cleaned, cooked, and washed clothing for her new family and Carpenter tended to the crops, livestock, and property. Winifred realized that the daily routine was manageable, but she wondered when would her new husband demand more from her? The days passed with the usual routine. The end of June approached and the days became longer and hotter. Winifred longed to hug her mother and see her father's beautiful calming smile. Winifred was often called a daddy's girl. She often finished her chores and searched the plantation for her father's location. Winifred would walk beside her father and ask how and why he performed certain tasks. She learned how to write her name in the dirt from her father before she attended Stevensville Academy. Winifred used to sit on her father's lap and hug his almond colored neck. She ran her fingers through his loosely curled dark brown hair. Before removing her small pale fingers from his head, Thornton always laughed and hugged Winifred. Thornton always told Winifred to go back to her mother and learn all that she could learn. She longed for those days, but she knew that her life with Carpenter would not be like the days she spent with her father. Carpenter was quiet, his house was quiet and days with him were uneventful. Days were uneventful until a quiet sunny morning on Friday, July 11, 1873. Winifred was placing the dishes in the cupboard when she heard a horse drawn wagon in the back yard. She did not bother to look out the window because she assumed Carpenter was working as usual. Shortly thereafter, the back kitchen screen door opened and a White man stepped into the kitchen. Winifred slowly placed the dishes she was holding on the counter and stepped back. She nervously rubbed her hands on her cotton apron as the five foot eight inch sharply dressed gentleman smiled and greeted her.

Winifred stared at the older gentleman's face in hopes of recognizing him. He stood in front of the kitchen wood box with a soft smile, graying temples, black hair, glasses, clean shaven face, and a black bowler in his hands. Her stomach muscles tightened as she wondered where Carpenter was and why he hadn't greeted the man in the yard. The gentleman slowly walked around the kitchen in his three piece black suit with a gold watch in his vest pocket. As he looked in the wood box, surveyed the windows and ceiling joints, he asked Winifred if Carpenter had been treating her okay. She replied with a simple "yes" as she nervously wiped her apron. The gentleman stopped at the end of the table where Carpenter usually sat as his shiny black leather shoes caught Winifred's attention. He told Winifred that if she needed anything, she should tell Carpenter.

The gentleman told her that he was Dr. Grunburg and that he was providing the farm. He told Winifred that he would be back from time to time. Winifred swallowed a mouth full of air as the doctor slowly walked toward her. He stopped about one foot from her, smiled, looked into her eyes briefly, and scanned her hair. He told her that her hair was still as beautiful as he remembered. The light from the window obstructed a clear view of both eyes, but Winifred could tell that his eyes were blue. She could also smell the fresh scent of Williams Shaving Soap. Winifred knew the smell of Williams Shaving Soap because Mr. Tate, the Plantation owner, used the same shaving soap. He made sure that Thornton, Winifred's father, used Williams Shaving Soap before he drove Mr. Tate to town or neighboring farms. Dr. Grunburg told Winifred that he would like a glass of water. She reached for the glass in the cupboard and dipped the water from the pail on the counter. Winifred handed the glass to Dr. Grunburg as their eyes met. He smiled and gazed into Winifred's hazel eyes as he slowly took the glass from her small pale hand. He gently slid his hand across her tender fingers as he smiled and took the glass. He drank the entire glass while watching Winifred's face turn to a pink blush. He finished the glass, licked his lips, and thanked her for the water. Dr. Grunburg handed the glass to Winifred and told her he would be back. As his leather shoes scraped the bare wooden floor, Winifred stood in awe as the tall kind gentleman pushed the back kitchen door open with his left hand. As he stepped out of the kitchen, he placed his hat on top of his head with his right hand. Winifred leaned onto the counter as the butterflies prepared for flight in her stomach. Shortly thereafter, she heard the horse drawn wagon leave the yard.

Winifred took several deep breaths, finished putting the dishes in the cupboard and began cleaning. She knew that she needed to follow the daily routine. After the doctor left, the day ended as the previous days had ended. At the end of dinner, Carpenter asked Winifred if she needed anything. Winifred told him the items she needed and within one to two days, Carpenter provided the supplies.

Several days later, Winifred awakened early in the morning and started the coffee. She noticed that Carpenter had left a goose among some fresh vegetables on the counter. She had learned from her mother that dinner's preparation began right after breakfast. Carpenter came in the back kitchen screen door just as breakfast was completed. Winifred served his plate and poured his coffee. As Carpenter ate his meal, she prepared her plate and sat at the other end of the table with a cup of coffee. Neither of them mentioned the fresh goose. After drinking the last of his coffee, Carpenter thanked Winifred, slid his chair back, walked toward the back kitchen screen door, took his hat from the hook beside the door, and today he did something unusual. He looked back at Winifred sitting at the table for a short moment and quietly pushed open the screen door with his left hand. Winifred noticed the change in routine and immediately thought that Carpenter was about to make demands upon her that any newlywed man would have already taken. Winifred quickly looked down at her plate and Carpenter slowly pushed the screen door open with his left hand. As he stepped out of the kitchen, Winifred cleared the table and began washing the dishes.

The scent of the baking goose filled the kitchen air. Winifred decided to cut the carrots before peeling the potatoes. As she chopped the hard orange vegetables, she did not hear the screen door open. As the shiny black leather shoes scraped the bare kitchen floor, Winifred turned quickly to see why Carpenter had returned before lunch was prepared. Much to her surprise, Carpenter was not standing at the door. Dr. Grunburg had returned and he greeted her with a smile. Winifred nervously greeted the doctor and asked if he would like something to drink. Dr. Grunburg told Winifred that he wanted a glass of water as he confidently walked toward the kitchen table and placed his black bowler at Carpenter's place setting.

As Winifred turned to reach for the glass in the cupboard, Dr. Grunburg stepped to the outside of Winifred's feet. The inside of his thighs cradled her hips. Winifred froze with her arms outstretched in the cupboard. The doctor fondled her breasts and pulled her petite body closer. As he breathed heavily onto her neck, the doctor told Winifred to let her hair down.

Winifred reached up and took the black hair pin out of her hair as the doctor slowly moved his manhood against her buttocks. Her long straight red hair fell over the doctor's hands as he fondled her erect nipples. Dr. Grunburg smelled and tasted her flaming red hair that draped the back of her pale neck and shoulders. The doctor removed his right hand from her right breast and unbuttoned the back of Winifred's cotton dress. He gently lowered the plaid green dress over her shoulders and pulled the dress from her petite body with his left hand. She stood motionless as her pelvic area began to throb and the hot July air felt like a cool fall breeze caressing her breasts. Winifred felt her dress cover the top of her feet. The doctor's breathing transitioned into a raspy moan in her ear. The doctor was beginning to sweat as he removed his hands from her breast and removed his coat. The doctor threw his coat on top of the kitchen table and unbuttoned his vest. As his vest fell to the floor, the doctor moved in closer to Winifred's body and placed her right hand on his manhood. Winifred stiffened as the bulge of manhood in her hand seemed to grow and harden.

In one sweeping motion, the doctor pushed his left forearm behind her knees and cradled her back. He lifted Winifred's petite body and carried her to the larger bedroom. He opened the wooden door with his left hand and quickly carried her to the large white bed. As the doctor caressed Winifred's body with soft gentle kisses, he passionately called her Winnie. For a fleeting moment, Winnie forgot that the doctor was not supposed to be in her marriage bed.

Winnie felt her nipples harden to the point of tingling. Her vagina grew moist and throbbed with anticipation. She did not know what to expect from this older man, but she could not stop her body from responding to his passionate kisses. She did not look at him until he gently pushed her legs apart with his right hand.

He placed his right knee between her thighs as he continued to kiss a path from the middle of her stomach to the base of her neck. He kissed a path up the right side of her neck and sucked on her chin. The doctor used his right hand to guide his erect penis over her pubic hair and between the lips of her vagina.

As he inserted his manhood, Winnie raised her chin and opened her mouth. As he journeyed into her virgin body, the size of his enlarged manhood caused her to moan. The deeper his penetration, the louder she moaned. As their pelvic areas collided, he engulfed her open mouth with his moist lips.

As the blissful pain of his full manhood stretched her body, she began to push up on his chest as if she wanted to be freed from the intensity of the moment. The doctor grabbed both of her hands and pinned them on the bed beside her ears. He slowly began to thrust his penis in and out of her. As the minutes wore on, the pain of his penetration began to transition into enthralling pleasure.

The doctor felt her body relax and he released her hands. He placed his hands on the bed and continued to thrust himself in a steady rhythmic motion. Winnie placed her hands on his buttocks as he gently kissed her lips and quickened the rhythm of his thrust. As he climaxed and released his bodily fluids into her vagina, she moved her hands up to his waist. She began to think that the doctor's visits may be intriguing and pleasurable.

As Winnie and the doctor lay exhausted on the double bed, he explained how he knew Winnie. The doctor told Winnie that he first saw her at the Tate Plantation in King and Queen County about two years earlier. He was accompanying a friend who was visiting Mr. Tate. The doctor saw Winnie take her father his lunch. He told Winnie that he later contacted Mr. Tate and asked him to make the arrangement with Thornton. Thornton was given the right to live on the Plantation as long as Mr. Tate was alive, in exchange for his daughter entering this arrangement.

Winnie realized that her new husband would not be the tall dark muscular man who stood before her parents and said wedding vows. She realized that her new husband would be the older graying doctor who provided for all of her needs. On this hot July day, Winnie consummated a relationship that lasted for about twelve years.

About every five days, Dr. Grunburg drove from the central part of Middlesex County to Winnie's house at the northern end of the county. The trip was about fifteen miles one way. As the doctor and Winnie became more familiar with each other, he began to spend more time at the house before going to his next appointment. They often discussed medical terminology, common practices, and many of his daily house call cases.

Around the second week of October 1873, Dr. Grunburg came to Winnie's house as usual. As he entered the back kitchen screen door, he noticed Winnie was holding her abdomen and leaning on the counter. Dr. Grunburg placed his medical bag on the table and rushed to her side. He pulled a chair from the kitchen table and guided her to the seat. Winnie's mouth was dry and her naturally pale face seemed even paler in the sunlight from the window. She told the doctor that she had been feeling poorly for the past three days. The doctor opened his medical bag and took out the small mirror and conducted a papillary test. He wanted to check how Winnie's pupils constricted and dialated in response to the bright light. He checked to see if Winnie had any neurological concerns. Dr. Grunburg asked Winnie to go to her bedroom and lie on the large white bed. He followed closely behind Winnie and conducted an examination. As he examined Winnie's breast, she flinched as he touched her tender nipples. He examined her abdomen with his hands, listened to her chest and listened to her abdomen with the stethoscope. Dr. Grunburg slowly took the cloth shoes from Winnie's feet and gently examined the soles of her tender feet. He took the stethoscope from around his neck, sighed, leaned over Winnie and proudly told her that she was pregnant. Winnie smiled and embraced her abdomen.

Dr. Grunburg slowly and gently began kissing Winnie's pink cracked lips. He unbuttoned his shirt and vest and tossed them onto the tan wooden frame wicker chair at the left of the mirrored dresser. He continued to unbutton Winnie's dress and pull the dress down the length of her petite frame. As the doctor slid down his white boxer shorts and exposed his erect manhood, Winnie took the black hair pin out of her straight vibrant red hair and tossed the pin on the bare wooden floor. The doctor told Winnie he needed to finish his examination. She had developed a deeper sense of security in sharing her body with the doctor. After sharing the most intimate act between a man and a woman, the doctor held Winnie close to his mixed gray hairy chest. He told Winnie that his wife had tried for many years to conceive, but had never been successful. Winnie listened without saying a word. The doctor told Winnie that he needed to make a home visit to a neighboring farm. The woman was due to deliver in six weeks. He told Winnie that he wanted her to prepare a ginger beverage and drink the concoction whenever she felt sick. He told her to rest a while as he dressed. Dr. Grunburg gathered his medical bag, gently kissed Winnie on her forehead and walked toward the kitchen. Winnie lay in bed and embraced her abdomen as she thought of the miracle growing within. She knew that her family would not be like her mother and father's family.

Chapter 2

Thornton and Sarah Tate started their family on the Tate Plantation in King and Queen County, Virginia. Thornton often spent days away on trips with the Plantation owner, but Sarah and Winnie expected his return. He was, in all aspects of the word, Sarah's husband. He slept in the same bed as his wife and his children expected him to show them how to do certain household chores. His children ran to greet him upon his return home. Winnie realized that her marriage bed would be unlike most marriage beds. She concluded that her parents knew her fate as she left the Tate Plantation on June 14, 1873.

Winnie wished for a moment that her marriage could be a marriage like her mother and father's marriage. She wished that her husband would come home at the end of the day with a smile, joke, and hug as her father had done. She wished that her husband would sharpen his knife, clean his boots, ask questions about her day, and even tickle and hug her as she cooked his dinner. She wished that her husband made the night enjoyable with his after dinner tales of the day's travel and humorous events. Just as she was rolling her head on the pillow and feeling good about having her own baby, she heard the screen door close. She knew it had to be Carpenter coming in for his lunch. Winnie grabbed her dress from the foot of the bed as she shoved her feet in the small cotton shoes. She sprinted through the bedroom door and rushed to the stove. Much to her surprise, Carpenter had already left the kitchen. She looked out the screen door just as Carpenter turned to enter the barn door. Winnie's shoulders slumped downward in disappointment. She realized that Carpenter was always kind, polite and kept the farm in good condition without making any improper comments or gestures toward her. All she had to do was prepare his meals and wash his dirty laundry yet she had let her need for pleasure prevent him from eating a meal. She quickly walked to the cupboard and took out a plate and glass. Winnie placed them on the counter as she stirred the cresses and great northern beans and ham. She spooned up the plate and poured the buttermilk into the glass. Winnie placed the plate and glass on the brown wooden tray and walked carefully to the kitchen screen door. She turned her left shoulder to the door, pushed and stepped out of the kitchen. She carefully carried the meal to the barn. As she entered the barn door, Carpenter quickly put the wrench on the plow and rushed toward Winnie. He told her that she shouldn't have brought the food to the barn. Winnie blushed and told him that it was no problem. Carpenter held the tray and watched her walk through the barn door. The sick feeling welled up in her throat as she approached the kitchen steps. Suddenly the acidic mucus gushed out of her mouth. Winnie knew she had to go inside and prepare a ginger drink. As soon as she was able to stop her stomach muscles from contracting, Winnie pulled open the kitchen screen door and walked to the spice rack. She needed to find the ginger and calm her upset stomach. She knew that it would be several months before she would deliver her baby and she had a lot of work to do. Winnie decided to make some hot tea with ginger. Her stomach settled and she was able to finish the rest of the day's chores.

Winnie appreciated the way Dr. Grunburg treated her. He treated her with respect. On the days that she expected him to visit, she planned meals with dessert. She baked a pie or cake and wore her best dress. Dr. Grunburg had an open carriage for the clear and warm weather. The carriage had a bench made for two with a black leather canopy. The carriage had no cover for the legs and feet. During the cold weather, Dr. Grunburg used a wool buggy lap robe blanket. As the cold weather approached, Dr. Grunburg's visits became farther apart. He didn't want to become ill from the cold weather.

As the months passed, Winnie's petite figure stretched around her growing fetus. By December 1873, Winnie's stomach prevented her from seeing her feet as she stood in front of her mirrored dresser. She caressed her abdomen each night while looking in the mirror and Dr. Grunburg caressed her abdomen during each visit. His cold weather visits were about every ten to twelve days.

Winnie greeted the doctor with a hot meal upon his entering the kitchen. He greeted her with a smile, placed his bowler on the kitchen table and sat at Carpenter's place setting. Winnie ate her meal with the doctor. Their conversations were primarily about medical topics. The doctor was impressed by Winnie's ability to comprehend and retain the detailed medical information. After finishing his meal, the doctor would give Winnie a medical examination. This always led to an intimate encounter. After the encounter, the doctor usually discussed and demonstrated examining techniques. Since the weather was cold, Carpenter had no crops to tend. He went to the wooded acreage each morning to cut and split firewood. If the weather was bad, Carpenter worked in the barn. Whenever the doctor visited, Carpenter stayed away from the house. He waited for at least an hour after the doctor's departure before entering the house. Carpenter treated Winnie as if she were the head of household.

With her due date days away, Winnie prepared breakfast and occasionally peered through the window at the blooming wild flowers and dandelions. Her once dainty feet were swollen and she now waddled her previously petite figure around the kitchen. Carpenter had been bringing baby items into the kitchen for about a month. He brought a large crib and a small cradle. Carpenter didn't tell Winnie that he made the items and she never asked him where the items came from. She placed them in her bedroom and cleaned them.

Carpenter always brought food items to the kitchen. About two months earlier, he started bringing cloth, thread, dresses and lately baby items. He didn't tell Winnie who the items were from. She didn't ask him who the items were from. She assumed the items were from Dr. Grunburg. Since Winnie had gotten married, she had not been to town. She used to ride to the town of Tappahannock in Essex County, Virginia with her father. Thornton Tate regularly drove the wagon to town in order to purchase/buy on credit/ barter items from merchants for the Tate Plantation. She missed laughing and talking with her father as they travelled to and from town.

On a cloudy morning in April 1873, Winnie managed to cover her swollen abdomen with the thin cotton dress, pin her straight red hair in a bun, and shove her swollen feet into the cloth shoes without tying the laces. When she reached the kitchen, Carpenter had already made the coffee and had left the kitchen. Winnie struggled to prepare the breakfast. Her only consolation was that the sickness had stopped about two months ago. As Winnie turned to place Carpenter's plate on the table, he pulled the door open and stepped in the kitchen. He told Winnie that he needed the food packed for a trip. Winnie stopped suddenly and looked at Carpenter. She wondered why he was going on a trip and she was due to deliver on any day. Her chest and face quickly turned blush red as she thought of delivering her first baby alone. Carpenter, who rarely spoke more details than necessary, told Winnie that he was going to the Tate Plantation to bring her mother back.

Winnie felt a piercing pain on the right side of her abdomen. She dropped the plate about three inches above the table. She rubbed the right side of her abdomen and held onto the back of the chair. Carpenter told Winnie that he would be back by sundown. Winnie turned and walked to the pantry. She picked up a burlap sack from the box on the floor. She placed the food in the sack with an apple and an extra piece of cornbread. Winnie slowly turned and walked back into the kitchen where Carpenter quietly and patiently waited for her return. She handed him the sack and told him to be careful. He nodded, took the sack with his right hand, turned to his right, and walked toward the kitchen door. As he pushed the screen door with his left hand, Winnie told him to hurry back. Carpenter nodded and stepped out of the kitchen. Winnie waddled back to her chair, pulled the chair back and slowly sat at the table. The thought of seeing her mother made her weep. After she could no longer hear the sound of the moving carriage, Winnie decided to prepare dinner. She wanted her mother's first meal in her home to be ready when she came through the door.

Just before sundown, Winnie heard the sound of hooves and thc jingling of the carriage. She lit the oil lamp on the kitchen counter and placed it on the center of the kitchen table. As Winnie turned to watch the screen door, her mother pulled the screen door open and stepped inside the kitchen. She quickly waddled to her mother and they embraced each other. They both wept as they slowly stepped toward the kitchen table. Winnie asked her mother how her father and siblings were doing. She told Winnie that her father was feeling good and all of her siblings were getting taller. Sarah slowly pushed Winnie back to arm's length so that she could see the full length of her five foot two inch once petite frame. Winnie smiled and bashfully looked down at the floor. Her mother took her right hand and slowly lifted Winnie's chin as she told her not to look down. Sarah told Winnie that Jesus loved her and that she loved her. She also said that her father sent his love. She told Winnie that she was going to be a mother and that mothers don't have time to look down. She said, "Winnie, you need to keep your head up, so that you can see where Jesus is going to lead you and your children." Winnie told her mother that she and her father always knew the right words to say. Sarah told Winnie that she learned from the elders as a child that women had to walk with their heads up and talk about Jesus in order to have a safe delivery. Winnie smiled and shook her head as if to say that she knew that statement was not true.

Winnie told Sarah that if she was hungry, dinner was ready. She told her mother to have a seat and she opened the cupboard and took out three plates. As Winnie prepared the plates, her mother asked her how Carpenter treated her. She said that Carpenter was always helpful, but he didn't say a lot. Sarah laughed and told Winnie that it may be a good thing. They both laughed as Carpenter pulled open the screen door and stepped into the kitchen. Carpenter placed the arm load of wood in the wood box and hung his hat on the hook beside the door. As he turned and walked toward the kitchen table, Winnie served the plates. Sarah said a prayer over the food and the three ate dinner as the women talked and laughed.

They talked about their family life while living on the Tate Plantation. Sarah recalled the afternoon on which Winnie, Thornton Jr., and little Sarah (Sissy) bursted a sack of flour in the grain shed. They tried to put the flour back in the sack before coming in to eat dinner. All three of them were covered with flour dust from head to toe. They decided to wash the dust off at the well. The more they tried to wash the dust out of their hair, the more the dust became a paste. The dust on their bodies became damp and formed a paste also. They finally decided to go into the house and ask their mother to help them get the flour out of their hair and off their bodies. All three entered the kitchen screaming and crying. Sarah said, "When I turned and saw the three of you covered from head to toe, I laughed until I wet my clothes. Winnie said, "Yeah, when you started laughing, our cries turned to laughter. We knew that you were going to spank us. But you just laughed and slapped the front of your apron with both hands. That was a crazy day. And then when you stopped laughing so hard, you hugged all three of us. You told us that you thought we were White children before, but now you knew it." Sarah replied, "Winnie, the three of you were so pale, but that day, the three of you were paler than I ever could have imagined." They laughed until tears began streaming down their cheeks. Carpenter continued to eat and made a half smile. After the women calmed down, Winnie asked, "How are Thornton and Betty getting along?" Winnie had talked to her brother many nights about his time in the war. Thornton Jr. served in the Civil War as a Confederate soldier. He entered the War in July 1863 and left on December 15, 1864. He cooked and maintained the wagons. Thornton Jr. told Winnie about the wounded soldiers and how much pain the men suffered. He told her that many of the soldiers caught a fever, stomach sickness or diarrhea. Thornton Jr. told Winnie that he would never forget the smell of the rotting arms and legs that were piled outside of the camp. He also said that he hoped he would never have to go to war again.

Thornton Jr. had returned home in a somewhat weakened state of mind. He did not like to be around a lot of people or loud noises. He would often cut and split firewood from sunrise to sunset. He would stop to eat meals and return to the woods. He did not eat all of his food at mealtime until after the community learned of the capture of Jefferson Davis on May 10, 1865.

Thornton Sr. was very worried about his son. He asked the plantation owner, Mr. Tate, if Thornton Jr. could travel with him. Mr. Tate agreed. Father and son often traveled to Essex to pick up supplies. During one of their trips, Thornton Jr. met Betty Ellis. They dated for several months across county lines and on March 21, 1867, they married in Essex County. Thornton Sr. and Sarah attended the wedding.

Sarah told Winnie that her brother was doing better and he seemed more friendly at night. She said that he had been spending more time in the fields and helping in the stable. Carpenter thanked Winnie for the meal and nodded at Sarah. He walked over to the wood box, lit the oil lamp and pushed the screen door open. Carpenter stepped out of the kitchen and walked to the barn. He checked the barn after dinner every night before going to bed. Winnie and Sarah cleared the dishes from the table and cleaned the kitchen.

Each morning, Sarah had awakened before Winnie and started making the coffee. She knew that her daughter would deliver any day. Winnie smelled the coffee and sat up on the side of the bed. She shoved her feet in the cotton shoes without tying the laces and slowly stood in front of the mirrored dresser. This morning felt different. Her back was aching on both sides and she felt more tired than previous mornings. As she slowly walked into the kitchen, her mother came over and hugged her before she sat in the kitchen chair. Sarah told her that she had the pots, clean rags and baby blanket ready for today. Winnie sat down, placed the open palm of her right hand on her forehead and asked her mother what event she was getting ready for today. Sarah laughed hardily and walked over and gave Winnie a hug. She told her that the baby was coming today. Winnie laughed and held her abdomen. She told her mother that she didn't feel like eating.

Carpenter pulled the screen door open and stepped in the kitchen. Sarah told him that the baby would be coming. Carpenter asked her if she needed anything. She told him that she needed plenty of firewood and plenty of water. As he turned to leave the kitchen, Sarah told him to eat first. Carpenter smiled and walked to the kitchen table, sat down and looked at Winnie. She did not look up and her mother prepared Carpenter's plate. As Sarah placed the plate in front of Carpenter, she asked Winnie if she wanted something to eat. She told her mother that she didn't want anything to eat and she was going back to bed. As Winnie stood up, a clear fluid rushed from her womb, down her legs, and onto her feet. Sarah turned and quickly supported her shoulders and told her daughter that the baby was coming. Sarah reached onto the kitchen counter, grabbed several clean rags and placed them between her legs from the rear of her dress. She pulled the kitchen chair back and asked Carpenter to bring one of the dry chairs to the bedroom. As he stood up to carry a dry chair, both women slowly walked to the bedroom. Sarah held her daughter's shoulders and told her that she wanted her to sit in the chair until the pain comes closer together. Carpenter placed the chair beside the bed facing the mirrored dresser. As Winnie slowly sat down, she felt the fluid dripping onto the rags. As she instinctively reached for the rags, her mother told her, "Don't hold the rags, they wouldn't come out."

Sarah pulled the black hair pin from Winnie's hair and her straight red hair fell over her shoulders. They both looked in the mirror and hugged cheek to cheek. As her mother walked back to the kitchen, Winnie caressed her abdomen as she had done each night for the past five months. She wondered if her baby would be healthy, if it would be a boy or a girl, if it would look like her, if it would look like Dr. Grunburg, or if it would look like her mother or her father. She was startled by an intense pain that caused her to push with her pelvic muscles and moan loudly. As she moaned and rocked from left to right, her mother rushed into the room and told her not to push. Her mother lifted her out of the chair and guided her over to the side of the bed. As she moaned and lay back on the pillow, her mother removed the wet rags and checked to see if the baby had dropped down in the birth canal.

Carpenter heard the moan and walked into the doorway of the bedroom. He asked if anything was needed. Sarah told him to keep the wood box filled and close the bedroom door. As he reached for the door knob, she told him that there was food on the kitchen counter. He nodded and pulled the door closed.

Shortly after the door was closed, another intense pain overcame Winnie and she moaned again. Her mother told her not to push until she got back with the rags, blanket and water. As she stood up with a broad smile and turned to go to the kitchen, she told her daughter that she was about to be a mother. She walked quickly to the door, turned the knob, pulled the door open and hurried into the kitchen. She gathered rags, a sharp knife, the baby blanket, and a pan of hot water. As she quickly walked back to the bedroom, she could see her daughter tossing her body from side to side. She told her to stop rolling and put her knees up. Sarah placed the pan of hot water in the chair. She placed the knife, rags, and blanket on the bed as she pulled the sheet back. She reached for the extra pillow. She placed the pillow under her daughter's shoulder blades and told her to get ready to push.

She watched with great anticipation as the brown hair on her grandchild's head appeared at the end of the birth canal. She told her daughter to wait until the next pain and then push. As the next moan grew in volume and length, Sarah guided and turned her grandchild's face to the up position. As her daughter breathed heavily and moaned, she cleaned the baby's eyes of mucus and blood. As the next moan filled the room, the baby's body quickly slid out of the birth canal into open hands. The proud grandmother announced that it was a baby girl. She tied the umbilical cord in two places, cleaned the baby, and then placed her on her mother's abdomen. The proud grandmother changed the soiled rags and cleaned her daughter's body as the afterbirth exited the birth canal. She cut the umbilical cord, wrapped all the waste material, and placed it on the floor.

The baby began to cry and both women laughed and cried with joy. The baby's face turned pink as she cried and opened her hazel eyes. Her mother tightened the blanket and raised her head up to her cheek. As she rubbed her tiny back, the proud new mother told her baby girl that her name was Betty. She told Betty that she was happy that she was finally here. As the baby stopped crying, her grandmother gathered all of the birthing materials and walked into the kitchen. Carpenter, who had been waiting in the kitchen, stood up and asked if he could have the rags. She handed them over and he said he would burn them. As he pushed the screen door open, she thanked him for helping. He nodded and stepped out of the kitchen. Sarah smiled and quietly walked into the bedroom to watch her daughter and granddaughter. She sat down in the kitchen chair beside the bed and quietly said a prayer. When she opened her eyes, her daughter lifted the baby toward her. She took little Betty and sat in the chair. She rubbed her straight brown hair and kissed her forehead. She prayed that Jesus would protect her, that she would be healthy and that she would live a long life. As she held her first grandchild, tears flowed down each cheek. Her tears were symbolic of the love, fear, hope, and promise of a better future for her innocent granddaughter. She kissed Betty and handed her back to her mother. She told her daughter that Betty's birth was a new beginning. She told her daughter to make the best of her father's arrangement and that she and her father only wanted the best for her.

Winnie told her mother that she understood why they made the arrangement for her. She said that Carpenter took care of the farm and Dr. Grunburg treated her with respect. She told her mother that she wished she could have dated and married the man of her choice, but that wasn't going to happen. She told her mother that she had gotten used to seeing Dr. Grunburg during the day. Winnie suddenly smiled and told her mother that the doctor had promised to train her as a nurse. She explained that the doctor showed her examining techniques on each visit and he was teaching her the proper names of instruments and body parts. She told her mother that the doctor didn't have any children and he was happy that she was able to get pregnant.

Sarah smiled, put her right hand over her mouth, and looked down at the floor. She told her daughter that she could tell when she was a little girl that her life would be different. She recalled memories of a pale little girl with a full head of red hair who always asked questions about how things worked and why she had to do chores. She said she always feared that her smart little girl would get into big trouble for being so smart. Sarah dropped her shoulders as she seemed to think out loud that now someone wanted her daughter to be smart. She told her daughter that her father would be so happy to hear about her new life. Sarah reminded her daughter to always do her best and let God handle the rest. At that moment, Betty began to cry. She walked over to the bedside and told her daughter that her new baby was ready to eat. As Betty turned her head to nurse for the first time, both women guided her mouth to her mother's breast.

Chapter 3

It was several days later when Dr. Grunburg returned to the farm. Winnie and Betty were feeling stronger. Sarah was preparing lunch and dinner when she heard a horse drawn wagon in the back yard. She looked out the kitchen window and saw a middle aged White man approaching. He wore a three piece suit with a black bowler. She told Winnie that the doctor was here to see her. She told her daughter that she would watch the baby. As she walked to the bedroom, the screen door opened.

Dr. Grunburg stepped into the kitchen as Winnie entered the kitchen from the bedroom. They both smiled at each other and the doctor jokingly told her that she looked as if she had lost someone. She told him that Betty was beautiful and getting stronger each day. She told him that the navel was healing nicely. He walked over to her and gave her a gentle hug. He asked her how she was feeling. She told him that her mother had been helping and checking her progress. He pushed her back to arm's length, smiled and told her that he wanted to examine both of them. He placed his hat on the table. She told him to examine Betty first. As they both turned to walk into the bedroom, she told him that Betty had brown hair and hazel eyes. When they entered the bedroom, Sarah stood up while holding her new grandbaby. She smiled and handed the baby to her daughter. Dr. Grunburg told Sarah his name and nodded. Sarah smiled and told him she was glad to meet him. She announced that she would be in the kitchen if they needed anything. She walked through the door and pulled it shut. Dr. Grunburg took his daughter into his arms, smiled, hugged her, and slowly kissed her on the forehead. As Betty squirmed in his arms, he turned and thanked Winnie. He told her that she had done a perfect job. They both smiled and he placed Betty on the bed. He affectionately told the baby that she needed to have her first examination. As he began the examination, her smiling mother sat on the bed beside her daughter. She watched and asked questions. The Doctor and Winnie used this examination as a teaching/learning opportunity. After the examination, he placed the baby in the crib. He turned and told Winnie that it was her turn to be examined.

As she undressed and lay on the bed, he turned and looked at the baby. He told her that she was the most beautiful baby he had ever seen. Again, both of them used the examination as a teaching/learning opportunity. He told her not to lift heavy items for about four weeks. He told her that he would bring her some leather shoes that most of the nurses wore. She smiled and looked at Betty sleeping in her crib. As he stood up, he told her that he was hungry and would love something to eat. As she sat on the side of the bed, the doctor turned and looked at Betty sleeping. He turned back to Winnie and hugged her as she stood up. They both walked to the door. They could hear plates, silverware and glasses rattling. He turned the knob, pulled the door, and stood as the woman who had given him his first child walked into the kitchen.

As she left the kitchen, Sarah told them that she would watch the baby. They both sat at the table. Winnie asked the Doctor where his next appointment was located. He told her that he needed to see a farmer who got his hand caught in rope as the mule pulled the plow. Again, he talked about monitoring the color of the injured area, and checking for swelling, and signs of infection. He told her that he would bring some of his books about childbirth on his next visit. After he finished his meal, the doctor took his hat from the table and smiled at Winnie. He stepped toward her and gave her a gentle hug. As he turned to walk to the door, Betty began to cry in the next room. They both laughed and he told her that someone was calling for an appointment.

As the doctor pushed the screen door open and stepped out of the kitchen, she turned and walked toward the bedroom. As she entered the room, her mother was holding the baby. Betty continued to cry as Winnie took her from Sarah. Winnie sat down on the bed and began nursing the baby. Her mother told her that she would go to the kitchen and clean the dishes. As she left the room, Betty opened her eyes and looked at her mother. Sarah announced from the kitchen that she would be leaving in the morning. She said that Thornton Jr. needed her to help with the spring planting. She told her daughter that she was pleased with the arrangement and she knew that everyone would be taken care of adequately.

Several months passed and Betty had learned to sit up alone. She was six months old and her straight brown hair was about three inches long. Her eyes were still hazel and her cheeks were a flesh pink. Her skin was the same almond color as her grandfather Thornton's skin. Her skin did not appear to tan even though her mother often took her walking under the large oak and walnut trees in the back yard.

There were two large oak trees to the left of the kitchen door. They were growing about fifty feet in front of the kitchen door near the path to the barn. The barn was about fifty yards from the house to the left. In order to get to the oak trees everyone had to walk past the surface well. The well had a stone curb and the top was covered with a wooden board top. In order to draw the well water, the top had to be removed. The farm had about fifty acres. Carpenter said that the farm used to be run by an older couple. The couple died and Dr. Grunburg started paying the taxes and asked him to work the farm.

Winnie embraced the concept of being a trained nurse. Dr. Grunburg had brought the leather shoes and medical books several months earlier. After she tucked Betty in her crib, she would read and study the books each night. She understood the concepts and asked the doctor for clarification when he made his visits. The doctor told her that he wanted her to help with his pregnant patients. The Depression had already lasted about two years. Some of his patients could not afford to pay him with money or pay the full price of a home visit.

Dr. Grunburg told Winnie that a nurse's home visit would be less costly than a doctor's visit. He told her that she could do some of the prenatal house calls for him. He said that he would drive her to the patient's homes. He wanted to introduce her as a trained nurse and then she would be able to visit the prenatal patients while he visited other patients.

Winnie often read and studied the medical books until she fell asleep at the kitchen table. She hadn't noticed that Carpenter was moving slowly and not eating the usual amount. One night, she was awakened to the sound of loud moaning in his bedroom. She listened for a while and then quietly walked from the kitchen table to his bedroom door. She listened again and then knocked softly. He did not respond. After the third knock, she slowly opened the door and looked at his bed. He was rolling from side to side. The moonlight coming through the window revealed the perspiration on his forehead. She asked him if he were alright. He did not answer. She moved closer to the bed and touched his forehead. It was cool to the touch and covered with perspiration. She decided to go back to the kitchen and bring the oil lamp into the room. As she left the room, he continued to moan and roll from side to side.

Winnie carefully picked up the oil lamp from the kitchen table and walked back to the bedroom. As she got closer to the bed, she could see a dark spot on the top sheet. She moved closer to examine the spot. It was obviously blood. She pulled the sheet back and revealed a cut on his abdomen. The cut was about six inches long. The wound did not look new, but she suddenly felt the need to go and check on Betty.

She turned and quickly walked through the bedroom door. She turned to the left and entered her room. She nervously approached the crib. As she lifted the lamp above the crib, she could see that Betty was sleeping peaceably. She turned and went back to the kitchen. She kept her medical bag that Dr. Grunburg had given her and supplies in the pantry. She walked to the pantry and picked up the medium size leather bag from the bottom right shelf. She turned and walked back to Carpenter's bedroom. She placed the lamp on his night stand.

She opened the leather bag and took out some small cleaning rags and a bottle of iodine. As she began to clean the wound, he flinched in pain. She dressed the wound with an iodine soaked cloth and covered it with a large bandage. She gathered the waste material from the floor and reached for the lamp. She took the soiled bandages to the kitchen garbage pail. She placed the oil lamp on the kitchen table and started a fire in the stove. She knew that he would not be able to make the fire in the morning. She didn't want the temperature to drop too low and possibly cause Betty to catch a cold. As she checked the wood box, she realized how important Carpenter's help was in ensuring that she had productive days. As the flames of fire grew in the stove, she decided to go back and check on his condition. When she entered the room, Carpenter had stopped moaning and seemed to be resting. She decided that since Carpenter was doing a little better, she would go to bed.

The next morning seemed like ten minutes later. Winnie sat on the side of the bed, pushed her feet into her slippers, and looked at Betty in the crib. As she stood up, she reached for her robe on the foot of the bed. She walked into the kitchen and got some firewood from the wood box. As she walked over to the stove, she could hear Carpenter snoring in his bed. She placed the wood in the stove and began making breakfast. She knew that this day would be busy. She knew that she would have to get firewood and feed the livestock. Betty was eating food from the table, so it would be easier to feed her. From the size of the wound, she did not think that Carpenter would be able to help out with farm chores for a couple of weeks. She knew that the doctor would not be able to help with the chores. She would have to get someone to come and work on the farm. She had not hitched a wagon in a long time. If she needed to drive the wagon, she could recall how to hitch it. She decided to wait a couple of days before asking for help.

Just as she finished breakfast, Betty started crying. Winnie served two plates and placed them on the table. She walked into the bedroom and Betty was sitting in her crib crying. As she walked to the crib, her daughter raised her arms as large tears fell from her hazel eyes. Winnie lifted her out of the crib, kissed her on the cheek and hugged her. She turned and pulled the right top drawer of the mirrored dresser open. She picked a cloth diaper from the drawer, closed the drawer, and turned toward the bed. As she laid her on the bed, Betty smiled at her mother. She changed the diaper and lifted Betty onto her shoulder. She rolled up the soiled diaper and tossed it into the pail at the foot of the crib. As she walked back to the kitchen, Betty hugged her neck. Winnie told her that she was beautiful and smart like her grandfather. When she reached the kitchen table, she picked up one of the plates and carried it into Carpenter's room. She placed the plate on the night stand. As she walked back to the door, he thanked her for bringing the breakfast into his room. She turned back while supporting the baby's back with her left hand and told him to let her know if he wanted more food. She told Carpenter that she would bring his coffee to him. She went to the kitchen stove and poured the coffee into the cups on the counter. She placed the coffee pot back on the stove and picked up one cup. She carefully turned and carried the cup into his bedroom. She placed it on his night stand.

Winnie took Betty into the kitchen and sat down to eat breakfast. As she was wiping Betty's mouth, she heard a male voice calling Carpenter's name. She stood up and walked to the window. As she looked toward the barn, a short dark complexioned man was looking in the door. He closed the door and turned toward the house. As he walked toward the house, he continued to shout Carpenter's name. She could see a revolver in his belt. She did not recognize the man's face. She decided to go into her bedroom and close the door. She and Betty stood to the left of the door. The man pulled open the screen door and knocked on the door. He called Carpenter's name. Winnie rocked the baby and tried to keep her quiet. After no one answered, the man turned the knob and pushed the door open. As he stepped into the kitchen, Carpenter yelled the name William from his room. The man answered and told Carpenter that he was coming in. He walked into Carpenter's bedroom and they started talking in a friendly manner. Winnie let out a sigh of relief as she realized that the two men knew each other. She decided to go back into the kitchen and clean the breakfast items. She wanted to know the identity of the man. She also wondered if she could ask the friend to do some of the farm chores. She wanted to know what happened to Carpenter. She turned the knob and pulled the door open. She let the door bang against the wall. She wanted the man with the gun to know that she was in the house. As she walked into the kitchen, she heard a click that sounded like someone cocking a gun. Carpenter shouted, "Put that gun away!" He told him it was Winnie. As her body tensed, Betty started to cry. She could hear the man laughing and telling Carpenter that he thought it was Big Jim.

She decided to go to the bedroom door and introduce herself. As she stood in the door, the man greeted her. She greeted him and asked Carpenter how he was feeling. He told her he felt better. She asked him his friend's name. He told her that the man was his younger brother William. She told William she was happy to meet him and asked what happened to his brother. William told her it was a long story. Winnie said that she would put the baby in her crib and return to hear the story. As she turned to leave the room, William told Carpenter that Big Jim was really mad. She entered the bedroom and walked to the mirrored dresser. She picked up the baby rattle and gave it to Betty. As she placed the baby into the crib, she reached for the rattle. She heard the screen door open. She heard the door squeak and William loudly told Carpenter to move. The next sound was a gunshot.

Winnie screamed in a very high pitch. Betty started crying and she heard a heavy thumping sound like a body falling. She heard a third man's voice. He yelled, "I will kill you nigger!" There were two more shots and she could hear furniture scraping across the floor. She grabbed Betty and ran to the corner of the bedroom adjacent to the kitchen pantry. As she ran with the baby, she heard two shots. She did not want to be near the wall adjoining Carpenter's bedroom. She heard a man's painful scream. As she and Betty huddled in the corner crying, she heard what sounded like a kitchen chair falling and two more shots. She heard what sounded like wood falling from the wood box and another two shots. She cradled Betty who was screaming to the point of losing her voice. At this point, Winnie realized why her mother prayed in times of trouble. She began to rock and pray. While praying, she heard a man's voice say, "I will kill you!" She continued to pray for protection and the man's exit from the property. Another male voice yelled, "I will hunt you down, nigger!" Two more shots were fired. It sounded like the bullet hit the wall next to her head. Betty continued to scream. The screen door banged against the house. Another shot was fired outside. She then heard the screen door close and the wooden door slam shortly thereafter. The baby continued to scream and she continued to pray. She could hear the sound of the shoes dragging across the wooden kitchen floor. The person slowly walked into the other bedroom. She could hear Carpenter moaning as William told him to grab his neck. Betty continued to scream as she prayed and rocked in the corner. She could not calm the baby. She decided to get up and change the baby's diaper. She could feel the wet spot on her abdomen. As she walked back to the bed, the urine on her arm felt sticky. As she looked down at her arm, she could see the fluid was not urine but blood. Betty continued to scream and Winnie began to scream and cry. She yelled, "They shot my baby! They shot my baby! Oh Lord have mercy! Oh Lord!" She grabbed a diaper from the footboard of the crib. She laid her on the double bed. The baby continued to cry and she dabbed the bloody area. After several wipes, she could see that the blood was coming from her abdomen. She left her crying on the bed and ran to the pantry to get her medical bag. She grabbed the bag and ran back into the bedroom. She did not worry about who was in Carpenter's room. She needed to attend to the baby's wound right away. As she reached the bed, Betty was still crying. She opened the medical bag and took out the bottle of iodine. She poured the iodine on the diaper. She cleaned the wound as the baby continued to scream. She could see that the bullet had cut an impression in Betty's side. The wound was about half an inch wide. No organs were exposed, but the wound was bleeding. She closed the iodine and placed it back in the bag. She dressed the wound with a small iodine soaked cloth and tied a cloth diaper over the wound. Her screaming changed to a cry. Winnie picked her up and sat on the side of the bed. She held her daughter and began to pray again. Winnie stood up and walked into the kitchen. She decided to pour Betty a bottle of milk. Winnie gave her the bottle and walked back into the bedroom. She sat on the bed and rocked her. Betty cried and chewed the nipple while looking in her mother's eyes. Winnie rubbed her brown hair and told her that she loved her. Betty whimpered, drank, and attempted to talk with the nipple in her mouth. She was calming down and her mother was calming down. Winnie rocked her daughter and said a prayer of thanks. Betty began to doze. When she fell asleep, her mother stood up and placed her in the crib. After placing her daughter in the crib, Winnie cleaned up the waste items and walked into the kitchen. She placed the items in the garbage pail and turned to look around the kitchen. Firewood was on the floor, the screen door hinge was pulled from the door frame, and the kitchen chair was lying on the floor. She turned and walked to the wall near the pantry. Winnie could see the hole where the bullet came through and hit Betty. She walked into the pantry, picked up a small clean rag and walked back to the hole. Winnie tore a small strip of cloth and stuffed it in the hole. She did not want the small hole to create a draft while Betty was sleeping. Her father had taught her to always cover as many holes in walls as possible. He always joked that many little cracks would feel like a big crack. She knew that the hole was small, but she wanted to get rid of any reminders of the horrible event. She sighed and patted the hole before standing up. Winnie wanted to get rid of the visual reminders of this violent attack. She turned and looked at the kitchen door. There were two holes in the door. She tore off two small strips and stuffed the clean cloth into the holes. She decided that she would go into the other bedroom.

As she stepped inside the doorway, the two men stopped talking and looked at her. She could see that the night stand was turned on its' side and it had a bullet hole. The window also had a bullet hole. Both men told her they were sorry about Big Jim shooting up the house. She told them that her baby had been shot. Both men grabbed their faces and murmured a few words. Winnie wiped tears and told Carpenter that her baby's life was more important than her own. Both men nodded and looked down at the floor. She told them that she did not want to live her life…

Before she could finish her sentence, she heard a horse drawn wagon coming into the back yard. She shouted, "Oh Lord!" and turned to run back to her bedroom. Without looking through the kitchen door window, she quickly stepped inside the bedroom. She closed the door and ran to Betty's crib. As she reached for her baby, she heard a female voice. The woman yelled, "Is anybody home? Is everybody all right?" Winnie stopped herself from waking the baby. She turned and listened. William shouted, "Hold on! Hold on!" She could hear him walking to the kitchen door. She heard the knob turning and the squeaking of the door. A woman told him that she and her husband were going back home when they heard the shots and shouting. She told him that she and her husband had never heard any commotion before. They just wanted to check and make sure everything was all right. She asked if the lady of the house was home. He told her that she was in her room. The woman asked if she could speak with her. He told her to wait while he checked. Winnie decided to go into the kitchen. She took a deep breath and walked toward the door. She turned the knob and slowly opened the door. She stepped into the kitchen and stood in front of the bedroom door. The woman smiled and told her that her name was Martha. William told her to come in. He held the revolver in his right hand behind his back. As she stepped into the kitchen, William smiled, nodded and stepped outside. She moved toward Martha and told her that she was Winnie.

Martha was several inches taller than Winnie. She was a cinnamon brown complexioned heavy set woman. Her wavy black hair was pinned up in a bun. She wore a plain tan long dress with a red ribbon tied under her breasts. Her flat black leather shoes appeared worn.

Winnie asked if she wanted some coffee. She nodded and Winnie told her to have a seat. At that moment, Carpenter coughed. Martha looked startled as she sat down. Winnie told her that her husband was under the weather. She told her that her brother-in-law was there helping out until he was able to work. Martha asked if she had any children. She told her that she had a baby girl and her name was Betty. Martha told her that she thought she had seen baby clothes hanging on the clothes line. She told Winnie that she had been after her husband Tom about coming over to visit. She said that Tom didn't want to come because he thought that she was different. Winnie quietly turned from the stove and looked at Martha. As she blankly stared at the wall, Martha shrugged her shoulders and told her not to worry. She spoke in a matter of fact manner and told her that men were funny sometimes. Winnie turned back to the counter and poured the coffee. As she handed her guest the cup, Betty began to cry. She told her she would be right back and quickly walked to the bedroom door and turned the knob. She hurriedly opened the door and told her baby that she knew it was time for lunch. The cry became softer as she got closer to the crib. She picked up the baby, gave her a kiss on her cheek, and hugged her. As she turned to walk back to the kitchen, she rubbed her straight brown hair and kissed the top of her head. Betty clutched the sleeve and collar of her dress. As she stepped into the kitchen, Martha asked Betty if she was hungry. Betty did not recognize the voice and quickly turned toward the voice. Winnie walked to the counter and uncovered a small pan of cornbread. She asked her guest if she would like some bread. Martha told her that she would love some. Winnie held the baby in her right arm and reached in the cupboard with her left hand. She placed the two plates on the counter. As she served the cornbread to Martha, she asked if she had any children. Martha said she had two boys. One boy was nine years old and the other was eight years old. She said she tried to have a third child, but she lost it. Martha said she hadn't been able to get pregnant since. Winnie told her that she was sorry to hear that she could not have more babies. She asked which doctor helped her deliver. Martha said there was no doctor. Her husband Tom had helped with all the babies. Winnie placed her coffee and plate of cornbread on the table. As she sat down, Betty reached for the cornbread. She placed a piece of bread in her mouth and took a sip of coffee. She broke a small piece of bread and placed it in Betty's hand. Winnie ate her cornbread and told Martha that she was training to be a nurse. She told her that she worked with Dr. Grunburg. She told her that she would be making house calls and deliveries. Martha asked how she knew the doctor. She told her that he knew the owner of the Plantation where she grew up. Betty reached for more bread as she broke off a small piece. Martha told her that they should go to Tappahannock together and shop. Winnie told her that she would love to go. She told her that her husband goes on Saturday mornings about twice a month. Both women heard Tom shout Martha's name from the back yard. The screen door opened and then the wooden door. William stepped into the kitchen and announced that Tom was ready to leave. Martha drank the last of her coffee and told them she had to go. She said Tom didn't like to wait. She thanked Winnie for the food and drink. As she stood up, Martha came over and gave her a hug. She told her to let her know if she needed any help. Winnie told her that she would and hugged her with her left arm. Betty looked at both women before smiling at her mother. Martha told Winnie that she had a beautiful daughter. She thanked her and walked her to the kitchen door. As Martha stepped out of the kitchen, she stepped to the center of the door and waved to Tom. He waved back as Martha walked quickly to the wagon. As she turned her body to shield Betty from the cool air, William walked into Carpenter's bedroom. As Tom drove the wagon out of the back yard, Martha and Winnie smiled and waved to each other.

Chapter 4

Several days later, the stillness of the cold January morning was broken by the sound of a horse drawn carriage coming into the back yard. William had started a fire before going to check on the livestock. Winnie was finishing breakfast. She looked out the window as Dr. Grunburg was taking the carriage lap blanket from his legs. She felt a sense of relief. She wanted him to check Betty and Carpenter's wounds. Treating their wounds was her first attempt at practicing the information she had studied and discussed with the doctor. She served Carpenter's breakfast and she placed the plate and cup of coffee on the wooden tray that William built. She grabbed the two handles and took the food into him. As she got closer to the night stand, Carpenter sat up in bed and thanked her. She told him to let her know if he needed anything. She placed the tray on the stand and returned to the kitchen. As she closed his door, Dr. Grunburg opened the kitchen door and stepped inside. He took off his bowler and greeted her with a smile. She smiled, greeted him and asked if he wanted coffee. He told her that he definitely needed it after such a cold ride. They laughed as he placed his bowler and bag on the table and sat down. He asked how Betty was coming along and she told him that she wanted him to check her. As she served the doctor his cup of coffee, she told him about the shooting incident. He took one sip and listened intently. His face turned beet red as he told her that he wanted to examine Betty. He took his bag and walked into the bedroom. She walked quickly to catch up with him. As he placed his bag on the bed, she took Betty out of the crib. He motioned for her to let him hold Betty. He sat on the side of the bed and rubbed her brown hair. Dr. Grunburg turned and laid his baby daughter on the bed. He took the bandage off and exposed a pink wound on her abdomen. He immediately told Winnie that the wound looked good and it appeared to be free from infection. Dr. Grunburg told her that he would leave her more iodine. He instructed her to keep the wound clean and dry. The Doctor instructed her to change the dressing each day. He told her that she had passed her first test as a pediatric nurse. They both smiled and looked at each other. Dr. Grunburg told her to give him a clean diaper. She raised her eyebrows in surprise and got a clean diaper from the mirrored dresser. As she handed him the diaper, she told him that she was going to get Betty a bottle of milk. As she walked into the kitchen, she could hear father and daughter giggling. When she returned with the bottle, he was standing beside the crib with a dry happy baby. She gave Betty her bottle and the doctor placed her in the crib. When he turned toward Winnie, he told her that she needed an examination also.

The doctor pulled her close with his right arm and systematically kissed the right side of her neck, up the right side of her jaw to her chin. As he pushed her chin back with his open mouth, he proceeded to gently kiss down the left side of her jaw to the bottom of her neck. She could feel his hard erection pressing against her abdomen. He unbuttoned the back of her dress as she unbuttoned his vest. He put his feet to the outside of her feet and slowly started walking toward the double bed. He lowered the cotton dress over her shoulders as she slid his vest down his shoulders. He caressed both breasts as he softly kissed her forehead and told her to let her hair down. As she lifted her arms to remove the hair pin, he lifted her body onto the double bed. She reached to place the pin on the night stand as he took his dress shirt off and threw it onto the foot of the bed. He unbuckled his belt and pulled down his pants and boxers. He took his shoes off and started kissing and sucking her toes. As he continued to kiss his way up her body, they both began breathing heavily. As he kissed her erect nipples, she felt his erect penis. As he kissed up her chest and neck, he slowly inserted his manhood into her. She moaned with pleasure and reached up to his neck. They both moved in harmony as each of them pleasured away the stress of the shooting incident. The cold January air added to the hot steamy atmosphere of the double bed. As he fell beside her in exhaustion, they both sighed and clung to each other.

As if she were waiting for them to finish, Betty immediately started to talk-cry. They both laughed as Winnie told him that she would get Betty. She also told him that she wanted him to check Carpenter's wound before he left. As Winnie sat on the side of the bed, Betty sat up and smiled at her mother. Winnie told her that she had fresh milk for her. As she put on her dress and shoes, the doctor sat on the side of the bed. He reached in his medical bag and pulled out a bottle of iodine. He handed the bottle to Winnie and told her to keep the bottle and he would bring more since there was so much excitement these days. She took the bottle and they both laughed. She walked through the kitchen and placed the bottle in the pantry. Winnie picked up one of Betty's clean baby bottles and a black nipple. She walked to the counter and poured some milk into the bottle. When she returned to the room, the doctor was dressing and Betty was playing with the rawhide and porcelain rattle that

Carpenter made for her. She gave Betty the bottle and she chewed on the black nipple before attempting to drink. She was teething and the nipple was always cleaned and soaked in used cooking grease. The nipple had a strong rubber odor. Winnie discovered that if she cleaned the nipple and then placed the nipple down in the used grease, the odor was less offensive. Betty did not seem to mind the oily nipple. The doctor told Winnie that he wanted her to observe his treatment of the wound. They both walked toward the kitchen and turned toward the door on the right. Winnie knocked on the door and Carpenter told her to come in. She opened the door and they both walked to the bed. Dr. Grunburg told him that he wanted to examine his wound. Dr. Grunburg pulled back the sheet and revealed a soiled bandage. The doctor asked Carpenter if his wound had been bleeding for several days. He told the doctor that Winnie had done a good job stopping the bleeding, but after the shooting it was really painful. He said that his brother had dumped him on the floor to keep Big Jim from shooting him. The doctor told him that he would look at the wound and see what he could do. As he took off the bandage, he could see that Carpenters' abdomen needed stitches. The doctor told Winnie that he would need to do two sets of stitches. He told her that he needed to stitch the inner wall and then the outer wall. He told her that he would use the iodine to clean the inner wound and then stitch. He told her to watch how he started the stitch and how it is tied and cut at the end. He sat on the bed, got the iodine, soaked the clean cloth, and cleaned the inner wound. As he began stitching the wound, she peered over his shoulder. He proceeded to clean the outer wound and stitch it. He soaked the wound with iodine and it seemed to numb the wound after an initial surge of pain. Carpenter thanked him for closing the wound. He told the doctor that he felt better. The doctor told Winnie to clean and dress the wound each day. She picked up the soiled rags on the floor and took them to the kitchen garbage pail. The doctor gathered his bag and walked into the kitchen. He placed his bag on the kitchen table and put on his coat. As he reached for his bowler, he told Winnie that she was a good mother and nurse. They hugged, he put on his bowler, and he walked to the kitchen door. As he opened the door, he told her to stay warm. As he closed the door, she realized that this arrangement was going to work. Sometime after the doctor left, William came into the kitchen with an arm load of firewood and placed it in the wood box. Winnie told him that lunch would be ready in a short while. William told her he would wait with his brother. She prepared the lunch and took the meals into the room.

Several months had passed and Carpenter was much stronger. William had decided that he would stay at the farm and help his older brother. Carpenter was feeling stronger, but the men were quite pleased with the amount of work they completed when they worked together. William wanted to give some grain to his mother and father. They were getting older and he wanted to give back to them.

Betty was a year old and eating more food from the table. She was able to drink milk from a cup. Her complexion was still almond and her brown hair was still straight, and about shoulder length. Winnie started feeling sick in the morning. She thought it was caused by the spring air, but she remembered that she had not had a menstrual cycle since the beginning of January. It was the end of April and she realized that she was pregnant. She knew that she would have to clean Betty's baby bottles and keep them in the pantry. She could put the new baby in the small cradle that Carpenter made for Betty. Since Betty had just turned a year old, she could continue to sleep in the crib. William had the bedroom upstairs to the left. Betty would sleep in the bedroom upstairs to the right. That bedroom was directly above her. Winnie wanted to be able to hear her at night.

Martha and Tom were going to town on Saturday. She decided that she would look for more cloth to make night gowns and summer dresses. She did not like to travel during the cold months, but she enjoyed warm travel days. Martha had visited several times since the incident in January. Betty seemed to like her and she loved having the opportunity to care for a girl. She had two boys who worked in the fields with their father. On light chore days, Martha came to spend afternoons with Winnie and the baby. They worked on sewing, canning, baking, and if time permitted, a little gossip. Martha attended church at least twice a month. She invited Winnie and Carpenter, but Winnie thought it might be best if she didn't go. After several visits, Winnie had to tell Martha about the arrangement.

Martha listened to the story of how Dr. Grunburg saw Winnie at the Tate Plantation with her father. He decided that he wanted her and made an arrangement with Mr. Tate and Thornton. Thornton got lifetime rights to stay on the Plantation as long as Mr. Tate was alive. Winnie got a life that provided a home and food regardless of how the economic conditions were for the area. She told Martha that it was not what she wanted for her life as a young girl. She wanted to marry a young handsome man who looked like her father and live on the Tate Plantation. She realized that the arrangement was good for her family and it was working out for her. Dr. Grunburg treated her with respect. He thought she was smart and he was training her to be a nurse. She felt that if she had married a young man on the Tate Plantation, she may not have had the opportunity to train as a nurse.

Winnie told Martha that she valued their friendship, but she did not want to attend church and endure the women of the church whispering about her.

She did not want her kids to see or hear such things. She told Martha that she used to go to church with her mother and she understood how church women talked.

Martha laughed and told her that it was the truth. As Winnie smiled, she told her that Tom did not want her to keep visiting, but she reminded him that his sister's skin complexion was as light as his skin complexion was dark. Everyone in his family was dark except his older sister. She reminded him that his father loved her even though he knew the child wasn't his child. She reminded him that the women at the church talked about his sister and his mother and he didn't like it. After that discussion, he told her that she could visit. Winnie asked her why she wanted to visit. She said that she could tell by looking in her eyes that she was a kind woman. Winnie laughed as she leaned her head back in the chair. She told her that no one had ever told her that a person's eyes could tell what kind of personality they had.

Martha laughed with her and pretended to dance as if in the church and feeling "the spirit". She told Winnie that there were some older women in the church who talked about the eyes being the window to the soul. She told her that the older women were able to predict who was good to their family and who committed a crime. Winnie asked if she had read anyone else's eyes. They both laughed and Martha told her that she had read about five other people. She told her that she had been right in all cases. She knowingly told Winnie that she knew nursing, but she knew eyes. They both laughed and continued sewing dresses.

Martha made dresses for women at the church in order to make extra money. Some of the women did not have the money to pay for the dresses. They would pay with butter, cheese, canned goods, or sometimes unused cloth. Martha asked Winnie to help her because she could make more money and Winnie would be able to make some extra money. She knew that Carpenter did all of the shopping, but she also knew that women liked to have a little money of their own. Both women agreed to help each other with house hold chores and sewing.

On a sunny Saturday morning, Tom and Martha came to the back yard and waited for Winnie and Betty. Winnie brought a quilt and an umbrella. The wagon did not have a cover over the rear. Martha helped Winnie spread the quilt and get Betty seated in the back with the boxes for merchandise. The women talked and laughed as Tom drove the wagon to town. It had been about three years since Winnie had been to town. She remembered most of the shops and shop owners. She wore a large off white cotton bonnet and Betty wore a smaller version of her bonnet. Martha and Tom went to the farmer's market and Winnie told them that she wanted to go to the General Store. They agreed to meet back at the wagon in about an hour.

She had gone to the store several times with her father. She had always been allowed to walk around the store freely. She entered the store carrying Betty in her right arm and she was politely greeted by the clerk. She greeted the clerk and proceeded to the far end of the counter. She asked to look at several fabrics for dresses, curtains, aprons, and table cloths. She purchased two fabrics for dresses and six sticks of hard candy. As she turned to exit the store, the clerk invited her to come again. She thanked him and told him that she would be coming back. One of the female customers made small talk with Betty as she exited the store. Customers entering the store smiled and greeted both of them. As she walked back to the wagon, she felt as if she were being watched. When she reached the wagon, Martha jokingly told her that she was going to be the talk of the community. She asked her why she would say such a thing. She asked Winnie if she had noticed the women from the church watching her. She said that she had a feeling like someone was watching her. Martha laughed and told her that she was definitely right about someone watching her. They both laughed as they put their items and Betty in the back of the wagon. She pulled Betty next to her and raised the black umbrella. The sun was very hot on Betty's tender skin and Winnie's skin did not take well to the hot Virginia sun. Since childhood, the sun had always burned her skin. She learned to wear long sleeves, a bonnet, and stay out of the direct sun. As they rode through the southern part of town, the church people and their friends looked and whispered as they passed. Martha waved and called some of the women by their names. As they left the town limits, Martha, Tom, and Winnie laughed heartily. Betty started to laugh because the adults were laughing. Winnie hugged her and kissed her on the forehead.

The next week Martha came over and told Winnie that all of the women in church were talking about how she walked in the General Store like she was a White woman. Winnie asked her what she was talking about. She told her that all of the Negroes had to walk in the store, go to the back, and wait for the clerk to come and ask, "What do you want?" Everyone watched you walk straight to the counter. They all knew that the clerk was going to fuss at you and throw you out of the store. They were laughing and guessing when it would happen, but you kept looking at fabrics, the clerk kept smiling and asking questions, and you kept looking. Everyone thought you put on the greatest performance in there. They all laughed at how fearless you were.

Winnie told Martha and Tom that it wasn't a performance. They both told her at the same time that she had to be telling a joke. She quickly told them that she had always gone to that general store with her father. They never had to go to the back of the store and wait for the clerk. Martha and Tom immediately turned to look at each other. They stared at each other for about three seconds. They realized that Winnie and her father were able to walk freely throughout Tappahannock because of their light complexion.

Chapter 5

Several months later, the leaves had fallen from the trees and the smell of scalding animal flesh filled the cold November air. William and Carpenter had begun slaughtering the hogs. The men from the surrounding farms formed the slaughter team. They travelled from farm to farm until each farmer's animals were slaughtered. Martha and several of the women from the church came to help make sausage and prepare the meat for curing.

They set up stations in the kitchen. The men brought buckets filled with entrails to the kitchen door immediately after they were removed from the animal. The first pair of women dumped the contents of the entrails into a second bucket. Once the bucket was filled, it was placed outside the kitchen door. One of the men would leave an empty bucket and dump the full bucket away from the yard and crop area. The next pair of women poured water into the entrails and lifted one end while holding the other end closed near the floor. The women alternated which hand was raised to eye level. The movement created a top to bottom washing technique. The entrails were cut to about three feet in length.

The second pair of women poured water into the entrails and lifted them in an alternating motion. They washed the remaining material from the inner wall. The waste was dumped into a bucket. Once the bucket was filled, it was placed outside the kitchen door. After the rinse, the entrails were placed in a bucket and passed on to the third pair of women. They pulled any hairs and particles from the entrails. The waste water was dumped in a bucket. Once the bucket was full, it was placed outside the kitchen door. They examined the meat and determined which wash would be the final cleaning. The meat was then placed in a clean bucket for grinding and curing.

The women volunteered to go from house to house until all of the animals in the area had been slaughtered. Other women would bring prepared foods for the workers to eat. Some of the women chose to take care of any children who needed supervision. If a man lived alone, the women would still go to his house and help process the meat. The entire community worked to help each other. Winnie knew that Martha had been speaking positively of her. The women did less whispering when they saw her and some even thanked her for making certain garments.

Winnie was in her ninth month of pregnancy. About a week after the slaughtering of the hogs, she decided to spend a day baking bread and making pies. The wind was blowing snow flurries on the window sill. Betty was sitting in the kitchen chair playing with the cloth doll that her mother had made. She was eating warm bread and watching her mother. As Winnie opened the oven door to put a rack with four pies in the oven, her water broke. Clear fluid gushed from her abdomen and soaked her feet. She immediately looked at Betty and rubbed her abdomen with her right hand.

William and Carpenter had been outside for a while. She knew that Betty was too young to go outside and call for help. She was also wondering if she could take the chance of running out in the yard to call for help and leave her baby sitting at the table. She wondered why this baby didn't come the previous week when so many women were in the kitchen.

As her wet feet slid in her black leather shoes, she decided to run to the bedroom and grab a quilt. Betty was startled by her sudden movement. She turned her head quickly and followed her mother's movement. She held the piece of bread in her tiny clinched fist as she held her breath. She was about to let out a cry when her mother rushed back into the kitchen and told her to come with her. She immediately started to smile and reached for her mother's neck. She was quickly wrapped in the thick blue heavy quilt.

Winnie quickly moved to the kitchen door as clear fluid continued to trickle down her legs. She stepped outside and immediately started calling for Carpenter and William. They both heard her and came out of the barn. She yelled for them to go and get Martha because the baby was coming. William quickly ran back into the barn. Carpenter walked hurriedly toward the house. Winnie turned and quickly walked back to the kitchen door. As she struggled to open the door, Betty snuggled against her chest. She was totally oblivious to the urgency of the moment. As her mother walked through the bedroom door, she spoke unintelligible phrases that mimicked complete sentences.

Winnie slid the quilt off her shoulders and walked to the crib. As she leaned to place Betty in the crib, she felt the muscles on either side of her abdomen tighten. As she moaned in discomfort, Betty giggled as if her mother were humming a song to her. Winnie turned and picked up the quilt as Carpenter stepped into the bedroom doorway. He asked if she needed him to get anything. She told him to bring in more water and firewood. As he turned to leave the room, she folded the quilt and placed it under the bed pillows. She looked in the top right drawer of the mirrored dresser and took out a clean night gown. Betty smiled and talked to her mother as she hurriedly gathered clean bed linen and towels from the closet. She placed the items on the foot of the bed and walked to the side of the bed where she took off the wet dress. She turned to the side and looked at her naked pale swollen abdomen in the mirror. As she caressed her unborn child, she slowly developed an adoring smile. She wondered whether her innocent new baby would be a boy or a girl. She wondered if it would look like Betty or totally different. She reached for the clean gown and sat on the bed. As she slid the sleeves over her arms, Carpenter brought in more firewood. She could hear the door open and close as he went to get more water. Betty had fallen asleep just as she put several towels under her buttocks and leaned back against the pillows. Her hips ached and her abdomen felt as if the inner tissue were tearing away. Her thoughts were interrupted by the sound of a horse drawn wagon. William had ridden a bare backed horse to Martha and Tom's farm. Tom hitched the wagon and drove Martha to the house. She could hear Martha giving orders to the men as she rushed to the kitchen door. As she opened the kitchen door, she yelled Winnie's name. Winnie answered and told Martha to get her medical bag from the pantry. Martha got the bag from the pantry, placed it on the table, and checked the wood in the stove. She went over to the wood box and brought several pieces back and put them in the fire. She filled two pots with water and placed them over the fire. As the water was heating, Martha picked up the medical bag and walked into the bedroom. She asked where she wanted Betty to sleep. Winnie told her to take Betty into the kitchen and put her in the small wooden cradle. As Martha picked her up from the crib, Betty stretched and yawned. Both women laughed and joked about her not being interested in a new brother or sister. Winnie felt another contraction and moaned in discomfort. Martha told her that she would be right back. As she walked into the kitchen, the men came in the kitchen door. Carpenter was the last one to enter the house and he placed an arm load of firewood in the wood box. Martha told the men that they had to watch the baby, keep the fire up, and keep the water boiling. All three murmured in agreement simultaneously. As she came back into the bedroom, Winnie felt the urge to push. Martha told her to stop pushing as she closed the door and hurried to pull back the top sheet. She wanted to check the baby's location in the birth canal. Winnie told her that it was time to push. For several seconds the two argued back and forth about whether she should push or not.

As Martha pulled back the top sheet, she could see the crown of the baby's head. She told Winnie that she could see the baby's head. She told her that the hair was brown like Betty's hair. Martha reached for more clean towels and a large rag that she would use as the baby's first blanket. On the next push, the baby's head cleared the birth canal. Martha turned the baby's face up and began wiping the baby's face with clean rags. The baby had a pale complexion, but she noticed an unusual color. The baby seemed to have a gray color with a blue overtone. She raised her head and looked at Winnie. Her face was blush red and her straight red hair was soaked with perspiration. The hair near her forehead stuck to her skin. Winnie looked at Martha's face and asked if the baby looked alright.

She did not answer and immediately started wiping the baby's nose to clear any mucus and fluid. Martha opened the baby's mouth and attempted to clear mucus from the mouth with her finger. She told Winnie to get ready to push as she looked for the strips of cloth to tie the umbilical cord. Martha did not feel comfortable with how the baby looked and she wanted to cut the cord as quickly as possible. She was not used to seeing babies this pale, and she didn't like the way the baby looked. She cleared some mucus from the mouth and told Winnie to push. As she pushed, she asked repeatedly if the baby was alright. Again, Martha did not answer and rubbed the baby's body with the clean towel. The baby's body had the same blue and gray color of the face.

Martha tied the umbilical cord in two places. She quickly reached for the scalpel that she had taken from Winnie's black medical bag. She cut the cord and continued to rub the baby's body. Winnie asked if it were a boy or a girl. Martha replied in a hurried manner that the baby was a girl. As the new mother breathed a sigh of relief, she heard Martha smack the baby's bottom. As she listened for the newborn's first cry in the new world, she could hear Martha whispering something. She leaned forward to see what she was doing and she could only see Martha leaning over the newborn.

Winnie repeatedly asked what was wrong. Martha did not answer and continued to rub the baby's body with the towel and gently rubbing the baby's chest. She turned the baby on her stomach and rubbed her back. The baby still had the gray color with the blue overtone. She lay perfectly still. Without warning, Martha screamed Tom's name. Winnie screamed because she knew that her baby must be dead. She passed the afterbirth out of the birth canal. There was the loud sound of several chairs scraping the kitchen floor. Betty suddenly began crying and Tom quickly opened the bedroom door and rushed in. As the door slammed behind him, Martha told him to check the baby. As she wrapped the afterbirth in the soiled rags, Martha repeatedly said, "Lord Jesus" softly. She got the bottle of iodine from the black medical bag and poured some on the clean rag. She removed the soiled rags that were near Winnie's body and cleaned her body with the iodine rag. She packed the area with clean rags and told Winnie to hold still. Winnie yelled for Tom to give her the baby. As Tom handed her the motionless little blue and gray baby, she quickly transitioned from the weeping mother to a trained nurse. She told Martha to dip the clean rags into the boiling water and bring them back to her. She began rubbing the baby's body with the rags. She smacked the baby's buttocks, but the baby did not respond. As Martha rushed back with the hot rags, Winnie told Tom to hand her some clean rags. She laid the baby on the bed beside her. She unwrapped the baby's body and took the clean rags from Tom. She could hear William and Carpenter trying to console Betty in the kitchen.

Winnie placed the clean rags over the baby's body. She told Martha to give her two hot rags. She placed the hot rags on top of the clean rags and massaged the baby's abdomen. The baby's blue and gray body lay lifeless on the bed. She took one of the hot rags that had cooled from the baby's body. She told Martha to give her another hot rag. She placed it on the baby's abdomen. She used the cooler rag to clean the baby's straight brown hair. Betty had stopped crying in the kitchen and Tom slowly walked out of the bedroom.

Martha shook her head and slowly gathered all of the soiled rags. As she slowly turned to leave the bedroom, Winnie told her that she wanted to see the umbilical cord. Martha told her that she had to move on and she shouldn't look at it. Winnie told her that she needed to see if the cord was alright. Martha reluctantly placed the afterbirth and cord on the floor. She asked Winnie what she was looking for. Winnie told her to bring the cord closer. She told Martha to hold up the curved cord. She pointed out a knot in the cord. She told Martha that the knot had caused her to lose her angel. She thanked Martha and told her that she could take it away. As Martha wrapped the soiled rags, Winnie asked her to get the baby's tan gown from the top of the mirrored dresser.

Martha walked over and picked up the gown. She stood at the dresser and began to sob. She told Winnie that she was so sorry. She told her that she knew her pain and it reminded her of the beautiful little boy that she lost. Winnie told her that she was so thankful that she was there with her. Martha told her that she hoped she wasn't bad luck for babies. Winnie chuckled gently and told her to stop talking like a crazy woman and bring her the little angel's gown.

Winnie told her that she had helped deliver her own little angel. I'm going to name her Fannie because that was the name of the woman who helped deliver me. As Martha turned and walked toward her friend, tears streamed down her face. She handed her the gown and watched as only a mother could gently dress the tiny blue and gray body. Winnie softly sang "Yes Jesus Loves Me" as she carefully put Fannie's arms in the sleeves of the gown. She kissed each tiny hand and foot. She took the large cotton cloth and tightly wrapped the baby's body. Her tiny arms were wrapped across her chest and her legs were wrapped straight.

Martha turned, picked up the soiled rags and walked into the kitchen. She put the soiled rags in the kitchen trash bucket. William asked how she was doing. She told them that she was doing better than she thought she would. Winnie called for Martha from the bedroom. She rushed in to see what her friend needed. Winnie told her to carry the baby out to each person and offer the opportunity for each of them to hold the baby. Martha took the tiny bundle and turned to walk to the kitchen. As she got closer to the door, Winnie told her to bring her back to her. Martha entered the kitchen holding the bundle and tears streaming down her face. She told the men that she wanted each of them to have an opportunity to hold the baby. They all bowed their heads as Tom reached for the bundle first. William looked at his brother and reached for the baby. Carpenter handed Betty to Martha and held the bundle. Martha held Betty tightly, kissed her forehead, and rubbed her hair. As she blankly stared out of the kitchen window, Tom told her to give Betty to him. She handed Betty to Tom and took the bundle from Carpenter's arms. As she walked back into the bedroom, she heard Carpenter tell William to burn the rags and dig a hole between the last walnut tree and the barn.

As Martha walked toward the bed, she could see Winnie's shoulders shaking as she mourned the loss of her newborn. As Martha got closer, she raised her arms to receive the bundle. Martha hugged them both and wept with her friend. Martha sobbed and told her that she was sorry that Fannie didn't live. Both women embraced each other with one hand on the baby's body. The kitchen door closed and Winnie asked who was coming in the door. Martha told her that the men were preparing for the burial. Winnie softly told her that the baby would stay with her tonight. Martha told her that she would stay tonight and let Tom go back home to see to the boys.

In an effort to get back to the normal daily routine, Martha told her friend not to worry. She told her that she would make some dinner and change Betty. As she stood up to walk into the kitchen, Winnie thanked her for being there. Martha told her that she knew she would do the same for her. As she stepped into the kitchen, she closed the bedroom door and told Tom that she was going to spend the night. She told Carpenter to give her Betty and bring some potatoes and onions in from the barn. As the men gathered their hats and coats, she talked to Betty and placed the frying pan on the stove. She told Betty that her mother was a strong woman and Betty giggled as if she had told the funniest joke ever. She placed her in the kitchen chair and gave her a piece of biscuit as she began cooking ham and cutting the potatoes and onions that were on the counter. Martha took a bowl and cup to the pantry to get some flour. She knew the men would want biscuits with their meal.

Chapter 6

About three days later, the doctor drove his horse drawn carriage into the back yard. Carpenter saw the wagon approaching and greeted the doctor as he tied the horse to the post. Carpenter usually gave the horse water and oats while the doctor visited. He also checked the carriage connections and horse shoes.

Winnie looked out the kitchen window and watched as Carpenter and the doctor held a conversation. She had not seen the two of them discussing matters before today. She assumed that he was telling the doctor about the baby. She recalled that the two men never talked about the shooting. In order for Carpenter to approach the doctor, an important issue must be unresolved. She saw the doctor lower his head and look toward the second walnut tree. Carpenter lowered and shook his head as the doctor placed his left hand on his right shoulder. The doctor turned and walked with Carpenter toward the barn. Winnie was somewhat confused because the doctor paid Carpenter to take care of the property. He never did any repairs or made any decisions about the farm. She watched Carpenter walk the doctor to the barn path. As they stood between the barn and the second walnut tree, she realized that they were standing before Fannie's little grave. The image caused the pain of losing her baby to rise to the forefront of her emotions. She could not bear to watch them. She turned from the window and decided to sit at the table and gather her emotional composure. Betty was sitting at the table watching her mother. As usual when she turned to sit down, Betty was elated to see her mother's face. She giggled at her mother as if she had heard the funniest joke ever told. The innocent joy of her beautiful daughter brought a tearful smile to Winnie's face. She realized that her daughter was always happy and a source of pure innocent love. For a short moment, she thought that God had taken one angel, but he left her Betty. She was an angel on earth. As she smiled at her little angel, the kitchen door opened.

The doctor pulled the door open and stepped into the kitchen. He usually stepped in with a smile and often times a witty joke. On this day, he entered the kitchen with a pale distressed expression. He took his hat off, walked over to the table, and placed his hat and black medical bag on the table. As he walked to the table, Winnie stood up and walked to the side of the table next to the stove. The doctor kept his head down and stretched his arms forward.

Winnie slowly moved forward to meet his outstretched arms. They slowly and tightly hugged each other. They both sobbed without saying a word. The doctor gently kissed Winnie's red hair as she continued to sob against his chest. Betty sat on the other side of the table and quietly ate her biscuit. As Winnie sobbed, she told him that her hair was straight and brown just like Betty's. She told him that she looked just like Betty looked as a baby. The doctor whispered that he was sorry the baby didn't live. She quickly told him that her name was Fannie. He gently kissed her hair and whispered that he was sorry that Fannie did not live. He asked her if she were alright. Winnie described how Martha came over to help with the delivery and how she continued to help by staying overnight. She told him that she used the iodine from the medical bag and that she felt good. He slowly pushed her away from his body and held her face in his hands. He told her that he wanted to examine her before he left. She looked down at the floor, nodded her head, and told him that she would put Betty in the crib. As she turned to get Betty, he asked if she felt alright the week before delivery.

She told him that she felt fine and she had no discharge. She said that she helped with processing the meat, but she didn't get too tired. She explained that the labor seemed normal. As she walked into the bedroom with the baby, the doctor picked up his medical bag and walked closely behind her. She placed Betty in the crib and unbuttoned her cotton dress. The doctor smiled and told her that she was the best looking post delivery woman that he had ever seen. They both softly chuckled as he pulled her close to his body. He gently kissed her forehead, down the right side of her face, and down the right side of her neck. She limply held his waist. He carefully nibbled at her ear and told her that she was beautiful.

As he slowly lifted her chin, he told her that he wanted to examine her and make sure that she could have more beautiful babies. They both smiled as she sat on the bed and he opened his medical bag. The doctor examined her breasts and pressed the upper half of her abdomen. He asked her if the afterbirth was intact. Winnie told him that she looked at the afterbirth and everything looked alright. She also mentioned that she remembered reading about checking the afterbirth if the stillborn had no visible defects. Her voice quivered as she told him that the baby was perfect. Winnie told him that she noticed a knot in the umbilical cord. As he pressed and tapped the middle and lower part of her abdomen, she moaned with some discomfort. He asked her if she was alright. She said that she was alright and continued to describe the knotted cord. He asked about the complexion of the baby. She told him the baby seemed more gray with an overtone of blue. Her fingers and toes were gray. There seemed to be more gray than blue. He grunted and told her that he was going to examine the birth canal. Winnie told him that Martha had smacked the baby's buttocks and that she had also smacked the baby's buttocks, but there was no cry. She began to weep as she told him that little Fannie never took a breath. As she softly wept, he told her that everything looked good and there were no signs of infection. He instructed her to try to keep the area clean and dry. He also told her to keep using the iodine.

He put everything in the medical bag, placed it on the floor, and picked up Winnie's dress. He carefully put the dress over her head and arms. As he pulled the dress down over her abdomen, he told her to move over. He laid down in the bed beside her. He gently kissed her forehead and told her that based on everything that she shared about the delivery, Fannie was not supposed to live. Her shoulders shook as she wept. He told her that the gray color, especially in the toes and fingers meant that she hadn't had blood in those areas for some time. The knot in the cord restricted the oxygen and there was nothing that she could have done differently to save her life. He explained that sometimes the cord develops a knot and the medical community doesn't know why this happens. He kissed her forehead and touched his forehead against her forehead. He softly whispered that they would have to try again as he gazed into her light brown eyes. He laid back down beside her and told her that she did everything that she could. He said that he was definitely confident that she would be able to handle any of his pregnant patient's deliveries. He asked Winnie if she would like something to eat. As he sat on the side of the bed, he told her that Carpenter was doing a good job. The doctor picked up his medical bag and they both started walking toward the kitchen. He explained that he had some doubts about him after the shooting. He said he was thinking about getting someone else to take care of the farm, but after this incident, he felt that Carpenter was the best man for the job. He felt comfortable with the fact that his brother stayed to help with chores. I trust that you and Betty are safe.

As he placed his bag on the table, she located his lunch. She told him that William and Carpenter had told her that Big Jim did the shooting because of a card game. They explained that William had convinced Carpenter to go play cards at the "Sing Shack". The doctor asked if that were the place near the Essex County line. She told him that it was the same place. The men said that Carpenter won all of his money and Big Jim got angry about losing a week's wages. They assured her that Jim wouldn't be back. The doctor told her that he knew that Carpenter would do the right thing. The doctor ate his lunch and left to finish his house calls.

A couple of days later, Martha visited the house to see how she was feeling. Winnie invited her in for coffee and cake. Tom went to the barn with William and Carpenter. Winnie told her that the doctor had checked her and said that she did a good job. Martha joked that maybe she should train to be a nurse. They both laughed and she told Martha that the doctor was concerned about Carpenter staying at the farm after the shooting incident. Winnie explained to Martha that Big Jim came to the farm to shoot Carpenter because he lost all of his money in a card game. As she continued to talk, Martha interrupted her and asked her to repeat the reason that Big Jim shot up the house. Winnie repeated her statement and Martha raised her eyebrows and told her that someone was not telling the truth. Winnie stopped talking, sipped her coffee and looked at Martha. Martha continued to sip the coffee with her eyebrows up and an expression that said she had talked too much. Winnie calmly told Martha that she needed to share. Both women laughed and Martha looked over both shoulders as if she were checking to see if anyone was nearby.

She leaned forward and told Winnie that a different story was being told by the church women. Winnie cleared her throat and asked what their story was. Martha told her that William spent a lot of time with a young girl named Bett. He talked Carpenter into seeing her friend Big Belle. It seemed that Carpenter had been seeing Big Belle for about a year when Big Jim showed up.

"Big Jim worked at the loading dock in Tappahannock. He used to travel with the boats a lot. He got hurt when a load fell on him. They say he went home to Baltimore, but he ended up staying with Bett and Big Belle. Big Belle had been running a house of ill repute for a long time. The word was that Carpenter had been messing with Big Belle for about ten years." Winnie nodded her head as she concluded that Carpenter never made any inappropriate comments or actions toward her because he had Big Belle. She felt a little better about Carpenter's role in the arrangement. She was relieved that he had someone who showed him affection. Martha told her that Big Jim came back to the house early and caught Carpenter there. "They say he cut him pretty good. They say Carpenter stops over there after he goes to the mill. The word was that Big Jim had been watching Carpenter." Winnie said she was happy that he didn't come to the house and wait for him.

Winnie shook her head and told Martha that she was glad he didn't come to the house. She said that since it wasn't about a card game, he might come back. She said that was probably why William decided to stay. Martha told her that William was extra protection. She nodded her head and glanced at the bedroom door. The thought of anything happening to Betty after losing baby Fannie was just too much to bear. She confided in Martha that she was glad that Carpenter had somebody. She knew it was a different arrangement, but she was happy and that he was a good man. She told Martha that William had a gun. Martha told her that Tom said William was good with his fists and a pistol. As Winnie's eyebrows went up, she told her not to worry. Tom said that William really didn't fight unless he felt like someone was coming after him. Winnie asked if Tom knew of anyone who might be coming after William. Martha told her that she had better keep the medical bag filled. They both laughed as Tom opened the kitchen door. He greeted Winnie and asked Martha if she was ready to leave. As she stood up, she jokingly instructed Winnie to keep her eyes open. Winnie told her that she was sure it would be alright. As they hugged, Betty started to cry in the bedroom. Martha told her that someone was calling her. They both laughed and Martha and Tom left. As she turned to get Betty from the crib, Winnie decided that she would not ask the men any questions about Big Jim and the shooting incident.

She decided not to ask any questions, but she started looking out the window whenever she heard a noise. Christmas came and left and there were no events. She noticed that both men stayed out late Christmas night, but no one followed them home. She also noticed that some nights, William did not stay at the house.

Chapter 7

As Winnie looked out of the kitchen window, she could see that the frequent April showers of 1876 had already begun to spur new growth. She spent most of her day in the kitchen. Each day began with making coffee, preparing breakfast and planning lunch and dinner. From the kitchen window, she observed, contemplated, and enjoyed her lot in life. Being a "kept" woman may not have been her choice in life, but she realized that her life was less stressful than most other women in the community.

Martha had become Winnie's best friend. When she and Tom heard the shots at the farm, they came to check on Winnie's wellbeing. Martha was a warm caring church woman who truly believed in helping her neighbors. She attended church whenever work on the farm was manageable. Martha respected the elders of the church and followed their advice closely. She shopped, ran errands, and performed chores for the elders of the church as well as community members who needed assistance. Martha had been born in Essex County Virginia. She was the youngest of six children. Her five older brothers helped her develop into the caring strong woman who took care of everyone she loved. Her mother died when she was ten years old. She started cooking, cleaning, sewing, and providing for her father and five older brothers. By the time she met Tom at age sixteen, she was an experienced house keeper. Her ability to run a household was one of the reasons that Tom knew she was the woman for him. He was the youngest in his family and he was used to an orderly home. Martha may be perceived as bossy sometimes, but she does not take charge in order to demean others, she takes charge in order to help. Martha developed into a surrogate mother to Winnie even though they were about the same age.

Betty had just turned two years old. Martha had baked a small birthday cake that she ate all alone. When Martha gave Betty the cake, she smiled and dug into the center of the cake with both hands. Martha and Winnie laughed as she dropped pieces of cake all over the table, inside her dress, on the floor, and occasionally in her mouth. Betty's straight brown hair touched her shoulders and her hazel eyes complimented her almond complexion. Whenever Winnie looked into her eyes, they reminded her of the times she used to sit on her father's lap as a child. Oftentimes Winnie would just sit and gaze into his calming hazel eyes. Betty had her grandfather's hazel eyes and his pleasant personality. She was quiet and often sat and watched as the adults went about their daily chores. Betty could speak in complete sentences, but she chose to point, say one or two words, and often just smile. Whenever she looked at her mother, Betty giggled as if her mother were holding her down and tickling both arm pits. She was quiet pleasant company for her mother. As Winnie completed chores during the day, Betty would quietly play with her doll and wonder from room to room. Winnie decided to sew porcelain beads on the top of her cloth shoes in order to track her movements. Little did she know that Betty would walk, kick her feet up, and watch the beads as they seemed to clank a tune as she moved her feet.

Even with a beautiful daughter, a devoted friend, and a secure living arrangement, Winnie awakened with a sick feeling. This was the third morning that a deep nauseous feeling seemed to control her stomach and her mind. She hadn't felt this way since her last pregnancy. Just as the doctor had ordered, she decided to mix some ginger in her tea. As with the previous pregnancies, the ginger slowly calmed her stomach and she was able to start her routine morning activities. As Winnie pondered the possibility of another pregnancy, she recalled that her last menstrual cycle was at the end of January. She instinctively lowered her head as she recalled the pain and anguish of trying to save little Fannie's life. As she leaned on the kitchen counter, she looked out the window and caressed her abdomen. She said a short prayer as her eye caught the small patch of light green grass beside the walnut tree. Young grass sprouts were growing on Fannie's small grave.

Winnie had always considered spring as a season of new growth for plants as well as human beings. As a child, her father always showed her signs of new growth in the fields and around the farm. She would then share her thoughts about new activities that she and her family could participate in simply because it was spring. For a short moment, Winnie thought she would make some baby clothes for the bundle of joy now growing in her womb. She suddenly remembered that she had some items she had made for little Fannie, so there was no hurry to make baby clothes. The strong smell of freshly baked biscuits jolted her back to the moment at hand.

Winnie took the breakfast biscuits out of the oven and placed them on top of the stove. She saw something white move near the barn door. She knew that Carpenter had hitched the mule to the plow and headed toward the field some time ago. Carpenter did not typically come back to the barn or house until breakfast was served. William could have been working in the barn, but she didn't remember him wearing anything white. For a brief moment she wondered if Big Jim or someone else was looking for William or Carpenter. At that moment, she noticed the white movement near the barn again. She stopped preparing the breakfast plates and peered at the moving object. She could see that William was carrying white sheets and rags to the wagon. William may have been Carpenter's younger brother, but he was not as quiet and reserved as his older sibling. He carried a gun, hung out at the "Sing Shack", and often smelled of whiskey. He was respectful, but he gave the impression that if pressed, he would defy all authority.

Winnie shrugged her shoulders and decided to prepare the men's plates and place them in the oven. She wanted to eat before Betty woke up. She fixed her plate and poured a cup of tea with ginger. The taste of fried potatoes and onions fresh off the stove reminded her of eating breakfast with her family at the Tate farm. As she savored the salty taste and vivid memories, the kitchen door opened.

William rushed in with an anxious look on his face. He cleaned his throat almost as if he wanted to prepare himself and Winnie for his communication. He exclaimed, "I hate to bother you, but I need your help." She took the cup of tea from her lips and slowly moved the liquid around her mouth as if she wanted to fully enjoy the flavor before hearing his request. As she placed the cup on the saucer, she asked William what he needed.

He told her that Bett was going to have a baby and she wanted Winnie to handle the delivery. Bett was a tall, narrow featured, dark complexioned woman who along with her older friend Big Belle, ran the "Sing Shack". It was common knowledge that the men from several counties frequented "The Shack" on a regular basis. Winnie's first obligation was to answer the call for a nurse. Since William lived in the same house, she had a few personal questions. She cleared her throat and said, "A lot of people have been asking if the baby was your child. Rumor has it that you have been spending as much time over there as you spend here. Is the baby your child?" William smiled, looked at the floor, and told her that it was his child. Winnie asked, "When do you think the baby might be coming?" William stuttered and said "You need to come now! The baby is coming now!" Winnie quickly stood up and told him that she needed to take Betty to Martha's house. She told him to bring the wagon up to the back door while she got Betty ready to travel.

Winnie quickly walked to the pantry and picked up her medical bag. She placed it on the kitchen table as she walked into the bedroom. She didn't like the idea of delivering a baby who may not have received the proper prenatal care. She wondered if the mother had eaten enough vegetables. It was times like these that made her feel good about the many nights that she fell asleep at the kitchen table reading medical books by the dim lantern light.

Betty was still asleep, so she changed her diaper without waking her. She got a pillow case from the closet and put Betty's dress, shoes, and cloth doll inside. She decided to walk into the kitchen, wrap an egg and cheese biscuit in a cloth napkin, and place it in the case. She knew that Martha had plenty of food and she would feed Betty, but her conscience as a mother prompted her to pack a meal. As Winnie placed the pillow case on the table, William appeared in the door. She told him to put her items in the wagon as she walked into the bedroom. Winnie got her coat, black umbrella, and the blue quilt from the closet and walked to the crib. She put her coat on placed the umbrella next to Betty and wrapped the quilt around her. With a sigh symbolic of her pride as a mother and nurse, she lifted her out of the crib, turned, and walked into the kitchen. William walked back through the door and took Betty from Winnie. She held the door as he carried her bundle of joy to the wagon.

On the drive to Martha's house, Winnie sat in the back of the wagon with the umbrella up. William told her that Bett would pay her for delivering the baby. Since Winnie had not examined or had any contact with Bett during the pregnancy, she decided to use the travel time and William's knowledge of the situation in order to gather some background information about her soon-to-be patient. She asked William if this were Bett's first child. He told her that it was not her first child, but it was the first time that she kept the baby for nine months. He went on to explain that none of the previous babies had lived. They had died after a day or two or they were born dead.

As they pulled into Martha's back yard, she came running out of the house asking if everything was alright. William told her that Bett was having the baby. She immediately stopped, put both hands over her mouth and glanced at Winnie. Winnie smiled back and winked at Martha to let her know that they would talk later. Martha had been relaying the community gossip about the women at the "Sing Shack" to Winnie. Neither one of them expected that Winnie would be asked to deliver the baby. Martha told Winnie that she would keep Betty until she came back as she patted her hand and formed a mischievous smile. William jumped down from the front seat and took the blue quilt into Martha's house. Betty did not wake up as William placed her on Martha's bed. He came out of the home as Martha jokingly told Winnie to be careful at the "Sing Shack". As William climbed up to the driver's seat, Winnie told Martha, "I'll be alright, you just take care of my baby." William drove the wagon and Martha waved as she went into the house to check on Betty. On the rest of the ride, Winnie caressed her abdomen, smiled about the conversations she and Martha shared, and mentally prepared for the delivery.

As they reached Bett's house, William told Winnie to let him go in first. He wanted to make sure that the house was presentable for a woman who didn't live the same lifestyle that Bett and Big Belle lived. Instinctively, Winnie clutched her black bag and told him she would wait. Winnie appreciated William's effort to make sure her visit was respectable.

When he came back to the wagon, he told her that she could come in. Winnie smiled and told him that she had a baby to raise and she needed him to make sure that she got back to her. He smiled and told her that she would get back.

As she entered the house, there were lots of lanterns, red curtains, red furniture, paintings, and red rugs. As she waited for William to show her where the mother-to-be was located, she was overwhelmed by the fancy bright fabric and alluring paintings in the hallway. He stepped past her and turned to the left. As he opened the door, she could see that a young lady was lying on a double bed. The quilt on the bed was bright red with a satin finish. Winnie felt as if she had walked into a hotel room in a big city. It was obvious that the young lady was in pain as she rolled from side to side. Winnie told William to build up the fire and boil two pots of hot water. She instructed him to find a quilt and as many white sheets and towels as he could find. As he turned to leave, she told him to make sure the towels and sheets were white. William smiled and repeated the word white. Winnie was beginning to wonder if there were any white items in the house.

As she walked closer to the bed, the young lady thanked Winnie for coming to deliver the baby. She softly said, "William had bragged about you being a good nurse, but I didn't think you would make a house call here." Winnie told the young lady that she was a nurse and she was trained to deliver babies and save lives if needed. The mother-to-be grabbed her hand and thanked her again and again. Winnie could see that preparation for the delivery had to move forward. She interrupted the young lady's gracious words and told her that she would need to change into a loose fitting gown. She instructed the young lady to position her waist closer to the pillows.Winnie started looking in the closet and in the dresser drawers for the items she needed. She found a red quilt, folded it, and placed it behind the pillows. She found a pink gown in the dresser drawer and helped her patient put the gown on. Winnie asked her to say her name so that she would stop concentrating on the pain. She told Winnie that her name was Bett. Winnie smiled and told her that William had told her some things about her. Bett smiled and said, "William is the best thing that ever happened to me." Winnie smiled and told her, "I hope we'll be able to change your mind about that today. I hope this new baby will be the best thing that has happened in your life." They both laughed as William entered the bedroom. He announced that the fire was up and the two pots of water were boiling. Winnie instructed him to look for more white towels and sheets. He shook his head in acknowledgement that he had forgotten to get those items. Bett moaned in discomfort and he quickly exited the room.

Winnie had learned from some of the European medical books that Dr. Grunburg had given her that keeping the medical area clean was important. She looked around the room and located a small white basin. The corner wooden chair was moved from the corner and placed beside the bed. It served as a perfect table for the white basin. William brought several white towels and sheets in the room and placed them on the foot of the bed. Winnie instructed him to put a little hot water in the basin and bring it back. She told Bett to try to relax and not to push yet. William brought the basin back and she asked him to stay in the kitchen or near the door. As he turned to leave, Bett felt another contraction. As she moaned in discomfort, she started to push. Winnie instructed her not to push until she checked to see where the baby was located. Bett ignored Winnie's instructions and pushed. Winnie pulled back the sheet and placed several towels under her buttocks.

She quickly washed her hands in the basin and dried them. As she reached up the birth canal, she could feel that the baby's head was not at the birth canal. She told Bett that the next few minutes would be uncomfortable, but she would have to turn the baby. She reached into the medical bag and took out the bottle of whiskey.

Winnie looked around the bedroom for a cup. She didn't see one, so she called for William to bring a cup from the kitchen. She wiped Bett's forehead with a clean rag. She told her that she was going to give her some whiskey to help her relax. Bett smiled and said, "I never thought a nurse would tell me to drink whiskey." They both smiled and William walked into the room with the white cup. Winnie took the cup and poured the whiskey. She shook her head and said, "You found one of the few white things in this house?" William asked, "Is everything alright?" Both women acknowledged that everything was alright and Winnie asked William to go back to the kitchen and wait. As she put the cork back in the small whiskey bottle, Bett finished the drink. Winnie took the empty cup and placed it on the chair as she put the small bottle back in her medical bag.

Winnie washed her hands in the small basin and wiped them dry. She instructed Bett not to push because she was going to turn the baby. The baby's head was not facing the birth canal and she needed to position the baby for a safe delivery. As she reached up the birth canal, Bett moaned in discomfort. Winnie pressed the top of the abdomen with her left hand as she manipulated the fetus with her right hand. As she moved the fetus, Bett's moans turned into screams. William immediately called from the kitchen in an anxious voice. Winnie ignored his panic response and continued to instruct Bett not to push. Bett yelled, "I have to!" Winnie sternly instructed her not to push. As she wiped her hands with a clean rag, she told Bett that she should push with the next contraction. The mother-to-be did not acknowledge the instructions as she moaned and turned her head from side to side. Winnie wiped her patient's forehead and told her that she was ready to deliver. As Bett moaned, Winnie told her to push. As she returned to the birthing area, Winnie joyfully said, "The head is on the way!" Again, William called from the kitchen. Winnie yelled and told him that all was well. Bett moaned and Winnie told her to push. As the baby's head cleared the birth canal, Winnie announced, "The head is out!" She quietly and sternly ordered Bett not to push. She could see that the umbilical cord was wrapped around the baby's neck. She kept telling Bett not to push as she quickly wiped the baby's face and ran her finger around the baby's mouth. Winnie needed to clear the mucus, but she also knew that she had to loosen the cord from around the baby's neck without tearing the afterbirth away from the womb too soon. She cautiously turned the baby's head to the side and gently placed the baby's arm over the umbilical cord. The baby's complexion seemed dark. The dark blue color indicated that the baby had lost oxygen. Winnie massaged the umbilical cord and turned the baby's face up. As Bett began to moan, the baby slid farther down the birth canal and the umbilical cord slid to the baby's side. Winnie continued to wipe the baby's face, head, and mouth. As she massaged the cord, the baby's complexion lightened. She told Bett that one more push should be enough. She moaned, pushed, and the baby slid out of the birth canal. Winnie announced, It's a boy!" She turned the baby on his side and spanked his buttocks. The baby cried and she began tying the cord. As she cut the cord and wrapped the baby, both women could hear William yelling and cheering in the kitchen. Winnie took the baby around to his mother and congratulated her. As Bett reached for her newborn, tears streamed down her face and she graciously thanked Winnie.

Winnie returned to the side of the bed in order to receive the afterbirth and tend to the mother. Bett passed the afterbirth and Winnie wrapped the waste in the soiled rags. The research in Dr. Grunburg's medical books was innovative for the time. They emphasized keeping the patient and work area clean. She reached in the medical bag and took out the small bottle of iodine. She cleaned the birthing area and dressed it with clean rags. The importance of keeping the area clean and dry was discussed. They both agreed that a follow up house call visit would be necessary in three to four days.

Winnie walked to the door and told William that he could come in to see his new son. As she opened the door, he slowly walked to the head of the bed. Bett asked, “Do you want to hold the baby?” He shook his head indicating that he did not want to hold his new son yet he leaned over the bed in an effort to see his face. As Winnie packed up her items and straightened the bed linen, she realized that William was beaming with pride and also afraid to hold such a small baby. Winnie smiled and told him, “Go ahead and hold your son. After all of the work to get him here, you may as well hold him.” He smiled and took the baby from Bett. William looked at his son, smiled, rubbed his check with his forefinger, and slowly turned and thanked Winnie for delivering a strong boy. She told him it was her job and pleasure to help bring a beautiful baby into the world. She continued to gather soiled rags and the basin from the chair. Winnie took the items out to the kitchen pail and came back into the bedroom. She instructed William to burn the soiled items in the kitchen pail before they left. He handed the baby back to Bett and said he would burn the pail right away. Winnie continued to clean and placed the chair near Bett’s pillow. She took her medical bag and coat into the kitchen. At this point, Bett’s ability to get up and do light chores was her concern. She searched the kitchen and found a tray with a cup, two pieces of cornbread, a jar of buttermilk, a jar of water, and a cloth napkin and brought them to the bedroom. She placed the tray on the chair and walked over to the dresser. A silver brush and a red scarf were near the center tray. She picked up the items, walked over to Bett, brushed her hair and tied the scarf over her hair. Both mother and baby were asleep. She quietly walked out to the kitchen and put more wood in the fire. Winnie put on her coat and picked up her medical bag from the kitchen table. As she left the house, she took a deep breath and thanked God for a safe delivery. Winnie did not consider herself to be a “religious” woman, but she had adopted a practice of thanking God before, during, or after deliveries.

On the wagon ride back to Martha’s house, William thanked her for coming to Bett’s house and delivering his son. He explained that the other women in the community would not come to the house and Big Belle was in Baltimore visiting her mother. William’s explanation refreshed Winnie’s feelings of rejection from the community that she had experienced since she was a little girl. As a child, some of the darker complexioned children pulled her straight hair and told her that the hair was not real. They also told her that she was too light complexioned to play with them. As an adult, the women did not want to associate with her because of her living arrangement. Winnie jokingly told William, “I am the only trained nurse in the community, so who else was supposed to deliver the baby?” They both laughed as an expression of relief and humor as he drove the wagon into Martha’s back yard.

Martha came out of the house to greet them and asked if the baby was a boy or a girl. Winnie smiled as William proudly announced, “It’s a boy!” She looked at Winnie and asked, “How was the delivery?” As she stepped down from the seat, she proceeded to explain, “The cord was wrapped around the little fellow’s neck.” Martha immediately shouted, “Oh my God!” Winnie continued to explain how she massaged the cord and moved it under the baby’s arm. She beamed with pride as she described how the color slowly came back to the baby’s face. As she listened intently and walked to the house, Martha shook her head in admiration and told Winnie that she was a really good nurse. Before entering the house, Martha hugged Winnie and told her that Betty was a little angel while she was gone. Winnie asked where Betty was hiding and Martha told her that she had just gone in to take a nap. Martha explained that the boys had come from the field after working with Tom. Betty and the boys ran around the yard until Tom yelled for the boys to return to the field. When they went back to the field with Tom, Betty ate some lunch and held her doll while sitting at the table. Within a few minutes she was nodding, so she went into the bedroom and lay on the bed. Betty curled up in the fetal position and fell asleep on the big blue quilt.

As Winnie stepped into the doorway and looked in the bedroom, Betty sat up and held her arms up for her mother to pick her up. They both smiled at each other and Winnie walked over to the bed and sat down on the quilt. She hugged Betty and kissed her forehead. In customary manner, the sleepy little girl snuggled against her mother’s chest. As her mother told her that she loved her and rocked, Betty fell asleep in her mother’s arms.

Martha knew that mother and daughter were exhausted from the day’s activities. As they consoled each other, Martha packed some buttermilk in a jar, four pieces of cake, four large sweet potatoes, and four pieces of beef in a burlap sack. She explained that she didn’t want Betty feeling hungry because her mother was too tired to cook dinner. Both women chuckled softly as Winnie thanked her best friend and laid Betty on the quilt. She felt a sense of pride in knowing that she had helped Bett deliver a baby who would be loved as she loved Betty. Martha tied the sack and yelled for William to come and take the baby to the wagon.

Shortly thereafter, the kitchen door opened and William walked through the kitchen. He entered the bedroom and picked up Betty. Martha held the door open as he carried the baby to the wagon. She hugged Winnie and walked her to the wagon. As Winnie climbed in the back with Betty, Martha told her to get some rest. She knew that performing the duties of a nurse was exhausting and the demands of running the farm were just as exhausting. As she smiled and nodded in agreement, Winnie knew that rest was not a likely option. William drove the wagon out of the yard and the women waved farewell to each other.

As the wagon neared the road, Winnie put the black umbrella up to shield the sun from her face. Shortly after reaching the road, Winnie noticed another carriage coming from the opposite direction. She peered at the approaching carriage, but she did not recognize the driver. William did not mention the approaching carriage and Winnie turned to face the rear of the wagon. As the two carriages travelled closer to each other, the driver of the approaching carriage seemed disturbed by William's presence on the road. The older bald White man stopped his carriage. Once William realized that the driver had stopped, he decided to stop his wagon also. He didn't want to show any disrespect to the other driver. As soon as the wagon stopped, the bald man asked in a stern voice, "Where are you going?" William began to nervously twist in his seat as he said, "I'm taking the lady home." As the bald man slowly leaned forward to look at Winnie, he asked, "Why do you have a White woman in the back of this wagon?" At that moment, Winnie realized the bald man did not mean any good will toward William. Before William could speak, Winnie smiled and quickly told the man, "He is taking me and my daughter home." The stranger asked, "Ma'am, are you alright?" This encounter reminded Winnie of her road travels with her father. She smiled and thanked him for asking. She assured him that she and her daughter were just fine. Winnie jokingly told him, "William is such a good driver that my daughter has fallen asleep and I am sure to follow." They both laughed and the stranger wished her a good day. Winnie thanked him and William ordered the horses to move. They rode in silence for a while as each realized that they had just experienced the same roles of the slave and the mistress of the plantation.

After an awkward length of silence, William asked, "How did you do that?" Winnie did not have to inquire about his meaning. She matter of factly said, "My father and I always had to answer such questions when I rode with him as a child. William shook his head as he reminisced about his childhood and adult experiences when confronted by White males about his travels. He always needed a note, another individual, or a crop that obviously explained the intent of his travels. William shook his head and continued to drive toward the farm. As they pulled into the yard, Betty sat up and pointed at the house. Her mother gently pulled her tiny pale hand to her mouth, kissed her hand and told her, "We are home." As the wagon stopped near the well, Carpenter opened the barn door and yelled, "Is everything alright?" William yelled back, "It's a boy!" He came around to the side of the wagon with a broad smile and lifted Betty out of the wagon. He helped Winnie step down and told her that he would bring everything inside. She grabbed her medical bag and the burlap sack filled with their dinner. Winnie smiled as she walked to the house and thought about what a good friend Martha had become. She opened the door and waited as Betty stepped up into the kitchen. There appeared to be two hours of sunlight left for the day. Winnie placed the medical bag on the counter with the food sack. She walked into the pantry, picked up the extra bottle of iodine, the bottle of whiskey and clean rags. She brought them back to the kitchen counter and restocked the bag for the next house call. Betty walked around the kitchen and bedroom holding her cloth doll. Winnie started the fire so that she could heat the green beans that she left on the stove as well as the food Martha sent. She could hear William and Carpenter laughing and talking as they walked to the house. When the two men stepped into the kitchen, William announced that he would be going back to Bett's house to stay and help with chores until Big Belle returned from Baltimore. Winnie asked, "When do you expect her to return?" William said, "She should be back in about three days. She knew it was about time for the baby to come. She told Bett to wait until she got back." The three adults laughed as Carpenter said, "Don't come back with ah apron on." The three adults chuckled as Winnie said, "Let's eat before you leave."

Chapter 8

The summer of 1876 was a very busy time for deliveries. Winnie delivered two babies for White patients in July and two in August. The babies in July were both girls. In August, the first delivery was a boy and the second delivery was a girl. Winnie was about to start her third trimester and the patients seemed to like the fact that she could personally relate to their aches, pains, and struggles. Dr. Grunburg had discussed the length of travel from his house to his patients' houses at the northern end of the county with Winnie on several occasions. They agreed that the patients seemed more comfortable sharing additional information about female body changes with a woman. They seemed to have more inquiries about trimester development for the baby as well as the mother during pregnancy when Winnie made the house calls. Winnie was improving her skills as a trained nurse. She was gaining more research based information and experience. At the same time, labor relations seemed to be deteriorating on the east coast. The summer of 1876 could have been considered the calm before the storm.

According to the National Bureau of Economic Research, the recession was three years old. Jobs were few, wages were stagnant, and the economy showed no signs of recovery. Several of the men from the docks in Tappahannock discussed labor events at the "Sing Shack." They had heard that the "Molly Maquires" had killed several owners, workers, and supervisors at the coalfields in Pennsylvania. The Molly Maquires were considered the core body of the Ancient Order of Hibernians. The Ancient Order of Hibernians was a group comprised mostly of Irish coalfield workers in Eastern Pennsylvania. The diverse group of workers (Welsh, Scots-Irish Presbyterians, English Protestant, Irish Catholic) created a lot of tension on a daily basis. Most of the Irish Catholics were unskilled coal workers. The majority of the mine owners were Scots-Irish Presbyterians. Many skilled miners and foremen were typically English Protestants and Welsh. They organized the Workingmen's Benevolent Association. Over twenty Molly Maguires were tried, convicted, and hanged for murdering owners, workers and foremen. The men at the dock also talked about wages being cut at the railroad yard. The men who worked at the Baltimore and Ohio yard reported that their pay had been cut for the past two years.

Many of the White farmers were renters rather than owners. Former Plantation and large farm owners reported losses in profits mainly caused by the loss of slave labor and a decrease in crop prices. Winnie and Carpenter witnessed and heard tales of hardship, but they were not directly affected by the prolonged economic hardships. Carpenter and William took care of the animals, maintained the property, and tended the crops. Dr. Grunburg paid the taxes and rent on the property. The prolonged recession had lowered the doctor's profit margin, but he was still able to pay for the property.

The cool September breeze had no effect on the temperament of some local farmers. The decline in their family's wealth and the rise of the Black farm worker's family wealth created tensions similar to the coalfields of Eastern Pennsylvania. On a cool mid September afternoon, Winnie decided to take Betty outside to play in the back yard. She knew that she would deliver the baby soon and would not be able to go outside with Betty for a few weeks. As Betty yelled and chased dead leaves blowing in the brisk breeze, Winnie walked around the yard and caressed her abdomen. She stopped at little Fannie's grave and said a prayer for a healthy baby and a safe delivery. As she turned to tell Betty it was time to go inside, she noticed an odd shadow on the walnut tree closest to the house. Winnie slowly walked toward the dark image. She could see that the shape was long and had a curved edge. As she looked closer, she could see it was a rope tied as a noose. She immediately yelled, "Oh my God!" and clutched her apron as the sensation of rushing hot waves engulfed her entire body. Winnie ran to Betty, grabbed her tiny hand and quickly walked to the back door. As Betty slowly climbed the steps into the kitchen, she suddenly felt the need to stay up all night and watch for the cold hearted person who committed this cruel act. Knowing that the baby was due for delivery on any day, she quickly reasoned that she couldn't stay up all night. Telling Carpenter and William about her discovery would be the best she could do. She would ask Martha if she had heard any information about who could have done this. Winnie washed her hands and began to prepare the dinner plates.

When Carpenter came in for dinner, Winnie told him of her unpleasant discovery. He immediately turned around and walked out to the tree. He took the rope down and took it to the barn. He knew the noose was a warning that the property was marked for destruction. The wind had blown the rope to the backside of the tree where it had gotten caught on a knot on the trunk. He knew he would have to let the other Black farmers know about the noose. As he stepped through the kitchen door, Winnie asked, "Did you see it?" in an anxious manner. He calmly told her, "Yeah, I took care of it." At that moment, Winnie realized that she needed to tell Dr. Grunburg about this incident. The baby was ready to come and she didn't want to be without a house to deliver the baby. They ate their dinner in silence as Betty talked to her doll and pretended to feed her dinner.

In 1876, the United States Supreme Court's ruling took the core out of the Ku Klux Act. They ruled that the United States Government could not prosecute individuals who committed acts of violence and intimidation against individuals in order to promote White supremacy. The ruling required states to prosecute any individuals who violated federal civil rights protections. The Black community felt that this ruling gave the Ku Klux Klan freedom to operate without federal oversight. Hanging a noose from a tree or other item on a specific property was one of the intimidation practices used by the Ku Klux Klan.

The Ku Klux Klan was organized by six confederate Civil War veterans. The organization was founded in Pulaski, Tennessee during the Reconstruction Era. The Ku Klux Klan primarily attacked the freedman and any of their allies. Klan activities were not common, but residents of Middlesex, Essex, and King and Queen Counties occasionally experienced intimidating acts from the Klan. William, Carpenter and many of the men at the "Sing Shack" had experienced intimidating encounters with White men, but this was more intense than the verbal exchanges.

The next afternoon, Winnie cleaned the lunch dishes and started the dinner as usual. She heard the sound of a fast moving wagon entering the back yard. As she leaned to look out the kitchen window, Martha was already reaching to open the kitchen door. She hastily entered the kitchen and asked, "Winnie, Tom told me about the noose! Are you alright?" Winnie smiled and told her, "Yes Martha, I'm alright." Martha walked over to Winnie and gave her a long hug. She inquired about the positioning of the baby. Winnie confirmed that the baby had dropped and was in position for delivery. As the two women talked, Tom, Carpenter, and William talked beside the walnut tree that held the noose. Martha asked Winnie if she wanted to bring Betty to her house to wait until the baby was delivered. Martha and Tom had allowed several church members to stay at their house in the past. Over the past ten years, several barns and houses had been burned while families slept during the night. Martha knew how important it was to the mothers to feel safe and have their children in a safe place. Winnie explained that she wanted to talk to Dr. Grunburg before making any moves. She told Martha that she wanted to give the doctor an opportunity to deal with the cruel acts. Martha nodded in acknowledgement and told her to send William to the farm when the baby was ready to come. Martha gave Winnie a hug and told her that Miss Ruth from the church was coming to try on a dress that she made for her. Winnie wished her good luck and told her that she was about half finished with the dress she was making for Miss Ada. Betty came out of the bedroom holding her doll and told Martha, "Bye" as she opened and closed her four fingers. Martha turned, smiled, walked over to Betty, kissed her on the right cheek as she held both cheeks in her hands and affectionately said, "Good bye baby." Martha turned and walked out to the wagon. As Tom drove the wagon out of the yard, Winnie shook her head as she thought of how Martha always treated she and Betty like family.

Winnie arose the next morning with a muscle ache on her right side. She had washed some clothes on the previous afternoon and she thought she had scrubbed too hard with her right hand. As she sat up on the side of the bed, she checked to see if Betty was asleep. While putting on her robe, she could see that Betty was fast asleep. As she walked toward the kitchen, the urge to urinate consumed her thoughts. She decided to start the coffee before urinating. As she put the coffee grounds in the coffee pot, her water broke. The clear warm fluid gushed from her abdomen and soaked her feet and slippers. She put the coffee pot down and walked into the pantry to get her medical bag and more clean rags. As the delivery date grew closer, she began stacking clean rags in the wicker chair in her bedroom. She placed several rags between her legs and dropped one rag over the wet spot on the kitchen floor. As she walked back through the kitchen, she looked to see how much firewood was in the wood box. She walked into the bedroom and placed the medical bag and clean rags on the bed. She went back into the kitchen to put more wood in the stove. She decided to place two pots of water on the stove also. As she looked out the kitchen window, she could see that Carpenter was walking toward the house. She decided to walk to the kitchen door and yell, "The baby is coming!" Carpenter waved and turned around and walked back to the barn. She knew that he would tell William to go to Martha's house and let her know the baby was on the way.

Winnie continued to get clean sheets from her closet and placed them on the bed. Carpenter stepped into the kitchen and asked, "Do you need anything?" She told him, "Bring in more water and firewood." As he left to get more firewood, Winnie took the soiled rags from between her legs and placed them in the kitchen garbage pail. The contractions were stronger, so she decided to lie down until Martha arrived. As she lay back on her pillows, she heard Carpenter put the wood in the box. She could hear the sound of the thin metal handle rubbing in the small rings on either side of the pail.

Betty turned over in the crib as Winnie turned on her side and caressed her abdomen. Shortly thereafter, Winnie heard a horse drawn wagon coming into the back yard. Martha yelled, "Winnie, I'm on my way!" She was instructing the men to make sure that she had enough wood and water. The kitchen door opened quickly and Martha rushed into the bedroom. She suddenly stopped at the foot of the double bed with a broad smile. She placed both hands on her hips as her mid knee flowing tan apron continued to move from left to right. She and Winnie made eye contact and they both felt a sense of relief. They knew the subconscious worry about this baby's health would finally be over. She mischievously asked, "You ready?" Winnie answered, "As ready as I'm ever goin' to be." At that moment, Betty sat up in her crib with a big pleasant smile. Martha jokingly said, "How's my pretty girl? Winnie, you goin' to have to take care of yourself for a bit while I get my baby straight." As she walked to the crib, Betty struggled to stand in the crib. She held out her little almond colored arms as Martha's robust biceps and voluptuous breasts engulfed her tiny body. Both of them laughed as Martha showered her cheeks and forehead with kisses and rocked from side to side. She carried Betty into the kitchen and put her in her chair at the kitchen table. Martha started cooking ham, eggs, and biscuits as she finished making the coffee. She poured some hot water and mixed some cold water in a small basin. She walked into the pantry and picked up a small clean rag and a bar of soap. She told Betty to stay in her chair until she came back. Martha walked into the bedroom as Winnie moaned in discomfort. She announced, "You ready to push!" Winnie answered, "Just about" as she tossed her head from side to side. Her fiery red hair was stuck to her perspiring forehead. Martha told her, "Hold on long enough for me to wash and dress my baby. Where is her dress and socks? Oh, here they are." Martha picked up the clothes from the mirrored dresser and rushed back into the kitchen. She washed and dressed Betty as she stood in the chair. Martha took the small basin to the kitchen door, opened the door, and tossed the soapy water into the yard. She yelled, "Y'all come on in here and watch Betty while I help Winnie deliver this baby!" The kitchen door closed and Martha told Betty, "Sit down baby, it's time to eat." She quickly took the biscuits out of the oven and served Betty's plate. She served three plates for the men and placed them on the table. As the kitchen door opened, she quickly walked into the bedroom with a small basin of hot water and closed the door. Winnie moaned with a contraction as Martha walked to the bed. Martha placed the basin on the floor as Winnie told her that she thought it was time to push. Martha picked up the wicker chair beside the mirrored dresser and placed it beside the bed. She picked up the small basin and placed it on the seat of the chair. Martha washed her hands and reached for a clean rag at the foot of the bed. As she dried her hands, Martha said, "Let's see what we have here." As Martha sighed and pulled the sheet back, she checked the birth canal. The baby's head was in the canal and she told Winnie she could push. Martha placed clean sheets under her buttocks and reached for the clean rags and medical bag at the foot of the bed. She placed the bag on the chair and pulled the small bottle of iodine and small clean rags out. She saturated the clean rags and cleaned the birthing area. As she cleaned the area, Winnie moaned and pushed. Clear fluid oozed from the canal as Martha rushed to place clean rags to absorb the liquid. She announced, "I feel the head!" She placed the small bottle of iodine back in the bag and continued to pull soiled rags and place clean rags at the end of the birthing canal. She told Winnie, "One more push and the head should be out." Martha leaned forward and wiped Winnie's forehead. She told her, "You're doin' a fine job." Martha didn't have to instruct Winnie to prop herself up on the pillows, keep her legs bent and open, or wait for the contraction to push. She told Winnie, "You're your own best nurse." Winnie showed a quick smile and told Martha she was ready to push. Martha wiped her hands with a clean rag and returned to receive the baby's head out of the birth canal. As Winnie moaned and pushed, the baby's head emerged from the birth canal. Martha announced, "The head's out!" She turned the baby's head up as she wiped the face with a clean wet rag.

Winnie immediately asked in an anxious manner, "What is the color like? Is the cord free? Do you see any blue? What…." Martha interrupted her and said, "Winnie, calm down! The baby looks good. The cord is free." At that moment, Winnie moaned and pushed. The baby slid into Martha's hands. She smiled, smacked the baby's buttocks, and wrapped a larger rag around the body. She continued to clean the baby's face and body as she announced, "It's a girl!" As the baby screamed in pain, Winnie cried, smiled, and chuckled as she thanked God for a safe delivery. She called to Martha, "Is she alright? How many fingers and toes?"

As Martha continued to clean the frightened little girl, she tied the cord and placed the baby on Winnie's abdomen. The new mother received her new daughter and told her, "Come to momma baby Mary." As she kissed her straight brown hair and examined her fingers, toes, and back, she thanked Martha for helping. Martha jokingly told her, "You know I wasn't goin' to let nobody else deliver my second daughter." They both chuckled as Winnie covered Mary from the cool air and passed the afterbirth. Martha reached in the medical bag, took out the scalpel, cut the cord, and wrapped the afterbirth in several rags. She placed the rags on the floor and asked Winnie what clothing she wanted to put on Mary.

Winnie totally ignored the question as she rubbed little Mary's straight brown hair. She softly said, "Martha, she has blue eyes." Martha excitedly said, "No she don't!" Winnie told her, "Look, her eyes are blue" as she turned the baby's face toward Martha. She leaned over the baby, nodded in acknowledgment and grunted. Both women knew that this baby's blue eyes, pale complexion, and the ethnicity of her father would make her life much easier than both of their lives. Martha asked, "Winnie, where are the clothes for Mary? What you want her to wear?" Winnie instructed her to look on the back right side of the mirrored dresser. Martha walked over to the dresser and picked up the material at the back of the dresser. As she examined it, she could see that the gown was made of a bright yellow cloth with tiny blue dots. Martha asked, "Winnie, did you know this baby was goin' to have blue eyes?" Winnie answered, "No Martha. Stop all that church stuff and give me my baby's clothes." They both laughed as Winnie dressed Mary and explained that the cloth caught her eye last spring when she went to the General Store in April. It was so bright that she felt it would make this delivery even more joyous after losing little Fannie. She explained that the bright color reminded her of the spring days that she used to spend with her father looking at wild spring flowers. Winnie carefully wrapped Mary's little arms close to her body with the tan flannel blanket that she made just for her. She handed Mary to Martha and announced, "She's ready to meet the family." Martha told her, "Winnie, you did a good job." Winnie thanked her as Martha sang "Yes, Jesus Loves Me" and walked to the door. As she opened the door, all eyes were on her. Martha announced, "Everybody, meet Mary!" She handed Mary to each man and then she held Mary down low enough for Betty to see her new baby sister. Betty pointed to Mary's chest and said, "Baby." All of the adults laughed as Betty looked at her tan cloth doll's face and then looked at Mary's face. Martha rubbed Betty's straight brown hair and told her, "You have a new baby sister." Betty smiled and walked away to play with her doll. Carpenter asked, "Is Winnie alright?" Martha told him, "Yes, she's alright. Tom, I think I should stay tonight and help with Betty." Tom said, "Alright, I'll let the boys know."

Martha turned and walked back into the bedroom. She handed Mary to Winnie and began cleaning the soiled rags and sheets from the room. She took the rags to the kitchen pail and asked Carpenter to burn them. She put the soiled sheets in a bucket with some washing powder. She poured some of the hot water from the stove into the bucket. Martha prepared a tray with a jar of tea, a jar of water, some slices of ham, a biscuit, and some great northern beans. She carried the tray into the bedroom and placed it on the seat of the wicker chair. As she took the basin from the chair, Winnie was rubbing Mary's brown hair and smiling. Martha took the basin to the kitchen door, opened the door, and threw the dirty water into the yard. She placed the basin under the sink and walked into the bedroom to look for the small cradle. She walked to the right side of the bed and picked up the small cradle. She placed it next to the wicker chair and told Winnie, "I'll check back on you two later." Winnie calmly replied, "Alright." Martha went back into the kitchen and began preparing dinner as Betty walked and played with her cloth doll.

A few days later, Winnie slowly awakened and put on her robe and slippers. She paused to take in the view of both girls fast asleep. Betty was asleep in the crib and Mary was asleep in the small cradle. Tears of joy, love, and pride welled up in her eyes. She sighed, wiped her eyes and slowly walked into the kitchen. She was thankful that Carpenter had put wood in the stove and had put a load of wood in the wood box. She started the coffee, put the ham in the frying pan, and walked into the pantry to get the flour for biscuits. She thought about how strong Mary's cry sounded and how well her appetite was picking up. As she reached into the oven and pulled out the biscuits, she heard a horse drawn carriage pull into the back yard.

Dr. Grunburg entered the kitchen with his usual pleasant smile. He looked at Winnie and asked, "Did you lose something?" They both smiled as he walked toward the kitchen table and placed his hat and medical bag on the right side. He held his arms out with a smile that boasted pride as she moved toward him. They embarrassed each other as he kissed her vibrant red hair and asked, "Who did you bring into the world this time?" They both chuckled as he gently lifted her chin with his left forefinger and she softly stated, "Mary. She has your blue eyes and straight brown hair like Betty. She's perfect." The doctor gently kissed her forehead, nose and lips as he whispered, "Thank you." After a long tender kiss, he said, "I want to see her. Let me examine her and then I'll examine you."

As he grabbed his medical bag and walked into the bedroom, Winnie told him that she seems to be quiet like Betty was at birth. The doctor placed his bag on the double bed and walked over to the cradle. As he reached for his youngest daughter, he smiled and told Winnie, "She's beautiful. She looks just like Betty." At that moment he glanced in the crib as Betty quietly slept. He laid Mary on the double bed and took out his stethoscope and listened to her heart, chest and abdomen. Mary frowned and squirmed as the cool metal touched her skin. As the doctor moved the tip of the navel, Mary opened her eyes and opened her mouth. The doctor wrapped the narrow rag around her abdomen as he said, "You do have beautiful blue eyes Mary." She frowned as he opened the diaper and checked her genitalia. As he fastened the diaper pin, Winnie asked, "So what do you think?" The doctor smiled and said, "Again, you have delivered a perfect baby." As he lifted Mary and turned to put her back in the cradle, the doctor told Mary, "Now you take a little nap while I examine your mother, okay pretty girl?" He gently kissed her forehead and placed her in the cradle. As he turned to examine Winnie, she told him, "I have to talk to you about something that happened a few days ago." He told her, "Relax and let me finish your examination first. I want to make sure I don't miss anything. You have to be strong and ready to take care of those two beautiful little girls. Now, relax." The doctor examined her breast, pressed her abdomen and then listened to her heart. He told her, "Let me take a look at how you're healing and we'll be done. Do you have any spotting or unusual pain?" Winnie answered, "No, I feel great." The doctor told her as he pulled her dress down, "And you look great. There's no sign of swelling or infection. Keep the area dry and clean. Everything looks good. Now, what was so important that you wanted to interrupt my most important examination?"

She sat on the side of the bed and put her feet in her slippers. As she stood and walked toward the kitchen, the doctor picked up his medical bag from the bed and followed. As she entered the kitchen, she explained that she and Betty were out in the yard a few days ago when she noticed a strange shape on the back side of the first walnut tree. She poured two cups of coffee and placed one cup at the end of the table. The doctor sat down as she took her cup and walked to the other end of the table and sat down. The doctor lifted his cup and asked, "What was it?" Winnie answered, "Well, as I moved closer, I could see that it was a rope. In fact, it was a noose." The doctor suddenly put down his cup as his face flushed pink. He asked, "What did you do?" She said, "I ran and grabbed Betty by the hand and came inside. I told Carpenter when he came in and he went right back outside and took it down. Carpenter said he was going to tell the other men about it, but I just don't feel safe. I…" The doctor interrupted her and told her, "Don't worry. I'll take care of this. Don't worry. I'll see someone today. This will not happen again. I promise you." Winnie served the doctor his food and he hurriedly ate. As he wiped his mouth, he told her, "In fact, I am going to leave now so that this may be dealt with today." Winnie told him, "Thank you." He picked up his medical bag and told her, "Don't worry, this will not happen again." He walked toward the kitchen door without saying good bye. Winnie called out, "Good-bye." He smiled, turned and walked back to Winnie. They both laughed as he hugged her and kissed her on the cheek. She told him, "Be careful." As he walked to the kitchen door he said, "I will. And don't worry, this will not happen again." He opened the door and quickly walked to his carriage.

Chapter 9

A few months later, Christmas and New Year's were celebrated as a joyous family occasion. Betty was almost three years old and this was the first year that she noticed the Christmas tree. She pointed at homemade stockings and stars. She marveled at the shiny metal ornaments. Winnie made a pink dress and another tan cloth doll for her. Martha made a blue dress and matching socks for Betty. She had made arrangements with Winnie to pick Betty up early on Christmas morning and take her to church. Since Winnie helped Martha make garments for several women at the church, she felt more comfortable allowing Betty to attend church events. She had gone to church on several Sundays, so going to Christmas Morning Church service was not an unusual activity. Tom and Martha wrapped Betty in several quilts in the back of the wagon as they drove to the church. Martha's two boys sat in the back of the wagon with Betty.

Mary stayed at home with her mother. Martha and Winnie made pastel blue dresses for Mary that matched her eyes. She lay in the cradle as her mother prepared the Christmas dinner. Carpenter slaughtered one of the male geese for Christmas dinner.

William and Carpenter celebrated the holidays at the "Sing Shack". Carpenter managed to return home late each night. William often times did not return. He stayed at the "Sing Shack" with Bett and his son. Martha had told Winnie that Bett's younger sister had moved into the "Sing Shack" in order to help take care of the baby. Winnie was hoping that 1877 would be a good year.

On a cold mid January day, Winnie awakened a little earlier than usual. She could feel the bedroom temperature dropping and she did not want the girls to catch a cold. As she sat on the side of the bed, she could see that both girls were snuggled under the quilts that she had made for them. Winnie put on her robe, put on her slippers and walked toward the kitchen. Even at this early hour, Carpenter had already filled the wood box. She got some wood from the box and put more firewood in the stove. As she began making the coffee, she could see snow flurries falling. As she went to the pantry with a cup for the flour, she could see that Carpenter was bringing the animals into the barn. He typically brought the animals into the barn before extremely bad weather.

As she placed the biscuits in the oven, she heard a horse trot by the house. As she closed the oven, she glanced out the window as William jumped off his horse at the barn door. It was apparent to her, at that moment, that William had spent the night at Bett's house. The two men talked in front of the barn door for a few minutes. William took his horse inside while Carpenter herded the two cows, mules, and goats inside the door. As Winnie finished cooking the eggs, she heard another horse drawn carriage pull into the back yard. She immediately thought that Martha had gotten Tom to bring her to visit before the bad weather arrived. She looked out the kitchen window and much to her surprise, Dr. Grunburg was stepping down from the carriage seat. She realized that he was about a couple of hours early. She assumed that he needed to visit a patient and she hoped that it was not an emergency call. Winnie looked out the window, but the doctor was already opening the kitchen door. Since it was snowing, he decided to bring the saddle blanket into the kitchen. As he walked through the door, Winnie asked, "What are you doing here so early? Is everything alright?" He smiled as he put the carriage blanket, hat, coat, and medical bag in the kitchen chair. He mischievously told her, "I came to give you a New Year's present." Winnie smiled, raised her eyebrows, and said, "Oh, what is it?" He unbuttoned his vest and pants. He put his glasses on the table and told her, "Me." They both smiled as he deliberately moved toward her and let his pants fall to his ankles. She instinctively finished unbuttoning his vest and lowered it over his shoulders. The doctor stepped out of his shoes and slacks as he reached for Winnie's buttocks.

As he pulled her petite body close to his, he kissed her neck and unbuttoned the back of her cotton dress. He slid the dress off her shoulders as he gently kissed her chest and each of her breasts. As her dark pink nipples hardened, she reached for his bulging manhood that pressed against her abdomen with her right hand. When she grabbed his penis, her body stiffened at the enormousness of his erection. Over their four year relationship, she could not recall an erection this full. The doctor seemed more aggressive in his advances. She wondered if he had taken a drink or something, but she could not smell alcohol on his breath. Winnie was pleasantly surprised and aroused by the feel of his full manhood.

The doctor pulled his shirt over his head and threw the shirt on the counter. As Winnie followed the path of the shirt to her left, the doctor bent his knees and kissed the back right side of her neck as he thrust the head of his penis back and forth across her clitoris. She softly moaned with pleasure as her nipples hardened to the point of icy stinging pleasure. She suddenly felt the lips of her vagina overcome with moisture. The doctor grabbed her buttocks and pulled her pelvic area to his as he gently tasted each breast. Without warning, he lifted her by the waist and carried her into the pantry doorway. He gently lowered her to the floor and slid his hands up her smooth pale back. He pulled her hair pin out of her vibrant red hair and grabbed both sides of her face as her hair gently swept across both breasts. He softly kissed each lip and gently bit her bottom lip as he pushed her head down. As her mouth ran down his chest, he leaned his head back as he continued to guide her mouth to his bulging penis. He breathed heavily through his teeth in anticipation of her hot moist mouth engulfing his manhood. As her lips covered the head of his penis, they both moaned as he slowly moved her head back and forth. He softly said, "Yes, yes, yes." His moans became louder as he ejaculated into her mouth. She was beginning to feel a sense of disappointment as she realized that she would not have intercourse. The doctor pulled his leaking softer penis out of her mouth and lifted her to a standing position. As he passionately kissed her, she could feel his penis rising against her abdomen. Without warning the doctor turned her against the brown wooden door and entered her from the rear. As she grasped at the door, he thrust his manhood slowly between her legs. As he entered her vagina, she moaned in pleasure while his manhood stretched her vagina to stiffness. He continued to move in and out like the top of an oil well as he sucked the left, back, and right side of her neck. He whispered sweet nothings in her ear until he told her to go to the bed.

As she walked naked to the bed, he followed her holding and slowly stroking his penis. As she lay on the bed, the doctor walked up to the bed and placed her left hand on his penis. He sucked through his teeth and watched as she clasped his manhood. He pushed her back on the bed and began kissing her mouth, her neck, her chest, her right nipple, her left nipple, the top of her stomach and finally her navel. He stuck his tongue in her navel and tasted her oils and skin. He moved down the center of her stomach with his tongue until he reached the straight red hair below her stomach. He kissed and sucked each side of her vagina and then slowly licked her clitoris. She moaned, tilted her head back on the pillow and gently pushed on the top of his shoulders. He proceeded to gently suck and lick her clitoris. He reached up and fondled each breast as he put one knee between her legs. As she felt his hairy thigh touch her inner thigh, she pulled his head up to her face. She kissed him as he inserted his penis slowly and deliberately into her moist vagina. He slowly and rhythmically thrust his penis in and out of her as she instinctively grabbed his gyrating buttocks. She moaned in pleasure as sweat dripped from his forehead onto her chest. He lifted her legs as he quickened the rhythm of his manhood thrusting in and out of her. He gently lowered his body on top of her as he pinned both of her hands above her head. He moaned and continued to thrust his scrotum against her genitalia.

His mouth filled with saliva as her vagina was filled with semen. They both moaned in ecstasy as her pulsating vagina clutched his throbbing penis. He gently kissed her lips as the pulsating muscles slowly pushed his softening penis out of her. He continued to kiss her as his leaking limp penis drained on her thigh. As he rolled to the window side of the bed, he began a low moan as Winnie thought that he had never been so aroused in the four years of their relationship. As she looked around the room for a clean rag to wipe her body, the doctor continued to moan and began slowly moving from side to side. When he turned over to face Winnie, his face was sweaty and pale. He reached for his left arm and continued to moan. Winnie put on her robe, and looked back at him. The doctor was still breathing in quick shallow breaths.

Winnie decided to go into the kitchen and search his medical bag. Perhaps a personal medication would explain his unusual behavior before and after making love. As she walked to the kitchen, he continued to moan. She hurriedly opened his medical bag that he left on the kitchen chair. She didn't see any medication that looked like it was his personal supply. She picked up the bag and rushed back to the bed. The doctor was tossing from side to side and moaning, "My back, oh, my back."

Winnie suddenly theorized that he was having muscle spasms in his back. She dropped the bag on the foot of the bed and walked to the side. She leaned over him and told him, "Turn over on your back." The doctor moaned and said, "I can't." She replied, "What do you mean, you can't?" He breathlessly stated, "I'm too weak." Winnie grabbed her forehead with both hands and said, "Think, think." She turned and ran into the kitchen. She picked up the tea pot from the stove and poured hot water into the small white basin. She walked into the pantry, gathered several clean rags, and placed them under her arm. She walked to the kitchen counter, picked up the small basin, and walked back into the bedroom. As she moved closer to the bed, she could see that the doctor was still sweaty and tossing his head from side to side. Winnie placed the basin on the floor and put the clean rags beside the pillow. She dipped a clean rag in the hot water and squeezed the excess water out. As she turned toward the doctor he said, "My chest, my chest feels so heavy." She placed the hot rag on his chest and looked out the window. The snow had completely covered the grass. With this bad weather, she did not think the doctor would be able to drive his carriage back home.

At that moment, Betty sat up in her crib and said, "Momma." Winnie turned and answered, “Yes, Betty.” Betty suddenly smiled her usual bright cheery smile and held out her tiny arms. Winnie smiled at her and lifted her out of the crib. She got her clean clothes from the top of the mirrored dresser. Since Betty was born, Winnie had always put the next day’s clothing on the top right side of the dresser.

She took Betty into the kitchen as the doctor’s moans began to quiet. She stood Betty in the chair as she filled her wash basin with warm water. She walked into the pantry and picked up a clean rag and a cake of soap. She washed and dressed Betty as she listened to the doctor moaning in the bedroom. As she left the kitchen, she gave Betty a plate with a biscuit, a piece of sausage, and a small cup of buttermilk. As she walked closer to the bed, the doctor was softly saying, “I’m so tired. I’m so tired.”

She took the wet rag from his chest and covered him with the sheet and quilt. Mary began to cry as she tucked the quilt under the doctor’s chin. She walked over to the cradle and lifted Mary out of the cradle. She turned and picked up a clean diaper on the back right side of the dresser. As she walked into the kitchen, Betty ate her food and watched as Winnie changed Mary’s diaper in the kitchen cradle. Carpenter had made a second cradle for Mary to lie in while Winnie worked in the kitchen. Winnie propped Mary up in the cradle and fed Mary buttermilk on the tip of a tablespoon. Betty ate and drank her buttermilk without wetting the front of her dress. Winnie lifted Mary out of the cradle and patted her back until she burped several times. She placed Mary back in the cradle and decided to pick up the clothes that she and Dr. Grunburg had thrown around the kitchen before they passionately made love. She took the clothes and shoes into the bedroom.

Even though all adults knew the routine when the doctor visited, she decided that she should dress him before William and Carpenter came in to eat breakfast. She pulled the quilt down to his waist and searched for his shirt amidst the pile of clothes on the side of the bed. She unbuttoned the crisp white dress shirt and began pushing the sleeve down his right arm. As she leaned across his body and pulled the shirt behind his head, she could hear his shallow quick breathing. Her stomach muscles tightened and her face turned blush pink as she realized the doctor was not well. She heard William and Carpenter come in the kitchen and drop firewood in the wood box. She could hear them talking to Betty and discussing who would take which parts of the meal out to the barn.

William and Carpenter always waited until the doctor left the house before coming in for breakfast, but the doctor stayed much longer than usual. They decided to get their food and take it out to the barn. Winnie pulled the quilt away from the doctor’s body and struggled to slide his boxers up his legs.

When she pulled the boxers above his knees, she realized that she needed to use the clean rags to wash his thighs and genitalia. She quickly dipped the rag in the room temperature water and cleaned his body. She tossed the rag on the floor and proceeded to pull the boxers over his thighs and buttocks. She called out, "William!, Carpenter!" They immediately became silent in the kitchen. Betty continued to talk about more milk as Winnie yelled, "Betty, you've had enough milk! Put that cup down!" The men remained silent and looked at each other. Winnie called again, "William!, Carpenter! Come in here!" She immediately heard their shoes scraping across the wooden floor. They both rushed through the bedroom door as she pulled the quilt up over the doctor's chest.

William asked, "What's goin' on?" as Carpenter asked, "Is everything alright?" Winnie took a deep breath and said, "Dr. Grunburg has taken ill. He is quite weak and he can't drive himself. I don't want to move him right now, but the snow is coming down pretty steady." Both men's eyes widened as they both said, "He can't stay here!" Winnie replied, "He is weak. He can't drive that carriage." Dr. Grunburg turned his head to Winnie and softly said, "Take me to John's." Winnie turned to both men and said, "He wants you to take him to Dr. Brennan's house." William asked, "Where is he?" Winnie told him, "Keep straight down the main highway and just outside of Saluda, on the left, sits a large white farm house. A large barn sits to the back right of the house. His wife and their helper James should be there. I know it's snowing, but I need you to wait another hour before you move him." Both men nodded their heads in agreement. As they turned to go back into the kitchen, Winnie told them, "Please watch Betty while you're eating." William continued walking and replied, "Alright." They knew that Winnie was letting them know that it was alright to stay in the house while the doctor was present. Winnie felt a sense of relief that the men could take him. She also felt a little ashamed that the man that she had just shared her body with, had to be removed in a state of illness because their relationship was forbidden. She quickly dismissed this thought because owning this thought would condemn her girls. She loved her girls and felt that they were a gift from God. She refused to let any person or thoughts convince her of anything differently. She decided to lift up the quilt and lay beside the doctor. As she turned and placed her head on his chest, he told her, "Thank you." His breathing seemed a little deeper and steady. Winnie said a short prayer and looked out the window as the snowflakes floated to the already covered ground.

She was interrupted from her thoughts when she heard the sound of the kitchen door closing. There was no time to wallow in thoughts of pity. She sat on the side of the bed, put on her slippers, and walked toward the kitchen. As she entered the room, Betty smiled and said, "Momma, I want baby." Winnie smiled, shook her head and told her, "Alright Betty. I'll get your baby." She turned and walked to Betty's crib. She picked up the cloth doll and quickly walked back to the kitchen. She gave Betty the doll and looked at Mary sleeping in the cradle. The men would probably have to spend the night at Dr. Brenan's house and return in the morning. They would need some food for the trip and she needed to make sure she had enough firewood and water until the men returned. She gathered the burlap food sack from the pantry and put several biscuits and salt cured ham inside. She placed the sack on the table.

William and Carpenter had walked the doctor's horse and carriage down to the barn. They put a blanket on the doctor's horse as they hitched Carpenter's wagon. The men had constructed a wooden frame over the back of the wagon. They tied a tan canvas over the frame. The doctor would be protected from the snow during the trip. Winnie decided to go to the bedroom and dress the doctor. As she walked closer to the bed, she could see that the doctor's forehead was dry. She picked up the pants and began dressing the doctor. As she fastened his belt buckle, William opened the kitchen door and put more firewood in the wood box. As she reached for the doctor's blazer, William entered the bedroom and asked, "Is he ready to go?" She replied, "Almost. I have to help him with his blazer and shoes. He should be ready shortly. Is the wagon ready?" He replied, "Yeah, Carpenter is bringing both buggies up to the door. He's going to drive the doctor in the covered wagon and I'll drive the doctor's carriage. We should get there before sundown. We'll try to stay in the helper's bunk overnight and come back in the morning. I just brought some firewood in and Carpenter is bringing more. I'll bring in a couple of buckets of water and you should be good until we get back." She replied, "Thank you." William continued, "Uh, we figured the best way to get him to the wagon is on a stretcher. We put some straw in the bottom of the wagon and covered the back with a canvas." Winnie interrupted, "Yes, I saw that canvas on the back of the wagon. Where did you get the stretcher?" William told her, "We made the stretcher with a wool blanket from the barn and two pine poles. It's the same kind of rig that we use if one of the smaller animals is hurt and can't walk." Winnie quickly turned her head and looked up at William. He stuttered, raised both hands with palms facing Winnie and said, "Now wait, now wait, the blanket is clean. Everything's alright." She did not respond as she slowly smiled and he reciprocated. The kitchen door closed and Carpenter placed a load of firewood in the wood box. William turned and asked, "Are you ready?" Carpenter replied, "Yeah."

Both men walked out to the wagon to get the poles and blanket. They brought the items into the bedroom and wrapped the blanket around the pine poles on the foot of the bed. Winnie got the blue quilt from the closet and handed it to William. Both men positioned the quilt under the doctor. They lifted the doctor onto the stretcher as Winnie searched for a second quilt. She pulled the green quilt from the top shelf of the closet and placed it on top of the blue quilt. She neatly tucked the doctor beneath the two quilts. She announced, “He’s all ready to go.” as she patted him on the right leg. He smiled and told her, “Thank you.” As William and Carpenter lifted the stretcher from the foot of the bed, she placed his hat on his head and the black medical bag on his legs. Winnie opened the bedroom door wider and walked to the kitchen door. She held the door open as they carefully stepped onto the snowy steps. Winnie thought of the burlap sack on the table and quickly walked to the table, picked it up and called to the men, “Don’t forget your food!” As Carpenter positioned the doctor in the back of the wagon, William trotted back to the kitchen door and took the burlap sack from Winnie’s hand. She told him, “Be careful.” He replied, “We will!” as he trotted back to the wagon.

Winnie closed the door, clutched the collar of her robe, and walked toward Betty. She was standing beside the kitchen chair with her head lying on the seat of the chair. Winnie picked Betty up and pressed her head against her chest. Betty snuggled against her mother’s chest and clutched the collar of her robe. Winnie thought of how blessed she was to have two beautiful daughters.

Chapter 10

Several months had passed since the doctor suffered his illness. He had begun traveling to see patients again, but his health was diminished. During his recovery, Winnie attended to all of the female patients in the northern end of the county. Occasionally, she gave medical attention to their spouses and children. Dr. Brennan attended to the patients in the Saluda and Harmony Village areas.

Winnie awakened on a cool mid April morning to the sound of birds chirping and roosters crowing. As she sat on the side of the bed and put on her robe, she felt more tired than usual. She pushed her feet into her slippers and looked at each of the girls. They slept quietly as she walked into the kitchen. She started the coffee and took the bowl out of the cupboard. She went into the pantry to get some cornmeal for the cornbread. As the odor of the ham spread throughout the kitchen, she suddenly felt sick to her stomach. As she swallowed and tried to stop her stomach muscles from convulsing, she realized that she had not had a menstrual cycle since January. Instead of drinking a cup of coffee, she decided to drink a cup of tea with ginger. In her previous pregnancies, a cup of tea with ginger always calmed her stomach. As she looked in the cupboard for the can of tea, she realized that the doctor had not been able to visit since his illness. As she sipped the cup of tea, she looked out the kitchen window at little Fannie's grave. The pain of her death often seemed as piercing to her soul as it was two years ago. As in the previous three pregnancies, Winnie's stomach began to calm as she sipped the ginger tea. She chuckled and shed tears at the same time. At that moment, Winnie realized that the doctor's emotional support was a very important component of her psychological welfare. Would he be able to visit and see this child? Would this child know his face? Would this child have blue eyes like the doctor? Would they be able to share medical experiences? Would they be able to share intimate moments again?

Winnie understood that her living arrangement was not that of a normal household, but she had grown to accept it. Now, she realized that she was unable to maintain the relationship as an arrangement. She had allowed herself to become emotionally attached to the father of her children. He had become her teacher, her lover, and her friend. The thought of losing stimulating medical discussions was crushing. Since she was a child, she always enjoyed conversations with her father about nature, the farm, and life. Those discussions were mentally stimulating. After entering into the arrangement, Dr. Grunburg had become the person who participated in mentally stimulating discussions. He also became the person with whom she shared sexually stimulating experiences. She knew that she had to remain strong for her two girls. If the doctor did not recover fully, she would still have to take care of her children. She continued to sip her tea and prepare breakfast. As she pulled the cornbread out of the oven, thc sound of a horse drawn carriage caught her attention. She placed the pan of bread on top of the stove and looked out the kitchen window. She thought that Martha might be going to town today. She was shocked to see Dr. Grunburg climbing down from the carriage. Her face turned blush pink as she prepared a plate for him. He slowly opened the kitchen door and stepped inside. He took off his hat and slowly walked toward Winnie. She could see that he had lost weight and his hairline seemed to have more gray hairs. He walked slowly with his head down and placed his hat and medical bag on the table. Winnie waited anxiously in front of the stove as he held his arms out for her to give him a hug. She walked to him and wrapped her arms around his waist. He wrapped his arms around her shoulders as he kissed her vibrant red hair and whispered, "Thank you." They both wept in gratitude that they were able to share another hug.

She stepped back and asked, "How are you feeling?" She wiped her tears as he removed his glasses and wiped his tears. He placed his glasses on the table and told her that he was feeling better, but he was not the man that he used to be. She interrupted and said, "You look a little thin, but I'm sure you will be fine." He told her, "No, Winnie. I'm not the same. I'm not sure that I will be able to function as I used to. At this point, I am unable to hold an erection. I….." She put her left forefinger over his lips and placed his left hand on her abdomen. She said, "I am carrying your child. I am certain. I have not had my menstrual cycle since January." He grabbed Winnie's buttocks and pulled her close to his groin. She could feel his manhood harden and then slowly soften. She told him, "Why don't you eat something?" He told her, "Let me examine you and then I'll eat. Are the girls alright?" She answered, "Yes, they're fine."

He grabbed his glasses and medical bag from the table and followed her into the bedroom. As Winnie undressed, he smiled and looked at both girls sleeping. He told her, "Winnie, you have given me a life that I never thought

I could have. I don't know what will happen in the near future, but I do want to thank you for everything. My wife wants me to give up half of my practice, but I'm going to hold on as long as possible. I think you will be able to handle most of the maternity cases in the northern part of the county. We'll have to adjust some things." Winnie interrupted, "Alright, that's enough business for now. Let's see if I'm right."

The doctor took his stethoscope out of the bag and listened to Winnie's heart, chest, and abdomen. He examined her breast, tapped both sides of her upper abdomen, and then tapped both sides of her lower abdomen. He slowly took his stethoscope off and placed it in the bag. He leaned over and kissed Winnie on her abdomen and said, "Three's a charm." He picked up his medical bag and walked into the kitchen. He placed the bag on the table and turned to face the bedroom door. As Winnie stepped into the kitchen, he grabbed her by the waist with his left hand.

He pulled her so quickly that she released a quick high pitched grunt. He pulled her buttocks toward his groin as his entire body quivered. He repeatedly kissed her red hair and neck. While breathing heavily, he slid his hands up to her face and aggressively kissed her lips, cheeks, and neck. He turned and leaned his back against the wall as he grabbed her buttocks and pressed her pelvis against his manhood. His body continued to quiver as he held her buttocks and sucked her collar bone. He began to moan as if he was having an organism, but Winnie never felt his manhood rise. His heavy breathing slowly subsided and his quivering calmed. He whispered, "I'm sorry. I'm sorry." Winnie realized that her intimate moments with the doctor may have ended. She told him, "It's alright. Come on over and have a seat. Eat some breakfast." She led him by the hand and he sat down at the table. She placed his plate in front of him and poured his coffee. She prepared her plate and poured a cup of ginger tea. She asked which patients he was going to visit and she filled him in on the progress of his maternity patients while he was out sick. The doctor finished his meal and stood up to gather his hat and bag. He told her that he would probably come every two weeks until he got stronger. He stood, adjusted his vest, and walked toward Winnie. They embraced in front of the stove and he quietly turned to leave. Winnie told him, "Next time, could you take off your vest?" They both laughed as he replied, "Alright, next time." The doctor opened the door and stepped out of the kitchen. Winnie leaned against the counter in an effort to gather her composure. She realized that her life had changed. The doctor was about fifteen years older, but she never expected his health to deteriorate at such an early age.

Several months later, Winnie awakened on a late July sultry morning. She sat on the side of the bed and gazed at her beautiful girls. Winnie slid her feet into her slippers and put on her robe. As she stood and walked into the kitchen, she knew that all cooking should be done as early as possible today. The moisture was very thick in the air at a very early hour. She made the coffee and walked into the pantry to get the cornmeal for the cornbread. The sound of a horse drawn wagon seemed to echo through the kitchen, but the sun had just risen. Visitors did not come to visit this early in the morning. As she placed the cornmeal on the counter, she decided to look out the kitchen window to verify that no one was visiting before she had dressed for the day. Much to her surprise, there was a horse drawn wagon in the back yard. As she looked out the window, there appeared to be a young White couple lifting two babies from the back of the wagon. Winnie decided to rush into the bedroom and put on a dress. As she walked back through the kitchen doorway, the couple was standing at the kitchen door. The male wore a broad straw farmer's hat and held a toddler wearing a yellow bonnet. The woman held a baby who wore a yellow and white bonnet. As Winnie approached the door, the man took his hat off. As he looked up to knock on the door, Winnie screamed, "Oh my Lord! Thornton! Is that you?" She quickly opened the door and hugged her younger brother. He softly said, "Winnie" with a big smile. As Winnie wept, she said, "Thornton, I'm so happy to see you. I have missed you. Are you alright? Let me look at you." She stood back and then kissed him on the cheek."This has to be Annie. She looks like Daddy. She has his light brown eyes." Winnie turned to face the woman and baby. She sobbed and said, "Betty, thank you for coming. You look good. Oh, this must be Marie. Betty, she is beautiful!" Winnie hugged and kissed Betty while reaching for Marie. As Winnie lifted her niece into the air, she could see her glistening hazel eyes. Winnie hugged the baby and turned to Thornton. She lightly hit him on his right arm and said, "She has your old hazel eyes." Thornton told her, "Yes, she's beautiful just like her father." The three adults laughed as Marie snuggled on her aunt's chest.

Winnie told them, "Come in out of the sticky air." Betty said, "Yeah, we left home early because Thornton said it was going to be stuffy today." Winnie asked, "You listen to this man? We're going to have to talk about that." All three adults laughed. Betty asked, "Where are the babies?" Winnie told her, "Come on in the bedroom." Betty walked to the crib and picked up little Betty and said, "Winnie, she is beautiful! Oh, there you are. Open your eyes and come to Aunt Betty, Betty." Both women laughed. Betty said, "Look at her blinking. She doesn't know who this stranger is. Oh, Winnie. She sees you holding Marie. Do you think she'll be alright?" Winnie answered, "Oh yeah, Betty is the best baby ever. She is always happy. They both are good babies." As Betty lifted little Betty out of the crib, she asked, "When is the baby suppose to come?" Winnie told her, "In a couple of months, another September baby."

Winnie asked, "Is Betty dry?" Her sister-in-law told her, "Yes, she's dry. She's a big girl." Little Betty started to smile as her mother kissed her on the forehead. Winnie handed her clothes to Betty and walked to Mary's cradle. Mary was frowning and putting her fist in her mouth. Betty dressed her niece and Winnie walked over to the dresser and picked up Mary's clothes. Betty walked into the kitchen and told Thornton, "Thornton look. Little Betty has brown eyes just like your father." Thornton looked at little Betty and said, "Winnie, she is a pretty little girl. She must look like her father." All three adults laughed and Winnie yelled, "Betty, hit him for me!" Betty handed Thornton his niece. He sat at the table and talked to Betty and Annie about their dresses, socks, and shoes. Betty came into the bedroom and announced, "I want to wake little Mary. Let me see you pretty girl." She reached into the cradle and lifted Mary out. Mary frowned, opened her right eye, and then her left. Betty kissed her on both cheeks and said, "Winnie, her eyes are blue! You didn't tell me! They both chuckled as Winnie said, "Yeah, she has blue eyes just like her father." Betty sat on the bed and began changing her diaper. Winnie paced the floor and hugged and kissed Marie's forehead. Both women took care of the other's baby with special attention. They both knew that visits could and would most likely be few and far between. Betty finished dressing Mary and they walked into the kitchen. Little Betty looked at her mother and said, "Momma, I want my baby." Winnie told her, "Betty, go get your baby from the crib." Betty slid down out of her uncle's lap and walked into the bedroom. Winnie handed Marie to her mother. She served breakfast to everyone. Betty came back into the kitchen and Thornton said the blessing over the food.

As they ate breakfast, Thornton seemed relaxed and Betty seemed happy. Thornton explained that he was expanding the crop area and he had three men helping. Winnie said, "I haven't seen you in town. When do you go? I normally go on Saturdays with Tom and Martha." Betty said, "Thornton usually goes to town during the week. I go sometimes to buy fabric, but most of the time, he does the shopping." Thornton added, "Yeah, I've been trying to get Betty to go with me, but she doesn't like to travel a lot." Betty told Winnie, "I'll take the girls into the bedroom." As she stood up, William and Carpenter came through the kitchen door. Winnie introduced everyone and served breakfast for William and Carpenter. Winnie told the men that she would leave them to talk and walked into the bedroom with Betty and the girls.

As Winnie closed the door, she asked Betty, "So, how is life with my younger brother?" Betty smiled and answered, "He is a kind man. We have been married for ten years and it seems like two. When we first got married, I was a little afraid at night." Winnie took Marie from her and asked, "Why? What happened?" Betty continued, "Well, at night Thornton would start sweating and talking like he had a fever. After about a year, I just told him that I felt afraid when he talked out of his head. He told me to wake him up, but sometimes he was moving his arms and I didn't feel comfortable shaking him. Finally, he gave me a cow bell to keep beside the bed. Whenever he started sweating and talking out of his head, I would ring the bell. At first, I think I lost more sleep than he did. After about two months, I would ring the bell and he would wake up. Sometimes, he would just ask me to hold him. He would cry himself back to sleep and then in a couple of days it would start all over again. If he got really tired, the nightmares would be closer together. I was going over to my mother's house every day and crying on her shoulder. After a while, she started coming to our farm and talking to me during the day. She helped with meals and making curtains. She even helped me make a sleep shirt for Thornton. I thought maybe wearing something soft would help." Winnie interrupted and asked, "Did it help?" Betty continued, "Well, I think it did after about a year. My mother told me that I couldn't get pregnant because I was so worried about him. After a while, I knew that Thornton would never do anything to hurt me or any living thing. I started to relax more. My father convinced Thornton to hire some helpers so he wouldn't be so tired. Annie was born in January of 1874. Last year, we had Marie. I know Thornton really wanted boys to help on the farm, but God wanted us to have two girls anyway. I told him, we'll have more children." Winnie asked, "Is he still having the nightmares about the war?" Betty continued, "Well, he does every now and then, but I can shake him, kiss him, or hug him and he calms down. I haven't used the bell for about a year. Being on the farm is really good for him. Sometimes, in the middle of the day, he will come to the house to give all three of us a hug and kiss. Now, tell me about this doctor."

Winnie sighed and said, "Well, he treats me with respect. He is gentle with the girls, and he pays for this place. It's not what I would have chosen, but I can live with the situation. My life is more secure than most women. But that's enough about me. I am so happy that you were able to help Thornton get over the war. Ever since we were kids, Thornton has always been kind. I knew my little brother would be a good husband and father just like Daddy."

At that moment, Thornton yelled, "Betty and Winnie, I'm going out to the barn with Carpenter and William!" They both answered, "Alright!" Winnie told Betty that she was going to start on lunch and dinner. Betty said, "Alright, I'll bring the other cradle into the kitchen and I'll help you." The two women took the children into the kitchen and prepared the meals.

Thornton Jr. and Betty stayed with Winnie for three days. He trusted the farm helpers and Betty's parents promised to check on the farm while they were away. Winnie felt better about her parent's welfare also. Betty shared her and Thornton Jr.'s plan of bringing Thornton Sr. and Mary to live with them if they ever reached that point in life, where they had difficulty caring for themselves. They had the same plan for Betty's parents. Betty expressed her appreciation to Winnie for listening to Thornton's war stories before they were married. In turn, Winnie thanked Betty for being patient, kind, and loving with her younger brother. Both women realized that their lives were less stressful than most people of color. Their parents had been allowed certain privileges and freedoms because one parent was White. The White parent provided housing, and food, and was allowed to travel throughout surrounding counties. Each child who carried the white or almond complexion received the same privileges. Thornton Jr., Sarah, and Winnie never spoke about these facts, but they observed the treatment that their younger siblings received. Edward and Margaret were not allowed to travel and shop freely. They were always stopped and asked to account for their presence and travel intentions. Thornton Jr., Sarah, and Winnie traveled without inquiries. Betty also traveled without harassment.

On a cool mid September morning, Winnie awakened and started her morning routine. The girls were asleep and Carpenter had started a fire in the kitchen stove. As she walked through the kitchen doorway, she could tell that coffee was needed. She felt unusually tired. She started the coffee and went into the pantry to get a cup of flour for the biscuits. The ham was cooking as she reached for her apron hanging beside the cupboard. She lifted the fabric off the hook and tied the light blue apron above her abdomen. She realized that she needed to get more butter from the well.

Her mother showed her how to store butter when she was a little girl. During the warmer months, her mother placed the butter in a small metal bucket that her father made. He punched holes in the bottom of the bucket so that water would drain out. He tied two small ropes on the handle of the bucket and tied the other end to a board that was nailed across the top of the well. The butter was placed in the bucket and lowered about eight to ten feet under water. During the colder months, the butter was stored in a barrel on the stoop of the kitchen door.

Winnie grabbed a spoon and a small bowl from the cupboard and she walked to the kitchen door. When she stepped onto the first step, the cool mid September air brushed her face. She walked quickly to the well. About three feet in front of the well, a clear warm fluid gushed onto her feet. The warm liquid created a mist in the cool air. She continued walking to the well and pulled up the butter. She dipped out a bowl of butter and lowered the bucket back into the well. While she was lowering the bucket, she saw Carpenter come out of the barn door. She yelled, "The baby is coming!" Carpenter answered, "Alright!" As Winnie turned to walk back to the kitchen door, the once warm fluid chilled her legs and feet. She opened the door and walked to the stove. She pushed the wet slippers beside the stove to dry. Winnie put the bowl on the counter and walked into the pantry. She picked up her black medical bag and several clean rags. She placed some of the rags between her legs and walked into the bedroom. The girls were still asleep when she placed the items on the bed and walked back into the kitchen. Winnie made the biscuits and placed them in the oven. As she scrambled the eggs, Carpenter opened the door and put a load of firewood in the wood box. He said, "William is on his way to Tom and Martha's. I'll get more water after breakfast." Winnie answered, "Thank you." That should take care of everything." She took the biscuits out of the oven and served Carpenter's plate. After Carpenter said the blessing over the food, Winnie told him that she was going to lie down until Martha arrived. She got two quilts from the closet and placed them on the bed. She moved the wicker chair next to the bed and put the quilts behind her pillows. Winnie placed the medical bag on the chair and changed the rags between her legs. She put on a clean gown and finally relaxed on her pillows.

Martha helped deliver Winnie's third baby. She had straight brown hair and light brown eyes. The delivery was uneventful and Winnie named her Nanny. Dr. Grunburg examined them on his next visit and both patients passed the physical examination. The doctor's health remained the same, but the United States economy showed signs of recovery.

Chapter 11

The National Bureau of Economic Research reported that the recession of October 1873 ended in March 1879. Although the United States economy was improving, much of the South's market share around the world was taken over by international markets. Black and White sharecroppers had to compete with low priced goods from India, Egypt, and Brazil. This competition lasted for several generations. This challenge forced the South to adjust its economic priorities. For the first time, the South was able to increase its population, manufacturing and urban growth at the same rate as the North. The railroad industry expanded westward, coal mining increased, financial entities networked, and farms began producing more crops. Investors bought stock in factories, international mines, and railroads. For the first time, companies in the United States began to dominate the Latin American economies.

Winnie and Carpenter stayed at the farm in Jamaica, Middlesex County, Virginia for ten years with no major challenges. By 1882, the doctor's health had not improved. Five years after his illness, he had difficulty meeting all of his financial obligations. He asked Winnie to help with maternity patients, but his poor health would not allow him to resume his frequent travel to the northern part of the county. Since the economy was recovering, patients had the money to pay for services; still Dr. Grunburg's health would not allow him to meet his patient's demands.

On a cool mid May morning, Winnie was cleaning the breakfast dishes and the girls were playing in the upstairs bedroom. She heard a horse drawn carriage come into the back yard. She assumed it was Tom and Martha coming to pay a visit. After a while, no one opened the kitchen door or yelled for her to come outside. She decided to look out the kitchen window to see who was driving the wagon. Much to her surprise, three White men were walking down to the barn and visually surveying the property. As they approached the barn, Carpenter and William opened the barn door and walked out of the barn. The man at the front of the group seemed to be asking questions. As

William and Carpenter answered the questions, the second man appeared to write information in a ledger or book. The third man continued to visually survey the property. After a lengthy discussion, the men turned and walked back toward the wagon. As they approached the wagon, Winnie could see that the man in the front was older and the other two men were younger. The younger men appeared to be close to her age. When the three men reached the wagon, they stopped and talked.

The man who walked at the back of the group, suddenly turned and walked toward the house. The younger man called to him and he turned and replied, "I'll be just a few minutes!" The man knocked on the door and waited with both hands in the pockets of a gray wool trench coat.

Winnie cautiously walked toward the kitchen door. She did not recognize the man and she wondered why he wanted to speak with her. He had heard the answers to the questions that were asked of Carpenter and William. He had to know that a female would be in the house. What could he want? As she approached the door, she could see that he had sandy brown hair, a clean shaven narrow face, a long straight narrow nose, and radiant blue eyes. As she opened the door, he slowly developed a cunning, alluring smile. Winnie suddenly felt vulnerable as they made eye contact. She instinctively clutched the collar of her green cotton dress as he visually scanned her body from head to toe. She did not speak and he said, "Y-e-s, I saw you looking out of the window. You're even more delightful close up. What's your name?" Winnie softly said, "Winnie." He replied, "Winnie, I like the way that sounds. Well, Winnie I think I'll be back." He turned to walk away and then quickly turned back to face Winnie. He stretched his left hand forward in a gesture to shake hands. Winnie slowly stretched her left hand forward and touched his hand as she clutched her collar with her right hand. As their hands touched, he slid his fingers up the back side of her hand and just over her wrist. He continued smiling and said, "Oh y-e-a-h. You do have beautiful soft skin. My name is Cyrus. Have a good day now." He turned away from the door and jogged back to the two men conversing at the wagon. She slowly closed the door and walked back to the kitchen counter. As she looked out the window, Cyrus smiled and looked at her as the younger man drove the wagon out of the yard.

Winnie prepared lunch for the girls. She climbed the stairs to see what they were doing in the upstairs bedroom. The girls slept and played in the upstairs bedroom every day. William stopped sleeping at the house about three months ago. He decided to live with Bett and his son. His parents wanted him to marry Bett, but he hadn't committed to marriage.

As Winnie entered the bedroom, the girls were pretending to be mothers. Betty had several dolls sitting on the floor, in chairs, and on the bed. Blankets and wooden spoons were spread on the floor. The tea set was on the floor and the books were on the bed. Winnie had taught the girls to read and write. She also taught them the value of books and education. The chalk and slate board were on the floor. Winnie announced, "Girls, lunch is ready! Thank you for making up your beds. Nanny, get the brush. Let me brush your hair. Betty, why didn't you tell Nanny to brush her hair? Mary, put your shoes on. Now, that looks better. Nanny, put this brush on the dresser and go on down to eat." As the girls giggled and talked, Winnie sat on the double bed. She took in a deep breath and blocked the thoughts of Cyrus' cunning smile. The scraping of the chairs across the kitchen floor cleared her thoughts.

Winnie went down to the kitchen and prepared for dinner as the girls talked and ate lunch. As the girls finished lunch, Winnie began to think about their safety. The visit from Cyrus and the other two men caused her to advise the girls about visitors. She told them, "Girls, if someone comes to the house, I want you to stay in your room or if you're in the barn, stay in the barn. Do not come out to greet visitors unless I call for you. Do you understand?" All three girls replied, "Yes, momma." Winnie smiled and replied, "Now, give me a hug and get on upstairs and practice your letters." She hugged each of them and began to wash their dishes. She knew the men would be coming in for lunch soon.

Carpenter and William came in to eat lunch. As they walked toward the kitchen table, Winnie prepared their plates. She asked, "Who were those men who were asking questions this morning?" Do you know them?" Both men answered, "No, we don't know them." Winnie replied, "Well, why did they come here? What questions did they have? What did they want to know?" Carpenter replied, "Well, the older man was sayin' somethin' about Dr. Grunburg not being able to pay somethin' and they had the land and I don't know all what else they were saying and….." William interrupted, "It seems like Dr. Grunburg was rentin' the land from the old guy. U-h, the younger guy, who was takin' notes, said that we would be able to stay here. The other guy didn't say anything. He just smiled and looked around. The guy takin' notes wanted to know who lived here and everybody's name. He wanted to know how much grain we took to the mill. The funny thing about it, he asked if you had four little girls before I told him you had three. He kind uh acted like he already knew who lived here. I don't know….." Winnie anxiously interrupted, "Did he tell you his name?" As her face turned blush pink, he replied, "Yeah, he said it was B, Buck, or somethin' that started with uh "b". I can't seem to remember. Carpenter, do you remember what that old guy said his name was?" Carpenter answered, "N-a-u-g-h, I don't remember what he said his name was. I do think you right. It started with uh "b", but I don't know what it was. From the way they was talkin', Dr. Grunburg will know 'em." Winnie sighed as the men began talking about fixing the fence near the back property line. She realized that William and Carpenter really didn't want to discuss the matter. Winnie began to think about how these men knew Dr. Grunburg and why he didn't tell her that they would be paying a visit. She also felt relieved that she had warned the girls about greeting visitors.

A few days later, Dr. Grunburg stopped his carriage in the back yard. He brought his carriage blanket into the house. As he placed his items on the kitchen chair, he asked, "Is everybody alright?" He walked toward Winnie and held his arms out as they embraced in front of the stove. He asked, "Are you alright? You seem a little tense." She stood back and answered, "Yes, I'm alright. We just had a few unexpected visitors a few days ago." As he sat down at the table, he said, "Oh yeah. Who were they?" As Winnie fixed the plates, she said, "I don't know. I was hoping you could tell me who they were. William and Carpenter said their last name started with a "b" and they owned this property?" She handed the doctor his plate and a glass of water. As she took her plate and glass to the other end of the table, she asked, "Why did they come here? What's going on?"

The doctor wiped his mouth with the tan cloth napkin and said, "Well, Thaddeus owns this property and several others. I was able to provide this place for you because he gave me a special rate on the rent. I'm his family doctor and he allowed me to pay when it was convenient. Sometimes I deducted medical services from the rental fee. His wife and my wife attend many of the same social functions. I've been thinking about this for some time. I can no longer pay for this place without my wife noticing the missing funds. This was a business decision that had to be made." As he took another mouth full of food, Winnie realized that she and her girls were a "business decision". As she fought back the tears of hurt, pain, disappointment, shame, and reality, she managed to sip some water. This was the painful and shameful aspect of the arrangement. This was the moment of reckoning that defined her as property. This was the moment of truth that reminded her that she should not have become emotionally involved with a married man, especially with a White man. This was the moment of shame that reminded her that she was not in control of her life. Her meal suddenly tasted like butcher's paper as she realized that the doctor would not and could not protect her from the property owner's decisions.

She also realized that Cyrus would definitely be coming back to visit. She suddenly understood his cunning smile. He knew that the doctor could no longer pay for the property. She wondered if her girls would be safe with Cyrus. The thought of sending her girls to Martha's house for safety was painful, but may have to be considered. Maybe a trip to Thornton Jr.'s farm could be arranged for them. Her thoughts were abruptly interrupted by the doctor saying, "Winnie! Winnie! Winnie! Are you alright?" Winnie picked up the glass and slowly drank the cool water. After placing the glass back on the table, the desire to eat suddenly left. She decided to focus on the business of nursing. She started cleaning the dishes and asked, "Who are you visiting today? Are there any new maternity patients?" Dr. Grunburg said, "There are three more maternity patients. I'll give you their location. Carpenter should be able to find the houses easily. And, how are the girls?" Winnie emotionlessly replied, "The girls are fine. They're just fine." The doctor finished his meal and wiped his mouth. As he gathered his hat and coat, the doctor stopped and looked at Winnie. She was cleaning the dishes and did not bother to look at him. He realized that she was distracted, preoccupied, and maybe even upset. He slowly placed his hat back on the chair and walked over to her. She continued to clean the dishes without turning to say goodbye. The doctor walked up behind Winnie and slowly grabbed her around the waist. He pulled her buttocks tightly to his pelvic area. He slowly kissed the left side of her neck, the back of her neck, and the right side of her neck. She slowly began to sob and brace her knees against the counter cabinets. He whispered, "It will be alright. It will be alright." She did not answer as she slowly regained her composure. She wiped her eyes with her apron and turned to face him. She cleared her throat as she patted the lapel of his coat. Winnie raised the pitch of her voice and told him, "You need to leave. I'll be alright. Everything will work out." The doctor gently kissed her forehead and walked back to gather his items. As he walked toward the kitchen door, Winnie announced, "Next time, I may have a goose prepared." The doctor smiled and replied, "Alright, and don't worry.....you'll have a place to stay. Don't worry about that." As he opened the door and stepped out into the warm May air, she fell back into the kitchen chair. She quietly sobbed as she realized that from now on, things really would be different. The security that she once felt had been shattered. No longer could she depend on the doctor to take care of life's challenges. She realized that she had allowed herself to be consumed by the arrangement. The future had to be different. Maybe she would have to spend more time at Martha's church. Well, maybe that wasn't a good idea, but she had to make more friends in the Black community. Nursing was not all that mattered in life. She realized that she had let her relationship with the doctor become the majority of her social life. The arrangement that once provided strength and security seemed to have ultimately weakened her. She did not recall these thoughts of doubt as a child. She felt that the only way to save herself was to make some changes. She could not allow the arrangement to make her a victim. She took a deep breath and began preparing lunch for William and Carpenter.

The men came in for lunch in their usual boisterous manner. Without realizing it, Winnie appeared solemn. William, who is always ready to face a challenge, looked at Carpenter and then at Winnie. He asked her, "Are you alright? You seem kinda' down. Did the doctor tell you something? Is it something we should know?" Winnie placed the plates before the men and did not say a word. They looked at each other and William slowly shook his head.

William began eating his food and then firmly placed his fork on the plate. Carpenter and Winnie stiffened their backs as the sound of the clanking porcelain rang throughout the kitchen. William sat back in his chair and placed his right arm over the back of the chair. He sucked through his teeth as he pulled a thin piece of straw from his shirt pocket. He poked between his teeth and announced, "Winnie, sit down. Carpenter told me to keep my mouth shut, but I'm goin' to say it." Winnie turned and sat in the kitchen chair. Her face was blush pink. She knew that William was going to talk about all of the disadvantages of an arrangement. She knew that he would talk about how she had not treated his brother fairly. He had asked several months earlier if she ever had any feelings for Carpenter. She had told him that her relationship with Carpenter was not as husband and wife and it never would be that way. She told him that Carpenter had Belle so he wasn't alone. She was jolted from her thoughts by William's stern voice, "Winnie! Winnie! You need to get over it! That doctor has to do what he has to do. He can't pay for this place and these new guys are gonna' take over. I saw that guy that was walking at the back of the group down at the mill. And….." Winnie interrupted, "What did you say?! Did you say you saw one of them at the mill?"

William sucked between his teeth and said, "Yeah, the one who looked all around, but didn't say nothin'. He made sure he came up to us. He wanted us to see him. He was telling everybody what to do. I think he runs the mill or owns the mill. He asked us how things were going on the farm. He was questioning us about which days we came to the mill, which days we went into town, which days we tended to the fields. It was almost as if he wanted to find out when we wouldn't be around. I told Carpenter, the doctor better watch out. That new young man is tryin' to get to know you. He wants to know where we are so he can be with you. Carpenter told me to stay out of it, but you always treated me nice. You took care of that White man that stopped us after Bett had the baby. You never said nothin' when Carpenter got cut and I moved in. You alright. You let me know if that young man bothers you." Winnie interrupted, "William, I'll be alright. I don't want you getting yourself into trouble. You need to help Bett raise that baby. And how is he doing? Does he still look like you?" William smiled and moved the thin straw around in his mouth and said, "Y-e-a-h, he looks just like me. Momma says he looks like I spit him out. You know, you the only one that helped Bett have a baby that lived. Bett thinks you walk on water. She always gettin' me up early to come over here to help Carpenter. She say she don't want you doin' no farm work, just nurse work." Winnie laughed and said, "Well, you tell Bett I appreciate the help. Listen, I appreciate everything that you and Carpenter do for me and the girls. I know I can count on you two and you two should know you can count on me. We'll be alright. Everybody knows we have the best run farm in northern Middlesex County." All three adults laughed and Winnie continued to prepare dinner.

Chapter 12

A couple of days later, Winnie decided to bake several deep dish apple pies. She remembered the warm cozy feeling of sitting on the stone fireplace mantel eating hot apple pie with Sarah and Thornton Jr. As a child, her father had showed her how to store apples for the year. She, Sarah, and Thornton Jr. gathered apples each spring. They gathered as many apples from the tree and ground as possible. Her father brought old newspapers back from his trips to town and other farms. He instructed them to wrap each apple in newsprint. They placed the fully wrapped apples in a wooden box. The box was always located in a dark section of the barn. Her father often dug the floor of the barn about two feet deep. Putting the box down in the ground allowed the apples to stay cool regardless of the air temperature. The box was then covered with canvas, metal, or animal skins. The apples did not rot and this allowed her mother to cook apples during the cold months. She wanted her girls to carry on the family tradition of cooking and baking delicious food all year. Meal time was always a celebration in the Tate home. She did not have a fireplace, but she wanted her girls to cherish the delectable aromas, savory flavors, and the luscious taste of homemade dishes and home baked deserts. She wanted them to experience the felicitous atmosphere of eating and sharing with family.

While the meat and vegetables were cooking, Winnie cut and sliced the apples. She always made at least one pie with the skin still on the apple slice. Suddenly, the sound of a horse drawn wagon caught her attention. As she looked out the window, Tom and Martha were stepping down from the wagon seat. Martha had several pieces of fabric in her hands. Winnie smiled as she thought about how Martha always tried to help her. She helped her make extra money by sewing garments for women in the church, she took her girls to Sunday school and other church events, and she convinced Tom to take her to Tappahannock on shopping trips. Martha was like a mother and sister to her. Martha knocked on the door and turned the knob as she yelled, "Coming in!" Martha and Tom came in and sat in the kitchen chairs. Martha asked, "Where are my girls?" Winnie smiled and said, "They're upstairs playing. I had to have a talk with them about not greeting visitors." Martha interrupted, "What are you talking about?" Winnie continued to explain that a few days earlier three men came to visit the farm. They looked around the property and asked William and Carpenter questions. At that moment, Tom stood up and said, "I'm goin' to the barn. I'll let you two talk." As he walked toward the kitchen door, Martha asked, "Did something happen? What are you talking about? Do you need the girls to come and stay with us for a while? Winnie, what are you talking about?" Winnie continued, "Well, it seems that Dr. Grunburg can't afford to pay the rent on this place anymore. Martha interrupted, "You don't say." Winnie explained, "Yes, since his illness, the doctor has not been himself." Martha said, "Yeah, you told me he can't perform, but what is he doin' with the money? How he goin' just let this place go and you got these three girls and ….." Winnie interrupted, "Martha, he is not my husband. This is the bad part about the arrangement. He said he can't continue paying the rent without his wife finding out about the missing money." Martha started pacing the floor and said, "Uh huh. I knew he would do this. I told Tom….." Winnie interrupted, "Martha, calm down. We ….." Martha interrupted, "And what about the three men? Who are they? You need to let me take the girls with me for a few weeks. I ….." Winnie said, "Martha, I was going to ask you if the girls might be able to stay with you for a few days. The three men that came to look at the farm own the property. Dr. Grunburg knows them, but two of the men were younger than I am. Betty is just ten years old and I don't want anything to happen to her because I didn't have my eyes and ears open." Martha said, "Alright. Winnie, you know I love the girls like I gave birth to them. With everything that's going on right now, I think I should take them to the house with me until you find out a little more about these new owners. I don't like the sound of things. If you have to pack up and move, the girls will already be at my house. Please don't fight me on this. I have a bad feeling about this whole situation. I can't believe that after ten years, he just goin' let you and the girls be put off the farm with….." Winnie interrupted, "Martha, you're getting all worked up and there's really nothing we can do about the situation. I would like for you to take the girls with you until I can figure out how these new owners are going to run things. I'll pack some food to go with them today and then I'll have William bring more food over later. Betty is almost ten and she can help with Mary and Nanny." Martha answered, "Winnie, you pack some food and I'm goin' upstairs to get some clothes together. The girls will have fun at the church. God works everything out in mysterious ways." As she climbed the stairs, Martha announced grumpily, "I told you my babies needed to go to church more often. Now I have to rush and get these clothes together. Girls! Aunt Martha is here and you are going to stay at my house for a few days. Your mother is packing some food for you and we need to pack some church clothes." As she entered the bedroom, the girls ran to give her hugs. Winnie wiped away her tears and walked to the pantry to find a couple of burlap sacks. She picked up three quart jars of applesauce, three jars of string beans, and three jars of collard greens. Winnie wrapped some salt cured ham in a cloth napkin. She placed all of the items in one of the sacks and walked into the kitchen. She decided to pack some biscuits and cake. The girls liked to eat cake after dinner each night. As she cut the slices of cake, Martha and the girls came downstairs. Martha carried the large leather bag and Betty carried the small leather bag. Nanny asked, "Momma, where we gonin'?" Winnie walked over to Nanny and held her face in both hands. She told her, "Baby, you are going to stay with Aunt Martha and Uncle Tom while I do some nursing work. You will be with Betty and Mary. Don't worry, Mommy loves you." She kissed Nanny on the center of her forehead. Mary asked, "Momma, are you coming to Aunt Martha's?" Winnie answered, "No, I have some work to do. You will be just fine." Betty said, "Momma I'll take care of them. I'll help Aunt Martha clean and take care of the girls." Winnie said, "Girls, come and give me a hug that will last me until you get back home." All four of them hugged as Martha went to Winnie's bedroom to get their hats and coats. As she walked through the kitchen doorway, Winnie tearfully said, "Martha, take care of my babies. They are ….." Martha interrupted, "Winnie, you know these girls are just as much mine as yours. Stop worrying about them. We are going to do lots of church work, cooking, and maybe even a little sewing. Give me a hug and stop worrying about these children." The girls giggled as Winnie and Martha embraced each other. Betty and Mary took the coats from Martha's arms as the two women continued to embrace each other. Winnie softly sobbed as Martha moved their bodies from side to side in a rocking motion. Martha softly said, "It will be alright. God will take care of everything. It will be alright." The women embraced and Winnie sobbed until Nanny said, "Momma, are you alright? Momma, are you crying? Momma, Momma." As the women loosened their embrace, Martha told Nanny, "Momma is just happy. She's not crying." Winnie added, "Yes baby. Momma is happy because Aunt Martha always takes care of me and she always takes care of everybody. Now, give me a kiss and let's put your hat and coat on. Betty, get the two quilts out of my closet. Mary, you take one of the socks with the food. Get the lighter one. I don't want you to drop the jars and break them. Nanny, go upstairs and get all of your dolls." Nanny turned and quickly climbed the stairs. Winnie told Mary, "Mary, I want you to help your sister with Nanny.

She may start crying after a couple of days, but I need you to play with her and let her help with some of the chores." Mary nodded and walked over to pick up the food sack from the kitchen counter. Betty came back into the kitchen with the two quilts. Winnie told her, "Betty, you are growing up so fast." As usual, Betty smiled and said, "Thank you Momma." Nanny came down the stairs with a bright smile and an arm full of cloth dolls. Winnie asked, Nanny, did you get all of the dolls?" Nanny replied, "No Momma. I left baby Nanny on the bed. I didn't want you to get lonely. I'm going to leave her here to take care of you. Okay Momma?" Winnie laughed and said, "Alright Nanny. Thank you for leaving her." Martha said, "I hear Tom, William, and Carpenter coming up from the barn. Come on girls, let's get these things in the wagon. The men can bring the heavy stuff. Betty, give me the quilts, I'll get the back of the wagon straight." As Martha stepped out of the kitchen into the cool air, Winnie told the girls that she loved them and they would only stay a couple of days. All three girls ran to hug their mother as Martha instructed the men to come in the house and bring the heavier items out to the wagon. She told them to be strong and help Martha with the chores. All three girls promised to help with chores. Martha came back into the kitchen with the men. As Carpenter and Tom took the heavy items out to the wagon, William looked at Winnie and said, "Is this what you want?" Winnie answered, "I have to do this. I want my girls to be safe." William shook his head and helped carry items to the wagon. Martha hugged Winnie and told her, "Your girls will be alright. Take care of yourself Winnie." Winnie nodded in affirmation and swallowed to hold back the tears. Martha gently pushed the girls toward the kitchen door. Just before stepping outside, Nanny clutched Martha's wool coat. She smiled, waved to her mother and said, "I love you momma." The tears welled up in her eyes and Winnie's throat stiffened. She managed to whisper, "I love you too Nanny." Martha interrupted, "Let's go girls. Don't let all of the heat out of the house." Winnie slowly closed the door behind them as tears streamed down her face. She stepped back from the door and began to openly sob. She slowly walked over to the window. She thought it might be better for the girls if they saw her smiling and waving through the window as they left home. She wiped her tears with her apron, forced a smile and waved as Tom drove the wagon out of the yard.

Winnie leaned against the counter and gathered her thoughts. She prepared lunch for William and Carpenter and went into her bedroom. She decided to lie down and rest before finishing dinner. She realized that she already missed the sound of the girls playing and scuffing furniture across their bedroom floor. William and Carpenter came in to eat lunch as she pulled the covers up to her chin. William noticed that she was in bed. After Carpenter said the blessing over the food, William yelled, "Winnie! You alright? The girls are gonna be alright and you goin' be alright. Don't be layin' around here gettin' sick. You the nurse. Me and Carpenter can't help you. You suppose to help us, hear?" Winnie replied, "Alright William. I just need a little nap and then I'll be alright."

William and Carpenter talked and ate their lunch. When Winnie awakened, the men had gone back to the barn. She walked back into the kitchen and began cleaning the lunch dishes. She wondered how the girls were settling in at Martha's house. As she prepared the dinner, she realized that she would have food to store after dinner. When she planned the meal, she made enough for the girls. The thought of them not being at dinner helped her realize that she wouldn't be able to leave the girls at Martha's house for more than a few days.

The next several days were uneventful. There were no new visitors and the new property owners did not return. After four days, Winnie asked William to go to Martha's and bring the girls back home. She felt that she couldn't prevent life from happening. She felt that God already had a plan and there was nothing she could do to stop the plan from unfolding. William left right after sunrise to pick up the girls. He and Carpenter had decided at breakfast to cut more of the fallen trees near the rear of the property, beside the stream. William committed to helping Carpenter after he returned from the trip. Winnie cleaned the breakfast dishes and started to prepare the lunch as usual. Again, she decided to bake some pies to celebrate the girls' return home. Winnie decided to work on some of the fabric that Martha brought to her. She had cut most of the patterns the previous night, so she wanted to start the stitching during the day. Winnie carefully stitched the fabric together and listened for the sound of the wagon.

After a while, she heard Carpenter open the kitchen door. He brought in one bucket of water and picked up the empty bucket. As he walked back to the kitchen door he announced, "William is coming with the girls." Winnie quickly gathered all of the sewing materials and took them into her bedroom. She placed them in the wooden chair to the right of the door. As she walked back into the kitchen, Nanny opened the kitchen door and ran to her mother. Nanny yelled, "Momma! Momma!" Winnie announced, "My babies are home!" She hugged and kissed Nanny on both cheeks. Betty and Mary walked through the kitchen door with quilts in their arms. Both girls said, "Momma, we're back." Winnie answered, "Betty and Mary, come and give me a hug. I missed you so much." Both girls dropped the quilts and rushed to hug their mother. Nanny joined the threesome and worked her body between her mother and sisters. Nanny asked, "Momma, is little Nanny still on the bed?" Winnie laughed and said, "Yes Nanny. Little Nanny is still on the bed." William and Carpenter brought their luggage into the kitchen. William said, "Winnie, we won't be in for lunch. We goin' take some ham and those biscuits from breakfast with us. We won't be back up to the house until dinner." Winnie asked, "Do you need me to pack the biscuits?" William answered, "N-a-u-g-h, Carpenter already got 'em." Winnie said, "Alright, I'll see you then. Girls, get these things up to your bedroom. Leave the quilts. I'll put those away." The girls laughed and talked as they carried the items up to the bedroom. Winnie stirred the food and then picked up both quilts from the floor. She placed the quilts on the bed and began to fold them on the bed. She decided to fold the sewing items in the chair before folding the quilts. She had pinned the name of each woman on the fabric that would be used for her garment. As she placed the projects in the wicker sewing basket, she heard the kitchen door open. She assumed that William had changed his mind about her packing the biscuits for lunch. As she turned and walked toward the kitchen, she said, "So, did you change your mind. You want….." She stopped her sentence abruptly. As she walked through the kitchen doorway, it was obvious that William had not changed his mind.

A White man, about five foot six, mid-calf gray wool coat, brown hair, and oh yes…..blue eyes, stood smiling at her. She recognized the cunning smile and clutched the collar of her green cotton dress. It was Cyrus. He said, "Yes, I did change my mind, and I do want." Winnie anxiously replied, "No, I thought you were William. I was talking about preparing lunch. I ….." Cyrus interrupted, "I'm talking about lunch also." He slowly started walking to the kitchen table as he slid the wool coat off his shoulders. Winnie cautiously backed toward the window. As he placed his coat and hat on the kitchen chair, he said, "I thought I'd come back and get a little more information. I didn't get your name the last time I was here." He continued smiling and watching Winnie. She looked out the window at his horse and carriage in the back yard. His carriage seemed more shiny and larger than the doctor's carriage. She looked at the wheels on the carriage to see if they were somehow different from the other carriage wheels. She did not hear the carriage roll into the back yard. She wondered if the girls heard the carriage pull into the yard. She wondered if they remembered her warning about not greeting visitors. She was shaken from her thoughts as Cyrus walked toward her and asked, "So, what is it?" She nervously asked, "What is what?" He continued smiling and said, "What is your name? You have to have a name to go with that beautiful red hair." She continued to clutch her dress collar and said, "I told you, Winnie." He answered, "Winnie. Now that's different. Winnie, always a winner or maybe I'll be a winner." He sat down at the table and said, "So, don't you believe in feeding folks? What do you have for a hungry man?" She answered, "I have some ham, great northern beans, and some biscuits." He interrupted, "Well, where is it?" She began to prepare a plate for him and listened for the girls. He asked, "So, do you have any kids?" She turned abruptly and looked at him. He smiled and said, "Oh, don't worry, I'm not interested in your kids. I'm interested in you. I don't have much time. I'm going off to school in a couple of days. I just had to see you one more time before I left. You know, kind of a going away visit."

Winnie's face turned blush pink as she listened for the girls and put his plate in front of him. She heard the floor creak above her as she moved toward the table. She felt a sense of relief because at least the girls knew that the visitor was in the house. She hoped that Betty remembered the warning. As she turned and pulled her hand away from the plate, Cyrus grabbed her wrist.

He smiled and said, "Don't be so quick to get away. Seems like you're just as fiery as that red hair." He turned and stood up beside his chair. He pulled her closer as he stood. Her chest heaved as she realized the intent of his visit. He mentioned that he was going away to school, so whatever he did to her would certainly never be spoken of again. She could feel his hands trembling as he caressed her buttocks. She did not move as he fondled her buttocks. She did not move as he pulled her body towards his with malice of forethought. He rubbed his manhood against her pelvic area as he caressed and squeezed her buttocks. He kissed the left side of her neck and breathed heavily. He clumsily moved her body back against the counter. He stepped on her feet and quickly unbuttoned his shirt. He told her, "Take your dress off. Hurry up." As Winnie slid the dress over her shoulders, he looked at her breasts and unbuckled his pants. As the green cotton dress fell to her ankles, he reached inside his boxers and fondled his penis. His erection grew outside of the front flap of his boxers. He touched each of her breasts with his right hand as he continued to fondle his penis. Suddenly, he instructed her to turn around as he pushed her left shoulder. She turned and leaned on the counter as he lowered his boxers. He quickly and aggressively entered her from the rear. He quickly thrust his manhood in and out of her as he moaned in pleasure.

Winnie moaned also, but for a different reason. It had been six years since her last sexual encounter with the doctor. This experience was painful physically and mentally. She felt violated and yet she felt she had to allow him privilege to her body in order to prevent him from looking at her girls. The tears ran down her cheeks as she tried to block the sound of his moans and heavy breathing out of her mind. The thrusting began to shake the tears onto the counter. Just as she thought he was finishing, she unexpectedly felt him grab her left arm.

Cyrus pulled her to the left of the counter. In the process, he banged her head against the cupboard. As she moaned in pain, he forced her head and hands through the pantry doorway. She stumbled forward and caught the top of the potato and onion box. The box was about two feet tall. Before she could gain her balance, he entered her from the rear and aggressively thrust his manhood in and out, time and time again. She did not respond, but the muscles of her vagina began to pulsate against his hardened penis. He thrust himself inside her until he collapsed in apparent exhaustion against her buttocks. He instructed her to go to the bedroom. As she walked to the bedroom, she quickly stopped in the kitchen and picked up her green cotton dress from the floor. Cyrus followed her while holding his pants and boxers. He continued to stroke his penis with the other hand and instructed Winnie to lie on the bed. He fondled his penis as he looked at her lying on the bed. As his manhood stiffened, he climbed between her legs and entered her a third time. He kept his arms straight as he thrust his penis in and out of her. His powerful thrusts shook her body and the bed.

As she lay on the bed watching this younger man take liberties with her body, tears ran down the sides of her face into her ears. She realized that he never looked at her face. He simply wanted to pleasure himself and her identity was not of importance. She lost track of the elapsed time as she stared out the window at the steely blue sky. She prayed that he would finish this ordeal and leave. She prayed her girls would not hear any of these activities. She prayed that once he went off to school, Cyrus would never return. Sometime later, Cyrus moaned and his penis softened and slowly slid out of her. He crawled back from her and stood next to the bed. He pulled up his boxers and pants. He did not look at her and slowly walked to the kitchen while zipping his pants. Winnie lay on the bed naked as the cool morning air stiffened her nipples. He gathered his coat and hat from the kitchen chair and slowly walked out the door. As he stepped into the cold air, Winnie slowly sat on the side of the bed and put her dress on. She felt numb and thankful. He left without bothering her girls. She silently wept as the carriage left the yard.

Chapter 13

A few days later, Winnie awakened and started the morning with a fresh pot of coffee. Carpenter had started a fire, brought in a load of wood, and gone to the barn. As she prepared the breakfast, Winnie fought back the thoughts of Cyrus violating her personal space as well as her body. She sliced the ham and began to think about the sewing jobs that she needed to finish. She knew that she could not let the negative thoughts control her mind set. Her girls needed to know joy in their lives before entering a cruel adult world. A happy childhood was all that she could provide. Her thoughts were interrupted by the sound of a horse drawn carriage entering the back yard. Before she looked out the window, she said a short prayer. She asked that anyone be allowed to visit except Cyrus. As she anxiously looked out the window, she recognized the doctor climbing down from the carriage seat. She dropped the ham and knife. As Winnie wiped her hands on her apron, she quickly walked into the bedroom and stopped to face the mirrored dresser. She leaned forward and took the hair pin out of her hair. She carefully lowered the hair at the right margin of her face. Winnie pinned her hair and returned to the kitchen. As she started slicing the ham, the doctor opened the door and stepped into the kitchen. He closed the door and removed his hat. As he placed the items on the kitchen chair, he asked, "And how are you doing?" Winnie continued cutting the ham and replied, "I'm fine." He slowly walked up behind her and rested his hands on her hips.

Without thought, Winnie stiffened her body and stopped slicing the ham. The doctor slid his face next to the left side of Winnie's face and said, "My, we are tense today. Let me take a look at you." He stepped back and slowly turned her body at the hips. She slowly tilted her head away from him and looked at the stove. He said, "Your color seems a little pale and your hair is almost over your eye. You know I like to see all of your beautiful face. Let me help you." He slowly lifted her hair from the right side of her face and pushed it back. He sternly asked, "What's this? What happened to your face? You have a bruise and a small cut. What happened? Did Carpenter or his brother do this to you? I will ….."

Winnie interrupted, "No, no. They didn't do anything to me." The doctor said, "Well, who did this? What happened?" She answered, "I hit my head on the cupboard. It will be fine in a couple of weeks." He replied, "Listen, when I touched you, your entire body went rigid. Now, I have been a doctor long enough to know a woman who has been hit or abused. I've examined women after an attack and Winnie, you reacted in the same manner as those women. I don't think you're telling me the whole truth. You may have hit your head on the cupboard, but I don't think you are telling me the whole story. I don't know who you're trying to protect, but if I find out ….." Winnie interrupted, "I'm not protecting anyone. I hit my head and I have a bruise. It's ….." The doctor said, "You have a bruise that's about two inches in diameter and a quarter inch cut that has scrapes going across your skin. You didn't just bump your head on the cupboard. Your head hit a hard surface and these scrapes indicate that there was some additional pressure behind the initial contact. Who are you protecting? What happened?" She replied, "I'm not protecting anyone. You know that I would tell you if I thought I had a problem that wouldn't go away. Please let's just stop talking about this. I ….." He interrupted, "I want to take a closer look at this. Sit down. Let me get my bag. I can't have my nurse looking like she needs a doctor." They both laughed as Winnie sat down in the kitchen chair and the doctor opened his medical bag. The doctor cleaned several paint chips out of the cut and cleaned the wound with iodine. The doctor told her to cover the wound with a hat when attending to patients. Winnie said, "Thank you doctor. Now, would you like your lunch?" They both smiled and the doctor answered, "Yes, I would. I definitely earned my meal today." The doctor ate his lunch and discussed some of the latest medical practices. He received frequent communications from his friends in Europe. The European medical community stressed keeping wounds clean as well as the working area clean. A lot of the medical community in the United States was not as aggressive in stressing the importance of keeping all areas clean. The doctor finished his meal and asked, "Has Carpenter been able to get grain from the mill as usual?" Winnie replied, "As far as I know, yes. He hasn't said anything to me about not being able to get grain. Is there something I should know about?" He said, "No, no. Thaddeus told me that everything would remain the same, so I was just checking." As he gathered his items, the doctor told her, "Thaddeus is a friend of mine and he assured me that you would have a place to live." As he walked toward the kitchen door, Winnie cleared the table and cleaned the dishes. As he opened the kitchen door, he turned and said, "Winnie, make sure you get some rest." She replied, "I will. I'll be fine." As the doctor stepped out into the cool morning air, Winnie felt a sense of relief. She had survived the barrage of questions. She would be glad when this whole incident was forgotten by everyone.

Martha and Tom came to visit the next day. As Winnie was cleaning breakfast dishes, she heard the horse drawn carriage come into the back yard. Martha knocked on the door and yelled, "Comin' in!" Martha walked toward Winnie and Tom followed behind her. As Martha and Tom sat down at the kitchen table, Winnie continued to prepare lunch. Martha said, "So, you feeling ….."As Winnie turned to face them, Tom said, "Umh!" and Martha stopped talking in mid sentence. She put both hands over her mouth and said, "Winnie, who did this to you. Oh my Lord! What is going on? What happened?" Winnie smiled and said, "Martha, calm down. Nobody did anything to me. I hit my head on the cupboard. That's all. Stop looking like you just saw a ghost." Tom cleared his throat and said, "I'm goin' down to the barn to check on the men." As he walked toward the door Winnie explained, "Dr. Grunburg cleaned the cut with some iodine. Iodine is good, but it really stains the skin. It's not that bad. It's just a little bruise." Martha interjected, "Winnie, my momma taught me not to do it, but I swear …..You are getting' yourself into some kind of situations lately." Winnie interrupted, "What do you mean situations? I'm not doing anything. I'm just trying to raise these girls the best I know how." Martha answered, "Well, I done told you time and time again, you need to come to church with me and bring my babies to church more often. God is trying to tell you somethin'. And Winnie, you the only one that can figure what God wants you to do." Winnie answered, "I know Martha. I am trying to figure this out. I'm trying to do the best I can. Martha, believe me when I say I am trying." Martha stood up and gave Winnie a hug. She asked, "And where are my babies?" Winnie said, "I think they went back to bed. It was pretty cold upstairs last night and I heard them talking and playing until late." Martha said, "Alright. I'll see them on my next visit. I have to get back to the house and finish cooking some ham for Miss Ida. I told her I would cook it today." As she walked toward the kitchen door, Martha said, "Winnie, take care of yourself. Let me know if you need anything." Winnie replied, "I will Martha. Thank you." Both women smiled at each other as Martha opened the kitchen door and yelled for Tom.

Several months passed and the summer showers once again provided moisture for the young sprouts, saplings, and wild flowers. Winnie awakened on a sunny late September morning eager to start the day's chores. Carpenter told her the night before that the salad greens were ready to be picked. She wanted to can at least two dozen jars from the first harvest. She had also promised to give Martha some greens for the church ladies. As usual, Carpenter had started a fire and brought in one load of firewood. As she started the coffee and looked out the window, she could see that the wild flowers behind the barn were continuing to bloom. After ten years, she could barely see the small mound on Little Fannie's grave. As she day dreamed about what Fannie would have looked like, her stomach muscles suddenly convulsed. She found herself grabbing her mouth and swallowing quickly to prevent the contents of her stomach from spilling onto the counter. In her mind, she repeatedly tried to suppress the possibility that this desire to vomit was anything other than a negative reaction to spring flowers blooming. In a hopeful prayerful manner, she whispered, "No, no, no. Oh no Lord, don't let it be. Please Lord no. No, no, no." She anxiously searched for a cup in the cupboard, tea, and some ginger. She had to test if the ginger tea stopped her urge to vomit. She hastily and repeatedly whispered, "No, no, no." As she spooned the ginger powder into the hot tea, she whispered, "Lord, I know I should go to church more, but I need your help. I just don't want to be pregnant. Please Lord. No one knows what happened. Jesus please." As she slowly raised the hot cup of liquid to her lips, she closed her eyes.

As a child, whenever she really needed or wanted something, she would close her eyes and make a wish. She knew it was superstition, but she felt she needed every power, good or bad, to chart her fate. She took a sip, opened her eyes, and looked at the blue sky through the window. As the hot liquid slowly trickled down to her stomach, it seemed to leave a calming trail through her digestive tract. She openly sobbed and placed the cup on the counter.

Winnie suddenly felt numb. She was thinking that her life would be shaken to the core. Martha and the doctor would know that she did not reveal the truth. They would know that she was deceptive. They would know that she lied. How could they forgive her? Would they forgive her? Would the doctor stop giving her new patients? How would he take this? How could she tell him that his friend's son forced himself on her. Now that Cyrus had gone off to school, would anyone believe her?

Winnie realized that she had been acting distant toward the doctor. Subconsciously she wanted to hurt him. After he made his "business decision" to stop paying the rent, she felt like she wanted to be less affectionate toward him. She wanted him to feel some of the lack of compassion that she felt when he announced his decision. And now, she would have to reveal that she was carrying someone else's child. The doctor had not fully undressed since he returned from his illness. He could not sustain an erection, so he had resorted to fondling her breasts and genitalia fully clothed. He usually rubbed, hugged, kissed, and squeezed until he released his sexual tension in an apparent orgasm. There was no way to imply that this baby could be Dr.

Grunburg's baby. She realized that she would have to share what happened. If she were pregnant, he would have to do an examination. The doctor was just beginning to accept the loss of their physical intimate relationship. Would he think that she planned this? Would he think that she wanted the physical encounter? What would Cyrus' family think? Would they put her off the farm for making false accusations against the family? Would the entire family have to move to Thornton Jr.'s farm?

She knew that she would have to present the appearance of normalcy. William and Carpenter knew nothing about Cyrus taking liberties with her body. As she continued to prepare the breakfast, she realized that she would have to reveal the truth to Dr. Grunburg first. He at least deserved the right to be the first one to know what happened. His reaction would determine how she revealed the truth to Martha. If he had a negative reaction, Martha would be able to help her plan solutions to the challenges. Martha always treated her like a mother and a sister. If anyone could and would understand that she did not ask for this situation, it would be Martha. Winnie realized that this could be a moment of truth in her life. Who were her real friends? Who would stand by her and support her in all circumstances?

Winnie called the girls down to eat breakfast. Since Betty would be ten years old in a few days, Winnie permitted her to serve the girl's plates. The weather was warm enough for the girls to wash the breakfast dishes in the back yard. While the girls ate breakfast, Winnie decided to go into her bedroom and work on the sewing jobs from Martha.

After the girls finished eating, Betty organized the smooth transition from the kitchen to the backyard. As they washed, rinsed, and dried the breakfast dishes, Winnie returned to the kitchen and prepared the breakfast plates for the men.

Several days later, Winnie awakened to the sound of the birds chirping and the toads creaking. As she walked into the kitchen, Carpenter had started a fire and brought in a load of firewood. She started the coffee and smiled as she thought of Carpenter's dependability. Ever since the first day that he brought her to the farm, he has provided the basic supplies to run a household every day. As she walked into the pantry to get some ham, the urge to vomit consumed her thoughts. She grabbed the side of ham and quickly walked back to the counter. She placed the ham on the counter, and began looking for the tea and a cup in the cupboard. She poured the hot water into her cup and looked for the ginger. As she spooned the ginger powder into her tea, she was rather certain that she was pregnant. She sipped the ginger tea and continued making breakfast. As she opened the oven door and removed the biscuits, she heard a horse drawn carriage enter the back yard. She placed the biscuits on top of the stove and looked out the window. Dr. Grunburg was stepping down from the carriage seat.

Winnie decided to prepare a plate for the doctor and herself. She poured the doctor some coffee and made herself some ginger tea. As the doctor opened the kitchen door, the table was already set. The doctor said, "Oh, I guess you did get some rest. It's a good thing because I am hungry this morning." As he placed his items on the kitchen chair, he said, "This looks delicious." He sat down and Winnie sat at the other end of the table. As he placed his napkin on his lap, she sipped the ginger tea. She mentally asked God to help her explain what happened without losing her composure.

He asked, "So how are all of the maternity patients doing?" Winnie took another sip of tea and said, "Well, all of your patients are doing as expected." The doctor nodded in affirmation and continued eating. She continued, "I think you may have one new patient." The doctor looked at her and asked, "Who do you think the new patient will be?" Winnie slowly picked up the cup of ginger tea and sipped. As she slowly placed the cup on the table, she said, "Me." She looked into the doctor's eyes as his face turned pink and he asked, "Well, how did that happen?" In a sarcastic manner he continued, "Are you telling me this was an immaculate conception?" He stopped eating, put both elbows on either side of his plate, and clasped his hands in front of his mouth.

Winnie explained, "I need you to remain calm and listen to everything I have to say. It all started with the bruise and cut on my head a few months ago. I did hit my head on the cupboard, but I wasn't alone and you were right about more pressure behind my head. I was doing some work in the bedroom when I heard the kitchen door open. I thought it was William changing his mind about me packing some biscuits for his lunch. So, when I came back into the kitchen, I said, "So, you changed your mind?" Tears began to run down Winnie's cheeks and her voice cracked. She continued, "And when I walked in the kitchen, it wasn't William. It was the new property owner, Cyrus." The doctor interrupted, "Cyrus! Thaddeus' boy?" Winnie continued, "Yes, he said he wanted something to eat and he was going off to school. He said he wanted to make a going away visit before going to school. I fixed him a plate, but he wasn't interested in the food. He never ate anything and he ….." She swallowed as the tears continued to flow and her nose started to run." He had his way with me. I was hoping and praying that I wasn't pregnant, but I have been sick for the past few weeks. And just like with the girls, the ginger tea calms my stomach. I'm sorry. I'm sorry, but he is young and strong. I ….." The doctor interrupted, "Winnie, I know there's nothing you could have done. I'm sorry this happened to you. Cyrus is young and I don't think you'll have any more trouble from him. I'll talk to Thaddeus. After a short pause he said,

"Well, I guess I'd better do an examination and then we'll know more. Come into the bedroom and let me have a look." The doctor sighed as he grabbed his medical bag and walked toward the bedroom. Winnie walked into the pantry and got a clean rag to wipe her face and blow her nose. She knew she needed the examination, but she felt like Cyrus was violating her body all over again. She suddenly felt dirty and ashamed. For the first time, she really didn't want the doctor to examine her. She wasn't sure that she could look in his eyes after he finished the examination. She really wished there were some other way to get through this. As she stood in the kitchen floor blowing her nose, the doctor came out of the bedroom and hugged her. As he wrapped his arms around her petite trembling body, Winnie lost her composure. She sobbed openly as the doctor caressed her back and whispered, "I'm sorry. This is my fault. I'm sorry. Let me examine you and see if I can hear anything." Winnie continued to sob as the doctor led her to the bed.

The doctor took his stethoscope out of his medical bag as Winnie lay down on the bed. He completed his examination and confirmed Winnie's fear. She was about three months pregnant. Winnie began to sob openly again. The doctor put his stethoscope in his medical bag and placed it on the floor. He sat on the side of the bed and asked Winnie to move over. As she rolled on her side, the doctor lay on the bed beside her and hugged her from behind. He held her until she regained her composure.

As if someone tapped her on the shoulder, Winnie blew her nose and told the doctor that she was fine. She asked him which patients he was going to visit. As she walked back into the kitchen, the doctor grabbed his medical bag and followed. She cleared the breakfast dishes from the table as he gathered his items from the chair. He paused and announced, "Winnie, I'm sorry this happened, but don't worry. I will speak to Thaddeus. You will have a place to live. Thaddeus won't put you off the farm. In fact, I think Cyrus will have to answer some questions." He turned and walked to the kitchen door. She continued cleaning the dishes as the doctor stepped out into the fresh spring air. Winnie knew that she had to hurry and feed the girls before William and Carpenter came in for breakfast.

Chapter 14

A few days later, Winnie awakened and sat on the side of the bed. She sighed and pushed her feet into her slippers. As Winnie put on her robe and walked into the kitchen, the thought of telling Martha about her condition caused some anxiety. The hardest task had been completed. The doctor knew the truth and he accepted the facts better than she could have imagined. Preparing breakfast seemed like a more pleasant activity since she shared the truth with the doctor. The incident with Cyrus had obviously caused anxiety.

As she served the plates for the girls, Winnie called, "Betty! You girls come on down for breakfast!" Betty replied, "Alright Momma! We're coming!" As the girls rushed downstairs to breakfast, Winnie walked to the pantry and placed items on the counter that she would use to make lunch. When the girls sat down at the table, Betty instructed Mary and Nanny to bow their heads for prayer. After the girls finished the prayer, Winnie walked into the bedroom. She wanted to work on a few garments for some of the ladies from the church. She also wanted to gather her thoughts before sharing the details of the incident with Cyrus. After the girls finished eating, Betty cleaned the dishes from the table and organized the washing, drying and storage of the dishes. Betty was old enough and responsible enough to run the household. She was also capable of supervising Mary and Nanny without incident. After the girls finished putting away the dishes, Betty called, "Momma! We're all finished! We're going back upstairs!" As Winnie walked back into the kitchen, she said, "Girls, I want you to work on the reading, math, and spelling in the new books that I got in town last week." All three girls replied, "Alright Momma." As the girls hurried to their bedroom, Winnie prepared breakfast for the men and started preparing lunch. As she took the biscuits out of the oven, she heard the sound of a horse drawn carriage in the backyard. She placed the biscuits on top of the stove and looked out the window. Martha and Tom were stepping down from the carriage seat. Winnie prepared the plates for William and Carpenter and placed them on the table. When Martha and

Tom stepped into the kitchen, Winnie said, "Good morning Martha and Tom." They replied, "Good morning." Martha said, "I see you're feeling pretty good today. You have the plates ready for the men and we came early." All three adults laughed as Winnie said, "Yes, I have a lot to do today and Martha, I have something I have to tell you." Martha raised her eyebrows and stared at Winnie without speaking. Winnie continued, "Tom, could you tell Carpenter and William that breakfast is ready?" Tom stood up, looked at Martha and said, "I'll be right back."

Winnie walked toward the bedroom and told Martha, "Come with me. We need to talk." As Martha walked into the bedroom, she shook her head in anticipation of the information Winnie would share. Perhaps the girls would need to stay with her for a while. Winnie turned and asked Martha to close the door. As Martha closed the door, Winnie sat on the bed and said, "Martha, I have something to tell you. Martha walked to the bed and sat beside Winnie. Winnie continued, "Well, there's something that I didn't tell you. When I had that scar above my eye, there was something that happened. You were right. I didn't tell you everything that happened. The new property owner, Cyrus, did come back without the other two men. He said he wanted something to eat, but he wasn't interested in food. I got that scar above my eye when he pushed me and I hit my head on the cupboard. He....he had his way....and.... now....I am probably going to deliver in January." Martha slowly shook her head and held Winnie's hand with her right hand. Both women lowered their heads and wept. Each woman knew that this incident defined them as equally vulnerable. They both realized that Winnie's arrangement could not protect her from the daily struggles of being a woman. Martha wiped the tears from each eye with her left hand. She slowly raised her head and looked up at the ceiling. She sighed, looked at the ceiling and softly said, "Winnie, we're goin' to love this baby just like the girls. You are going to eat right, get your rest, rub your stomach, and talk sweet to this baby, just like you did the girls." Winnie leaned on Martha's large soft arm and quietly wept. She said, "Martha, I should have told you right after it first happened, but I was just so ashamed. I felt so dirty. I know how the women at the church feel about me and then I end up being treated just like every word they whisper about me." Martha interrupted, "Winnie, stop it. You know I love you like a sister. Stop it. I don't want to hear another word about this. Now let's get back out in the kitchen and get started on lunch." They both knew that this would have to be the last occasion of "crying over spilled milk". Life was not fair, but self pity was not an option.

Several months had passed and Winnie's petite body was stretched to its' limits. The late January wind blew through every crack in the house. The air felt like icicles stroking her skin. There were only two days left in January and Winnie knew that the baby was due for delivery at any moment. She felt that this baby seemed heavier than the girls and if it weren't delivered before the end of January, it would be the only late delivery. As she sat on the side of the bed, she wondered if this baby's temperament would be different from the girls. She pushed her swollen feet into her slippers and walked into the kitchen. Just as he had done every morning, Carpenter had started a fire and brought in a load of firewood. Winnie started the coffee and caressed her abdomen. As she glanced out the window, the bare tree limbs swayed in the cold January wind.

She walked into the pantry to get some flour for the biscuits and some salt ham. As she lifted the meat onto the counter, the all familiar warm fluid gushed onto her feet and slippers. She returned to the pantry and retrieved several rags. She placed a large rag over the wet spot on the floor. She also placed several rags between her legs as she walked into the pantry. She picked up more rags and her medical bag. As she walked back to the bedroom, she yelled, "Betty, the baby's coming! Go down to the barn and tell Carpenter!" Betty replied, "Alright Momma. I'm going!" Winnie walked into the bedroom and placed the rags and medical bag on the wooden chair. She pulled the chair next to the bed and walked to the closet. She managed to reach the two quilts on the top shelf. As she lifted the quilts from the shelf, warm fluid continued to trickle from her abdomen. She placed the quilts under her pillows as Betty ran down the stairs and opened the kitchen door. As Betty pulled the door open, she yelled, "I'm going to the barn Momma!" As Betty closed the door, Winnie sat on the side of the bed. She was thankful that Betty was old enough to help with chores. She had not finished preparing breakfast, but Betty was capable of finishing the meal.

Betty ran to the barn and announced, "The baby is coming! The baby is coming!" Carpenter and William came out of the barn. William told Betty that he would go to Martha's house and bring her back. Carpenter told Betty to go back in the house and he would bring more water and firewood. Betty ran back to the kitchen door and rushed inside. The cold January wind chilled Betty's face and caused her eyes to fill with fluid. She opened the door and ran to stand beside the hot woodstove. Betty rubbed her hands in front of the stove and rubbed her cheeks in an effort to warm her skin.

Winnie called, "Betty is that you?" She replied, "Yes Momma, it's me!" She turned and ran to her mother's bedside. As she sprinted to the bed, her shoulder length dark brown hair flowed behind her head. Winnie said, "Betty, I need you to finish cooking breakfast. Cut the ham, mix the biscuits and scramble some eggs. And make sure you don't have any shells in the egg."

Betty interrupted, "Momma, I know. You taught me how to make everything. Don't worry. I can do this. Is it alright if I go and wake Mary? She can help make the biscuits. I'll make sure I'm quiet. I won't wake Nanny. Will that be alright Momma?" Winnie replied, "Yes Betty, go ahead. Let Nanny sleep until you're ready to serve the plates." Betty leaned down and gave her mother a big hug and said, "Thank you Momma." As she quickly tip toed to wake Mary, Winnie smiled as she thought of her first baby becoming a young lady. Betty had been a source of joy and comfort for Winnie since birth. She always had a beautiful smile and always wanted to learn new skills. Once she learned a new skill, Betty had always volunteered to use the new skill in order to help her mother.

As Winnie relaxed on the pillows, her back began to ache on the right side. She rubbed her back and the muscles on the front left of her abdomen violently contracted. Unlike her previous pregnancies, the contractions seemed to be more severe earlier in the delivery. These contractions seemed intense at the start. The nature of this conception had caused anxiety throughout the pregnancy. Winnie realized that she needed to relax and let the labor take its' natural pace. She knew that she could not rush this baby's delivery. She heard the girls trying to move quietly through the kitchen. She called, "Mary, is that you!" She answered, "Yes Momma." Winnie called, "Mary, come in here!" She heard the light tapping of Mary's slippers on the wooden floor as she ran into the bedroom. Mary ran to her mother and laid her head on her chest. Winnie hugged her and kissed her on the top of her head. She said, "Mary, I need you to be a big girl and help Betty. Aunt Martha will be here shortly. I need you to listen to Betty. Do you understand?" Mary said, "Yes Momma, I'll do it." She hugged her mother at the neck and skipped back into the kitchen. Winnie moaned as another contraction distracted her thoughts to the immediacy of the moment. She tossed from side to side seeking a more comfortable position. She did not want to attempt pushing before Martha arrived. The anxiety caused by the contractions made her think that either the labor would be short or Martha had delayed her arrival time on purpose.

Shortly thereafter, she heard the sound of a horse drawn carriage stop in the backyard. Before she could ask, she heard Martha instructing the men to make sure there was enough firewood in the wood box. Martha entered the kitchen and hugged both girls. She told them that they were doing a good job making breakfast. She entered the bedroom and placed her coat on the chair to the right of the bed.

As she walked toward the side of the bed she said, "Winnie, are you ready to have this baby?" She smiled and put her hands on her hips as Winnie moaned in discomfort. Winnie replied, "Martha, this one is different. This baby is ready to come here." Both women laughed as Martha announced. "I'll go get the hot water and then we'll see what's going on." As she walked back toward the kitchen, Winnie moaned as another contraction began. Martha returned with a small white basin of hot water and placed it on the wooden chair. As Martha sat on the bed, Winnie said, "Martha, this baby is different from the girls. I think it's larger. I have more discomfort. I thought it seemed larger these last few months, but I definitely feel it now." Martha smiled, rubbed her forearm and said, "Winnie, you must be getting' old and tired. You never said this with the others. You just tryin' to hurry and deliver this baby. You just want to see what it looks like. You...." Winnie interrupted, "No Martha. This one feels larger. I do have a small bottle of whiskey in my medical bag. I use that with a lot of first time mothers, if the labor just keeps going on and on, or if the baby is a little too large for the birth canal. I hope we don't have to use it, but it's there. I ...." Martha replied, "Alright Winnie. I always said you were your own best nurse. I'll keep that in mind." At that moment, Winnie felt a strong contraction and moaned in discomfort.

Martha washed her hands in the basin of hot water. She dried her hands on a clean rag and told Winnie, "Alright, let's see what's goin' on." Martha pulled the sheet back and examined the birth canal. As she reached up the birth canal and pressed Winnie's lower abdomen, she raised her eyebrows. Winnie asked, "Martha, what's wrong? Is the baby's head first? Is...." Martha interrupted, "Winnie, I think you're right. The baby's head is a tight fit. Do you want that whiskey or do you think you can do this without it?" Winnie moaned and said, "I'm going to try without it." Martha said, "Alright on the next contraction, go ahead and push. It's about half way down the canal now."

Shortly thereafter, Winnie released a high pitched moaning scream. It took three more hard pushes before the baby's head cleared the birth canal. Martha cleaned the baby's nose, mouth and hair. She turned the baby's face up. Winnie asked, "What color is it? How does the color look?" She suddenly had a thought that this baby was the blue gray color of Fannie. She didn't want to think that this baby would be born dead because of the violent nature of its' conception. She asked, "Martha what...." Her words were abruptly interrupted by the intense pain of the contraction. She pushed and Martha caught the baby in both hands. Martha announced, "It's a boy! Winnie, it's a boy! He looks good." She smacked the baby's buttocks and he began to cry. Martha cleaned his body, tied the umbilical cord and placed him on his mother's abdomen. As she waited for Winnie to pass the afterbirth, Martha exchanged the soiled rags with clean rags. She placed the rags on the floor and picked up some clean rags. Winnie passed the afterbirth and Martha cut the umbilical cord. Martha said, "Winnie, I'm goin' to clean the birthing area, but I think you may need some stitching. You were right. That boy's head was certainly bigger than the girls. I think the doctor will have to give you some stitches. Winnie replied, "I know it. He should be here in a couple of days. I'll be alright. I think I'm going to rest. Betty will be able to make the meals and help out." Martha said, "Winnie, do you want me to take Mary and Nanny with me? They could stay with me for a few days." Winnie replied, "No, no. The girls will be fine. We'll be alright. Soon Tom is going to stop you from helping me deliver." Both women laughed as Martha gathered the soiled rags and took them to the kitchen garbage bucket. Martha told the girls that they had a new baby brother. The girls asked, "What is his name? What are we going to call him? What does he look like? Can we see him? Martha put her finger on the front of her mouth to indicate quiet.

Martha walked back into the bedroom and picked up the yellow gown on the mirrored dresser. She turned and asked, "Winnie, how are you? Are you gonna' be alright?" As she handed her the yellow gown, she said, "Martha, he's beautiful. He looks just like his father. He has blue eyes and a large forehead just like Cyrus. He …." Martha interrupted, "Winnie! Are you goin' to be alright with this baby. Are you going to be able to love him like the girls?"

Winnie replied, "Martha, I know why you asked, but this is my baby. He will be loved. I decided to name him Gruen." Martha replied, "What? Gru….what?" Winnie said, "Gruen. I am naming him after the doctor. He will probably take care of him and I don't know if I'll ever see Cyrus again. His name will be Gruen for Dr. Grunburg." Martha said, "Alright, Gr-oo-en it will be. Did Cyrus have light brown hair? Winnie answered, "Yes, he had light brown hair, blue eyes, a long straight nose and deep set eyes. I think he's going to look just like Cyrus. The good thing is, his family will know when they see Gruen that he is Cyrus' son." Martha said, "Winnie, let me take him to the girls. They want to see their new baby brother." As Winnie handed Gruen to Martha, he frowned and moved his clinched hands. Martha said, "Winnie, he looks like he's goin' to be tough." Both women laughed as Martha turned to walk into the kitchen. As Martha walked through the doorway, she announced, "Girls, meet your baby brother Gr-oo-en." Martha sat in the kitchen chair as the girls kissed his cheeks, rubbed his hair and lifted his fingers. He frowned and blinked his eyelids as he struggled to look at his sisters. Martha stood up and said, "Alright. Enough kisses for the first hour. I'm taking him back to your mother. Now …." Nanny interrupted, "May I see Momma? I want to see Momma." Martha told the girls, "Go in quietly and see your mother. She's tired and she needs some rest. Keep the noise down and then you three come back to the kitchen." As the girls went in to see their mother, Martha looked out the kitchen window. The men were working on a wagon in front of the barn door. Martha smiled as she thought that soon Gruen would be down by the barn trying to help fix things. Carpenter was beginning to show signs of aging. A pair of young hands around the farm would really be a help to Carpenter in about eight years. She looked down at Gruen's little pale face and smiled as he squirmed from the sunlight shining through the window. She raised his head and kissed his cheek. As his cheek brushed against her large soft breast, he turned and opened his mouth. Martha laughed and called, "Girls! Come on out to the kitchen. Your brother is hungry and I can't help him. Winnie, you had better get your rest because this boy is ready to eat and looks like he is full of energy." She walked toward the bed, the girls giggled and walked back into the kitchen. As Martha approached the bed, Winnie reached for her newborn son.

Chapter 15

Gruen continued to thrive through the winter months. His appetite was good and he gained weight. He had sparkling blue eyes and his nose continued to grow narrow and long. His deep set eyes and large forehead identified him as a smaller version of his father. When all of Winnie's children were gathered at the table, it was obvious that Gruen had a different father from the girls. His energy level was also different from his sisters. Gruen slept fewer hours than the girls did at his age. He spent a lot of time in the girl's bedroom. Winnie often smiled as she listened to the girls caring for their brother.

Gruen became the living doll for his sisters. The girls dressed, undressed, held, and passed Gruen to each other all day. He seemed to enjoy the attention as he sucked on several fingers or his tiny clinched fist.

The doctor regularly visited the farm about every seven days. He continued to share medical information and European medical practices with Winnie. The doctor continued to attempt sexual encounters with her. Since his illness, he remained unable to sustain an erection. He remained fully dressed during his attempts and eventually resorted to performing oral sex. Winnie was uncomfortable and disappointed by the deterioration of their physical relationship, but she realized that there were no other options.

The doctor and Winnie's physical relationship had deteriorated and so had the United States economy. According to the National Bureau of Economic Research, March 1882 marked the beginning of a recession. The sagging economy did not help the unstable and often violent labor relations of the time. The railroads had helped develop a national economy. Urban areas had increased as well as the demand for industrial workers. Many of the organizations that fought against slavery also fought against poor labor relations and the increased number of slums.

President Chester A. Arthur and his administration were also concerned about labor relations. The Arthur administration believed that government should provide an educational and ethical role in citizen's lives. In 1883, union leaders testified in Senate hearings in support of a national Bureau of Labor Statistics.

The initial movement for a Department of Labor began in 1867 at a national labor convention. The National Labor Union dissolved shortly thereafter, but the movement continued. In 1869, the state of Massachusetts established the first state level bureau of labor statistics. A former state legislator was appointed by the governor to stabilize and promote the organization. Carroll D. Wright reformed the organization and testified in the 1883 Senate hearings as an expert witness supporting the establishment of a Federal Bureau of Labor Statistics. Both houses passed a bill and the Bureau of Labor was created within the Department of the Interior. President Arthur signed the bill on June 27, 1884.

The Bureau of Labor Statistics was established in 1884 in order to help stabilize labor relations. While labor relations were stabilizing, Cyrus' family was destabilizing. While Cyrus was away at school, his father became ill in 1884. After a year of declining health, Thaddeus died in December of 1885. Naturally, Cyrus came home to attend his father's funeral.

On a cold windy December morning, Winnie awakened with a chill in the bedroom air. She sat on the side of the bed and looked at Gruen in his crib. He was fast asleep and she wanted to build the fire and raise the room temperature. She put on her robe and pushed her feet into her slippers. As she walked into the kitchen, she could feel the warmth from the fire that Carpenter had started. The wood box had wood and Carpenter had brought a new piece of salted ham in from the smoke shed. Winnie put on her apron, started the coffee, and sliced the ham. As she mixed the biscuits and the aroma of the ham drifted into the bedroom, Gruen began to toss and turn in his crib. Winnie continued to prepare breakfast and hoped that Gruen would remain asleep until the meal was prepared. He would be two years old in a month and he loved to run in the yard as well as in the house. As Winnie opened the oven door and took out the biscuits. Gruen began to cry. She placed the biscuits on top of the stove and called to Betty. "Betty! You girls come on down and eat breakfast!"

Gruen understood that his mother's loud talking meant that it was time to get out of his crib. As Winnie walked back into the bedroom, Gruen's cry changed from an angry cry to a pitiful cry. She wiped her hands on her apron and said, "Gruen, stop your fussing. I'm coming." She lifted him out of the crib and kissed him on his forehead. She lifted the corner of her apron and wiped the tears from his cheeks. Winnie decided to get back in bed and nurse Gruen. As she sat down and took her slippers off, Betty, Mary, and Nanny walked into the kitchen. As Gruen began to nurse, Winnie called, "Betty, there's some hot milk on the back of the stove!" Betty replied, "Alright Momma!"

Gruen nursed from both breasts. As he finished nursing, he looked up at his mother and smiled. She laughed as she looked at his upper and lower gums. She told him, "Gruen, you are a real charmer. You can't just grin with those pretty blue eyes and get your way." She kissed him on both checks and sat on the side of the bed. She put on her slippers and walked back into the kitchen. As she walked toward the kitchen, she placed Gruen on her shoulder and patted his back. Winnie stepped into the kitchen and Gruen released a loud burp. The girls giggled and Mary stood up and held her arms out. Winnie handed Gruen to Mary and walked over to the kitchen counter. As she prepared breakfast for Carpenter and William, Mary took Gruen back into the bedroom to change his diaper. Betty cleaned the dishes and Nanny put the dishes in the cupboard. When the girls finished the dishes, they took Gruen up to their bedroom.

William and Carpenter came in for breakfast and each man put a load of firewood in the wood box. William said, "It's goin' to be pretty windy today, so you may need to use more wood than usual. We'll bring more after lunch. "Winnie replied, "Thank you." William continued, "Yeah, Winnie we saw that property owner down at the mill yesterday. You know, the younger one, the one that didn't say nothin'." Winnie prepared her plate and sat at the table.

Winnie asked, "Has he been at the mill all year?" William replied, "No, I haven't seen him down there since he came to the farm. Now, he may have been there, but I never saw him." Winnie asked, "Well, why do you think he was at the mill?" Carpenter interrupted, "Somebody said his daddy died. I don't know if it's true or not." Winnie continued, "Well, I'll ask the doctor about it when he comes." Winnie slowly sipped her coffee as the feeling of several butterflies attacking her stomach consumed her thoughts. The terror that she experienced after Cyrus' physical assault surfaced as she thought of his possible return to the farm. As a child, some of the boys on the Tate Plantation treated her cruelly. They told her that her skin was too pale, her hair was too long, and her hair was too red. Those comments made her feel different, paltry, and unworthy. The thought of Cyrus terrorized her. There was no one to protect her from his desires. Her experiences with Cyrus helped her understand what the elders on the Tate Plantation talked about just before sundown. They talked about asking God to help you, letting God take care of it, and leaving it in the hands of God. As a child, she thought these statements were funny and at least unreal. Encounters with Cyrus caused her to pray and repeat the same statements that the elders discussed. There was no human who could stop Cyrus from committing an act. Her thoughts were stopped when William interrupted, "Winnie! Winnie! Are you alright? We been talkin' to you and you just starin' at the table. 'You alright?" She replied, "Yes William.

I'm alright. 'Just saying a little prayer." William replied, "As long as you prayed, that's not a little prayer, that's a big one. You just saved us all with that one." All three adults laughed as the men stood up and walked toward the kitchen door. William said, "Winnie, we'll see you at lunch. We may have a new calf before morning."

Winnie cleared the breakfast dishes and started cutting some potatoes for dinner. She decided to have great northern beans for lunch, so she had more time to prepare for dinner. She walked over to the wood box and picked up a couple of pieces of firewood. On windy days, she used a lot more firewood. As she placed the firewood in the stove, she heard a horse drawn wagon stop in the backyard. Her body stiffened at the thought that it may be Cyrus. Winnie anxiously walked to the window. She looked at the carriage and recognized the doctor. Her shoulders slumped in a sense of relief. She was thankful that Cyrus had not come to visit and she knew that the doctor would share information about Cyrus' location and perhaps intentions.

Winnie prepared a plate for the doctor and poured cups of tea. As the doctor opened the door and stepped into the kitchen, the raw cutting December wind swirled around the room. As the wind hit her face, Winnie said, "Look who the wind blew in." He replied, "Yes, I was literally blown this way today. The wind is coming from the southeast." As he placed his items on the kitchen chair, he said, "It was an easy ride here, but the ride back may be a little rough."

As the doctor sat down to eat, Winnie placed his plate and hot cup of tea on the table. She picked up her plate and tea. As she walked to her chair she asked the doctor about a few of his patients. After the doctor had eaten several forks of his meal, Winnie asked, "So, how are the property owners doing?" The doctor took a sip of tea and said, "It's funny you should ask that. Thaddeus passed about six days ago. The funeral was yesterday." Winnie asked, "Had he been sick?" The doctor said, "Well, he had several ailments over the past year, but things really turned downward around the end of October. Thaddeus had fallen while inspecting one of his properties about a year ago. After the fall, he suffered from swelling and pain in his lower right leg. We started with cool wet rags on the back of his leg, but that resulted in little improvement. He noticed that his leg felt better when he sat by the fireplace. We tried hot wet rags and that seemed to help for a short period. During the month of October, the entire right leg was full of fever. He told me it felt like it was on fire. Near the end of November, he started experiencing difficulty breathing. We started boiling water and keeping hot steam in the room. He stabilized for a few weeks, but his heart could not sustain the prolonged ailments. Thaddeus was a fighter." Winnie interrupted, "Well, who's going to take over his properties?" The doctor took a sip of tea. As he placed the cup on the table he continued, "His oldest boy Lester will take over. Cyrus is still in school and ...." Winnie interrupted, "Did Cyrus come home for the funeral?" He said, "Yes. He seems to have matured. I think school has been a good thing for him. Lester will make sure that everything is provided for Margaret. Cyrus said he has two more years of school. I think he's planning on running the mill." Winnie asked, "Well, when is he going back to school?" The doctor answered, "I don't think he's going back until sometime in January." Winnie felt like someone dropped an anvil on her abdomen. She had a feeling that Cyrus would return to the farm.

Several days later, the wind had calmed and the frozen ground reflected the sounds of the crows' caws. William and Carpenter had finished eating lunch and returned to the barn. As Winnie placed the beef in the oven, she decided to make some apple pies. She walked into the pantry and picked up ten apples and placed them in a small metal basin. As she walked through the kitchen doorway, she heard a knock at the door. She looked out the window, but she did not see a carriage or horse. As she walked to the kitchen door, she did not see anyone. She thought she must have been mistaken because no one would walk to the farm in such cold weather. She walked back to the counter and unwrapped the newsprint from each apple. The kitchen door opened and Winnie continued washing the apples. She assumed William or Carpenter was bringing in more firewood. She dried the apples with a clean rag. Without looking from the apples, she said, "Thanks for the wood."

There was no answer. Winnie froze at the counter. She knew that William and Carpenter would have answered. Martha always yelled before entering the house. The only person who was bold enough to enter the house would be ...." A male voice interrupted, "Winnie, how are you?"

It was Cyrus. Winnie could not move and she could not think. Her face, chest, and abdomen felt warm and tingly. Her neck muscles tighten on each side and her mouth suddenly felt like cotton. It was difficult to swallow and her knees felt weak. She immediately leaned forward on the counter. Her sudden movement caused Cyrus to rush to her side. When his hands touched her waist, she gasped for air and buried her mouth between her right breast and her armpit. Her knees buckled and Cyrus led her to the kitchen chair. She closed her eyes and put her hands over her mouth as she attempted to muffle her sobs.

Cyrus quietly sat down in the chair at the opposite end of the table. He quietly said, "Winnie, I am very sorry for what I did to you. I was overcome with emotion. I totally lost control. When I saw you peering through the window that day........, I knew you were the girl from the Tate Plantation."

Winnie tearfully said, "What? The Tate Plantation?" He continued, "Yes, my father had meetings over there and I decided to come along on one of the trips. I saw you and I knew that I wanted you. I tried to go down where you and a bunch of kids were playing, but my brother wouldn't let me go. He said it would embarrass father. Your red hair burned a soft spot in my heart. I spent many nights dreaming about you. I have courted other girls, but they don't have the same effect that you have on me. I know what I did was wrong. I knew that I was going off to school and I couldn't take the chance that you would move or something before I got back. I never wanted to hurt you. I hope I didn't hurt you, but I couldn't help myself. I was totally out of control and I never want to act like that again. Please believe me when I say I am sorry. Please accept my apology. My brother has taken over the properties and I told him that I wanted you to stay in this house. I am not the person who took advantage of you. I was out of control and I hope that we can start our relationship over. I would like to start with today. I ......" Winnie interrupted, "How did you get here?" He answered, "I drove father's small carriage." Winnie asked, "Where did you put it? I looked out the window and I didn't see it." He answered, "I tied the horse to the bush on the side of the house. He likes to eat shrubbery and he decided to stop there. I tried to move him, but he wasn't having it." Winnie asked, "Why did you stand to the side when you knocked on the door?" He answered, "Well, after the way I left the last time I was here, I didn't think you would let me in. I needed to talk to you and apologize for my inexcusable behavior. I'm not a bad guy. I made a horrible mistake and I am very sorry for any pain I may have caused you. My brother told me not to come here, but I'm not letting anyone keep me away from you again." A loud thump was heard from above. They both were startled and Cyrus asked, "What's that?" Winnie said, "That's just the kids. I guess they're getting up from their nap." Cyrus answered, "Well, I have to go now. I don't want mother worrying about me. I will be back before I leave for school. And this time, I really will eat your food." Cyrus smiled as Winnie anxiously watched him. He stood up and said, "You probably need to put some wood in the stove. Maybe I can taste some of your apple pie next time. I'll see myself out. Thanks for listening." Cyrus put his hat on and slowly walked toward the kitchen door. He turned the knob and looked back at Winnie. She was still sitting at the table with both arms resting on top of the table. She sat motionless as he smiled and said, "Goodbye Winnie."

Chapter 16

Several days later, Winnie cleaned the lunch dishes and decided to check the metal grate in the oven. Each time she placed a roaster or pan on the bottom grate, it rocked from side to side. The early January cold air continued to lower the house temperature, but she knew that early afternoon was the best time to check the oven. She did not put more firewood in the stove because she wanted the oven temperature lowered. She wanted to take the grates out and look at the brackets. If any were broken, Carpenter and William would have to repair or replace the stove.

Winnie used several rags and pulled the top grate from the brackets and placed it on the door of the oven. As she used both hands to remove the bottom grate, it seemed to be caught at the back left corner. She walked around to the right side of the oven with her back toward the kitchen door. She knew that her position would block some of the sunlight, but that position would allow the best view of the back left corner. She squatted to allow more visibility and wiggled the grate. She detected that the heat had warped the grate at the rear left corner. She thought that rotating the grate ninety or one hundred eighty degrees could solve the problem. She turned the bottom grate and picked up the top rack. She straightened her knees and bent over the door in order to slide the top rack back into the oven. As the grate reached the mid-point of the oven, a male voice said, “Now that’s a beautiful view.”

Winnie immediately stood up and banged her head on the underside of the cast iron frying pan handle. She loudly said, “Oh!” She grabbed the top of her head as a hand grabbed her waist. The hand pulled her away from the stove and against a body. The hardness of the body indicated that it was a male. With her right hand on her head, she quickly turned to face the person. It was Cyrus. He kept his hand around her waist and said, “I didn’t want you to fall on that hot stove.” Winnie glanced at the kitchen door. He stepped back and said, “Oh, I let myself in. I could see through the door that you were pretty involved with the stove. I also have something for you.” He stepped back one more step and held up his right hand. Hanging from his hand was a full grown turkey. He moved the lifeless bird toward her. She slowly removed her right hand from her head and reached for the turkey.

When her hand clasped the turkey's legs, Cyrus' fingers clasped her hand. She looked into his pale blue eyes and said, "Thank you." He smiled, softly caressed her right hand and said, "You're welcome." He suddenly stepped to her right side, took the rag from the oven door and closed the oven. He said, "Now, you're going to need some firewood in here. The temperature probably needs to be a little higher." As he quickly walked to the wood box and picked up several pieces of firewood, Winnie slowly turned and walked to the counter. She was trying to figure how Cyrus had come into the kitchen without her hearing his carriage enter the yard. Again, had he left the carriage in some strange hidden location of the property? She looked out the window and much to her surprise, the horse drawn carriage was there. She knew she wasn't losing her hearing. How could this be? She turned to her right and curiously asked, "How did you drive that carriage into the yard without me hearing it?" As Cyrus put the wood in the stove, he smiled and stated, "Father had the carriage built to reduce noise. He liked to work on things and try to make them easier to use. He had the stable help replace the chains with leather straps. The carriage is faster and makes less noise than the typical horse drawn carriage. You have to replace the leather straps about every third trip. It's a very nice ride." He smiled, looked at Winnie and said, "I'll have to take you for a ride sometime."

Winnie nervously jerked the feathers from the turkey's body as Cyrus sat at the opposite end of the table. He placed his hat on top of the table and slid his coat over his shoulders. He watched Winnie snatch the feathers from the carcass. She could feel that he was watching her and her face, neck, and abdomen began to tingle. At this point, she could not discern whether the tingling sensation was good or bad. She didn't know if fear or attraction was causing this reaction. She thought, "I could never be attracted to a man that…."

Her thoughts were interrupted as he asked, "Winnie, could I try a piece of your sweet smelling pie?" Winnie froze. The pie was two feet to her left, but did he really want pie? Was he setting up another physical encounter? She had told herself, " I won't let him get to me emotionally. How could …." Cyrus asked, "Winnie, are you alright?" Winnie washed her hands in the basin and said, "Yes, I'll heat the pie in the oven. Winnie picked up the pie pan and placed it on the bottom grate of the oven.

As she turned to walk back to the counter, Cyrus quickly stood up and grabbed her left wrist. She immediately stopped and her body stiffened. He slowly turned her body to face him. As they stood between the kitchen table and the woodstove, she felt trapped.

He reached with his left hand and lifted her chin. He said, "Winnie, you have beautiful brown eyes. Please let your hair down." She swallowed, closed her eyes, and reached up with both hands and took the black hair pin out of her hair. As her hair fell over her shoulders, he smiled and shook his head. He said, "Winnie, I want you to feel relaxed around me. I want to be your friend. I want you to consider me as a friend." Winnie sighed as he placed both of her hands on his shoulders. He asked, "May I hug you?" Winnie turned her head away from the heat of the woodstove. He gently slid his left hand down the left side of her face and stopped at her chin. He slowly turned and lifted her face so that he could see her eyes. He quietly asked, "Winnie, may I hug you?" She slowly nodded her head in affirmation. He slowly reached for her waist and pulled her body in toward his pelvic area.

Winnie could feel his hardened manhood pressing against her lower abdomen. She loosely rested her hands on his shoulders. He slowly moved his hands up and down her back. As he applied more pressure to her back, she began to feel a sense of fear building. He seemed to be advancing beyond a request for a hug. Her thoughts were confirmed when his hands slid down over her buttocks. He shifted his weight from left to right and sighed. He slid his hands up to her waist and whispered, "Thank you, thank you for the hug." He stepped back and covered his crotch with both hands. As he shuffled backward to his seat, Winnie opened the oven door and removed the apple pie. She placed the pie plate on top of the stove. She walked to the cupboard and picked up a saucer, cup, and plate. As she poured the tea and cut the pie, Cyrus continued to fidget with the crotch of his pants. She turned and placed the tea and pie on the table. As she turned back toward the counter, she heard the tapping of little feet on the wooden floor. As he reached the table, Gruen called, "Momma! Momma! Pie! Pie!" Gruen jumped beside the chair and his blond hair bounced freely. Winnie gasped and turned toward the table. Cyrus dropped his fork and the clanking of the porcelain plate caught Gruen's attention. He turned and looked at Cyrus. Winnie quickly moved toward her son. Cyrus smiled and said, "My, young fellow, you have some bright blue eyes." Gruen nodded his head in affirmation. Winnie grabbed his hand and said, "Gruen,…." She was interrupted as Cyrus said, "Wait, young fellow, I tell you what …." Cyrus picked up the fork and cut off a piece of pie. He ate the slice of pie and placed the fork on the plate. He said, "I'll give you the rest of my pie. Take it." Gruen looked up at his mother's face. She nodded in affirmation. Cyrus slid the plate in front of the chair next to Gruen's chair. Winnie attempted to move the plate farther away, but Cyrus leaned over and held the plate in place. She looked at Cyrus and pulled the chair back for Gruen. As Gruen happily climbed into the chair, Cyrus smiled and asked, “How old is he?” Winnie walked to the other end of the table and looked back at Cyrus. He smiled at Gruen as she walked toward the counter and continued pulling the feathers from the turkey. Cyrus continued, “I see he’s left handed. Are any of your other children left handed?” Winnie stopped pulling the feathers, looked out the window, and replied, “No.” She commenced pulling the feathers more rapidly and aggressively. Cyrus said, “Winnie ….” Gruen interrupted, “Momma! Momma! I go see Betty! Momma! ….” Winnie answered, “Alright Gruen, go see Betty.” As Gruen climbed out of the chair on Cyrus’ side, Cyrus rubbed his hair. Gruen motioned with both hands to remove his hand and ran back upstairs. Winnie washed her hands in the white basin and dried her hands on a clean rag. She sighed and walked toward Gruen’s plate. Cyrus stood and met her at the back of the chair. She avoided making eye contact with Cyrus. She picked up the plate and walked back to the counter. Cyrus followed her to the counter and pressed his body against her buttocks. He slowly wrapped his arms around her waist and said, “He looks great. You have taken good care of him.” He moved her hair on the left side of her neck with his chin and kissed her neck. He whispered, “Thank you.” He slowly stepped back and walked toward the kitchen table. He picked up his hat and coat. As he opened the kitchen door, he buttoned his coat and said, “Thank you for the pie. I’ll have to return the favor.” Winnie stood at the counter as he smiled and stepped out into the cold January air.

In January of 1886, it appeared that Winnie and Cyrus’ relationship had advanced from a relationship of terror to a friendship. The rest of the country was advancing also. On May 8, 1886, a carbonated beverage was invented by a pharmacist in Atlanta, Georgia. On May 29, 1886 he placed an advertisement in the Atlanta Journal. He referred to the beverage as Coca-Cola.

On a warm August morning, Dr. Grunburg stopped his horse drawn carriage in the backyard. Winnie had just come into the kitchen after the children had eaten. The second batch of biscuits was ready to be removed from the oven. As the doctor opened the door, she placed the biscuits on top of the stove. He came into the kitchen with two bottles filled with dark fluid. She prepared the doctor’s plate and poured two cups of tea. He seemed to walk faster than he had in several years. He sat down at the table with a big smile. He placed the two bottles on the table and removed his hat. He pointed to the two bottles and asked, “Do you know what these are?” She replied, “No, I have no idea.” He proceeded to explain that he had gotten the bottles from a medical convention in Richmond. Dr. John Stith Pemberton from Atlanta, Georgia had invented the elixir. He was a pharmacist who originally made the drink like a French wine. The county he lived in was a dry county, so he changed the purpose of the elixir to a medical application. The liquid was used to treat morphine addiction and dyspepsia. Dyspepsia was the feeling of fullness in the upper abdomen.

Winnie poured herself a cup of tea and sat at the table. Dr. Grunburg continued explaining that the liquid was used as treatment for headache and neurasthenia. Neurasthenia was identified as a combination of headache, neuralgia, anxiety, depressed mood, and fatigue. Many of Dr. Stith's female patients had fainting, weakness, and dizziness. Dr. Grunburg took a deep breath before identifying the last medical condition. Dr. Stith had also shared his personal results for treating impotence. Winnie took a sip of tea and raised her eyebrows in anticipation of the results. Dr. Grunburg was excited because he drank a bottle after returning home from the convention. He was elated because he was able to sustain an erection for about two to three minutes. Winnie lowered her eyebrows and took a long sip of tea. The doctor explained that his wife was elated that the elixir had shown promising results. On the other hand, Winnie realized that the doctor needed more than the dark fluid in the bottles to fulfill his duties as a husband and rekindle their physical relationship. The doctor further explained that the liquid was a major development for men's health.

Coca-cola being a major advance in medical history may have been questionable, but the President was making political history. On June 2, 1886, President Grover Cleveland made history by marrying his younger bride (27 years younger) in the White House. President Cleveland was the only President to ever marry in the White House. He was also the only non consecutive two-term President. President Cleveland continued to make history on October 28, 1886 when he dedicated the Statue of Liberty in New York City.

The industrial workforce continued to increase. Railroads continued to connect the United States workforce and economy. President Cleveland continued to fight against high tariffs during 1887. This was Cyrus' last year of school and he finished all of his requirements in December. He came to visit Winnie during the second week of December and he told her that he would be in charge of the mill. His brother Lester was in charge of the properties.

Christmas of 1887 continued to follow the advances of the year. Gruen would turn five years old in about a month and Nanny was now in the double figures. She was ten years old. This was the first year that Betty had helped with the Christmas shopping, decorating, cooking, and baking. Betty often took Mary to town while Nanny cared for Gruen. Martha carried the children to church functions more often. All of the children were learning to be more accountable and accept more responsibility.

The day after Christmas was still exciting for Nanny and Gruen. Carpenter and William had made Gruen a wooden wagon. He sat on the wagon and drove through every room on the first floor at least thirty times on Christmas Day. On the day after Christmas, he convinced Nanny to go outside with her baby carriage as he sat on his wagon and drove around the property for about an hour. He ate dinner, took a bath, and fell fast asleep shortly after his bath. Just before sundown, there was a knock on the door. The girls had gone upstairs, Carpenter was in his bedroom, and Winnie was working on her sewing jobs in her bedroom. Carpenter called, "I'm coming!" He walked to the kitchen door and said, "Good evening. Come on in sir. Let me get the lady of the house." Carpenter knocked on Winnie's open bedroom door. He stepped forward and announced, "There's someone here to see you." Winnie looked up from her sewing and slowly walked toward the kitchen. When she stopped at the kitchen doorway, she could see it was Cyrus. Winnie rubbed her apron with both hands and took a deep breath. Carpenter asked, "What would you like for me to do with your horse?" Cyrus replied, "Put him in the barn." Carpenter answered, "Yes sir." As Carpenter put on his coat and hat, Cyrus brought his arms from behind his body. In his right hand he held a bottle of wine and in his left had he held a small box. He placed the tall bottle on the table and handed the small box to Winnie. As she reached forward he said, "Merry Christmas." He smiled and asked, "Where are the wine glasses? Where is the cork screw?" Winnie ignored him and sat down at the kitchen table. She carefully opened the small box. It was a bottle of perfume. The back label read, "Made in France". She looked at Cyrus and said, "Thank you. I have never had a French perfume before." He smiled as he popped the cork and said, "Put some on. I think you'll like it."

The small dark blue bottle had a glass applicator attached to the top. Winnie smiled as she applied some perfume behind each ear. The perfume smelled of sweet powdery magnolias. Winnie could not contain her joy and feeling of instant feminine prowess. She applied a small amount to her right wrist and rubbed her wrists together. Cyrus handed her a short juice glass filled with white wine and said, "My, you do smell heavenly. Could you please let your hair down, just for me?" Winnie took a sip from her glass and placed it on the table. She smiled and took the black hair pin out of her hair. Cyrus refilled his glass and placed the bottle on the table.

He raised his glass and said, "Winnie, I would like to make a toast. A toast to us, a toast to friendship, a toast to being together." The two touched glasses and drank the wine. Cyrus continued, "I wanted to spend Christmas Night with you, but mother wanted me home with her. I want to spend the night with you. I want to be with you. I hope you can forgive me and one day, love me." Winnie responded, "Cyrus, we can't be together. I'm already ...." Cyrus interrupted, "Listen, I've already spoken with Doc. He knows I want you. I had a long conversation with mother about what's going on in the community. She told me that Doc can't perform. I can take care of you. I can perform. Winnie, I will protect you." He put both knees on the floor beside her chair. He kissed her left hand and up her left forearm. He kissed back down her forearm and sucked each of her fingers. He laid his head on her lap. She slowly rubbed his sandy brown hair. He stood up next to Winnie's chair and helped her to a standing position. He handed her the glass of wine and picked up the wine bottle. He grabbed her hand and led her into the bedroom. As she walked toward the bed, he closed the door and picked up the oil lamp from the table by the window. He placed the lamp on the mirrored dresser and walked over to the bed. Winnie took her shoes off and continued sipping the white wine.

Cyrus slowly undressed and told Winnie that he was going to give her the second part of her Christmas gift. Winnie giggled and handed the empty glass to Cyrus. He put the glass on the floor and kissed his way up her right arm. When he reached the sleeve of her dress, he skipped to kissing her neck. He unbuttoned the back of her dress and slid the dress over her shoulders. He kissed her right breast and fondled her left. As the white wine relaxed her body, she began to moan as he kissed her left breast and fondled her right. Cyrus proceeded to pull her dress and panties down to her ankles. As he looked at her body, his erection forced his penis out of the flap on the front of his boxers. As his penis brushed across her leg, she instinctively grabbed his manhood and pulled him to her body. The wine relaxed her jaw and she kissed him with an open mouth. He returned the favor and stretched his tongue deep into her mouth.

He passionately kissed her and gently fondled her breasts. He opened her legs and rubbed the head of his penis across her clitoris. She moaned in pleasure and tossed her head from side to side. He sucked each of her breasts and left a puddle of saliva on each nipple. He kissed down her stomach and tasted her navel. He kissed down to her clitoris and gently kissed, licked, and sucked until she begged him to stop. He left a large deposit of saliva on her clitoris and he slowly slid his penis down into her vagina.

She moaned in painful pleasure. He was the last man to penetrate her vagina and that was almost six years ago. He rhythmically thrust his penis in and out of her vagina. She climaxed to an orgasm and he continued to thrust his manhood until she climaxed a second time. He quickened his movements and lowered his mouth to her mouth. Each released their moans of ecstasy into the other's mouth.

He released saliva in her mouth as his penis released semen into her vagina. He continued to kiss her chin, neck, and breasts as they gasped for air. He slowly lowered himself to her right side. He turned on his back and pulled Winnie over onto his chest. Cyrus awakened once in the middle of the night and started to make love again. He pulled Winnie onto his chest until they awakened for the morning. Winnie tried to get out of bed to make coffee, but Cyrus pulled her back into the bed and made love to her a third time before breakfast.

Cyrus walked into the kitchen after the coffee was made. Winnie had sliced the ham and started the biscuits. Her body seemed relaxed and she prepared the meal with a sense of contentment. She believed that Cyrus had reestablished their relationship as a friendship and a physical relationship. Whether he would share the information that he had learned at school with her, remained to be seen. She had grown accustomed to sharing medical information and research with the doctor. She secretly hoped that Cyrus would share some of the information from school as well as information about the mill. Her thirteen year relationship with the doctor helped her realize what she wanted and needed in a relationship. She realized that a man would have to be her friend, lover, and intellectual mentor. She needed intellectual stimulation as well as physical stimulation. After the doctor's illness, she had adjusted to not having a physical relationship. It wasn't easy and it wasn't pleasant. She still had respect for the doctor and their relationship, but a piece of the relationship was missing. Cyrus now filled the void of the physical relationship with the doctor. She wanted that relationship that she once shared with the doctor, but perhaps fate wanted another plan for her life. Ever since the doctor described her world as a "business decision", she had drifted apart from the doctor. She no longer regarded him as a protector and lover. She now considered him a very friendly boss. Perhaps fate had sent Cyrus to change the course of her life.

Chapter 17

Cyrus was very comfortable at the farm. Carpenter and William used Cyrus' visit as an opportunity to spend more time at the "Sing Shack". On the nights that Carpenter planned to be away, he filled the wood box and stacked the equivalent of a second wood box on the floor. Betty and Mary drew water from the well and Nanny watched Gruen. Cyrus and Winnie had many opportunities to share emotionally, intellectually, and physically. Cyrus was kind and patient with all of the children. He seemed to have developed a noticeable closeness to Gruen.

On the fifth morning, Winnie awakened and felt blissfully exhausted. Cyrus was almost six years her junior, but she felt that he had the energy of someone at least ten years younger.

Winnie put more firewood in the stove and sliced the ham. She walked into the pantry to get flour and shortening to mix the biscuits. As she walked back through the kitchen doorway, she heard a horse drawn carriage stop in the backyard. It sounded like the wagon was moving rather quickly and stopped suddenly. Even on a cold December morning, a cloud of dust slowly drifted past the wagon. She peered out the window in hopes of identifying the driver. The driver was already walking quickly toward the house. He frowned and his face appeared to be blush. He quickly and forcibly knocked on the door.

Winnie cautiously walked to the door. As she opened the door, the carriage driver hurriedly asked, "Is Cyrus here?" Winnie grabbed the collar of her robe and said, "Yes, he's …." The man quickly interrupted, "I need to see him! I need to see him right now!" Winnie stepped back from the door and said, "Please come in from the cold." As she walked toward the bedroom, the man quickly opened the door and stepped into the kitchen. Winnie walked through the bedroom door and announced, "Cyrus, there's someone here to see you." Cyrus slowly raised his head and sat on the side of the bed. He picked up his pants from the floor, his shirt from the headboard and clumsily put them on. Winnie looked in the closet for a clean dress. As Cyrus walked past Winnie, he playfully spanked and rubbed her buttocks. Winnie quickly released a high pitched scream and immediately cupped her mouth with her right hand. They both giggled as Cyrus walked through the kitchen doorway.

Cyrus buttoned his shirt and looked up at the man. He smugly said, "Well, if it isn't big brother coming to make a visit. To what do we owe the privilege of your presence?" Winnie stepped into her blue cotton dress and whispered, "Oh, my Lord." She gently closed the closet door and listened at the doorway.

The man walked toward Cyrus and said, "You need to get home now. Mother has been asking about you." Cyrus replied, "Well Lester, Daddy left you in charge of everything. Why don't you just tell her I had to go out of town, ...on business? She'll believe you." Lester replied, "Cyrus, that's not the issue and you know it. Our family reputation is on the line. Our ancestors came to Essex County in 1655. They helped Governor Berkeley distribute land! They signed the Charter that created King William County! Daddy was the Commissioner of Revenue in Essex County and for God's sake, we own over 600 acres in Middlesex County alone! You will not tarnish this family's name and you sure as hell will not hurt Mother! Cyrus ...." Cyrus interrupted, "Well Lester ...."

Lester charged Cyrus, grabbed his neck, and yelled, "I've had it with you!"

The two men wrestled each other and fell onto the table. Lester pushed Cyrus against the stove and burned a hole in the right sleeve of his of his dress shirt. Cyrus yelled, "Damn it!" Cyrus pushed back and the two knocked over three kitchen chairs. Gruen began to cry and yell, "Momma! Momma! I want Momma!" Winnie heard the smacking of skin and deep throaty moans. Shortly thereafter, Cyrus slid on his back through the bedroom doorway. He moaned, rubbed his jaw and tossed from side to side on the floor. Winnie gasped and covered her mouth with her right hand. The smoke from the burning ham had filled the ceiling and begun to come through the bedroom door. Lester straightened his clothes, pointed at Cyrus and said, "Cyrus, if I have to come back, there will be hell to be paid! This little nest egg that you have here just might disappear! Cyrus slowly lowered his hand from his mouth and angrily said, "Lester, don't fuck around! This is my life!" Lester replied, "Cyrus! You can't stay here! That's life! Daddy is not here to protect you! We all have to do things that we don't want to do! You'd better get your fucking life in order! Have you been to the mill? You wanted that new steam engine down at the mill and you haven't even fucking been there! Make it right Cyrus! Don't make me come back here! Lester picked up his hat from the kitchen floor and stormed out of the door. The cold December air blew the smoke through the bedroom doorway. Gruen's crying seemed to be coming closer as Winnie rushed to help Cyrus sit up. She left Cyrus and rushed to take the smoking frying pan from the stove. She grabbed several rags from the counter, grabbed the handle of the frying pan, rushed to the kitchen door, and threw the frying pan into the back yard. As she turned to walk back to Cyrus, Gruen ran downstairs yelling, “Momma! Momma! Smoke! Smoke!” Winnie yelled, “Gruen! Get back upstairs with your sisters! Everything is fine!” Gruen’s cry became louder as he turned and ran back upstairs. Cyrus had managed to stand in the bedroom doorway. Winnie lifted the chairs to their four legs. As Winnie approached Cyrus, the chair closest to the stove tumbled to the floor. Winnie held Cyrus’ left arm and guided him to the kitchen chair. As he sat in the chair, she opened the kitchen door in order to let fresh air in and let the black smoke out. She rushed back toward the bedroom doorway and closed the door. Winnie walked past Cyrus and opened the kitchen window. The smoke followed the air stream out of the window. Winnie wet a clean rag with cold water. She walked over to Cyrus and gently wiped the bloody wound at the right corner of his mouth. After cleaning the wound, she slowly pulled his head to her abdomen. He wrapped his arms around her waist and said, “Thank you Winnie. I’m supposed to take care of you and ....” Winnie interrupted, “Sh-h-h-h.” After about fifteen seconds she softly said, “Cyrus, it’s alright. I believe you, but your brother is right. You can’t stay here. You know, the doctor always comes just before lunch. Maybe you should check your schedule at the mill and work out a good time to come here. We’re not going anywhere. Well, that is .... if you listen to your brother.” They both laughed as Winnie walked toward the door.

She said, “If I don’t close this door, we’ll all freeze to death. I’m glad Carpenter left extra wood. “She closed the door and turned to the stairwell. She called, “Betty, I need you and Mary to come down here!” She rushed over to the window and pulled it down. She said, “Cyrus, let me see your shirt. You may not be able to wear it to the mill anymore, but you may be able to wear it around the farm.” As he held out his arm, Betty and Mary stepped into the kitchen. Winnie said, “Betty start some biscuits and Mary, go out in the yard and get my frying pan. Now let ....” Mary interrupted, “In the yard? Momma, did you say....” Winnie sternly interrupted, “Girl, did you hear what I said?” Mary said, “Yes Momma.” As she walked out to retrieve the frying pan, Gruen ran downstairs and hugged his mother. Winnie said, “Gruen, everything is alright. We are making breakfast, but I need you to stay upstairs with Nanny.” As he turned to run upstairs, he said, “Alright Momma! Nanny, here I come!” Cyrus started to smile and then suddenly grabbed his mouth. He said, “That boy has a lot of energy. I could use him down at the mill, “Winnie laughed and said, “I’m going to hold you to that when he turns thirteen." Mary quickly opened the door and stepped into the kitchen. She announced, "Momma, I threw the burnt meat down by the barn." As she cleaned the pan, Betty laughed and said, "Mary you're going to bring the biggest opossum ever to the barn." They both laughed as Winnie pulled open the hole in Cyrus' shirt sleeve. She grasped, "Oh my Lord! Cyrus! Your arm has been burned. Go into the bedroom. I'm going to get my medical bag. Betty and Mary, finish making breakfast and call Nanny and Gruen down." The girls answered, "Alright Momma."

Cyrus walked into the bedroom and Winnie walked into the pantry to get her medical bag. When Winnie walked into the bedroom, Cyrus was slowly removing his shirt. He said, "Big brother still has a pretty good punch." Winnie replied, "He has a pretty good kick too, 'cause my kitchen chair is broken." They both laughed and Cyrus said, "Don't worry, we'll order a new one and then Carpenter can pick it up at the general store." Winnie answered, "Now Cyrus, don't go drawing attention by buying furniture that won't go to your mother's house." He replied, "Don't worry, once they find out that I'm paying, well, Lester will be paying, there will not be a problem. Nobody questions our family." Winnie replied, "Well, the only thing I know is ....this wound needs to be cleaned and dressed. Oh my goodness, it's on your right arm." As she poured the whiskey on the rag, Cyrus asked, "Why does it matter that the burn is on my right arm?" Winnie replied, "Well, you'll be doing most things with your right hand. You're ...." Cyrus interrupted, "Winnie, I'm left handed, just like Gruen." He looked up at Winnie and slowly smiled until Winnie intentionally rubbed his burn a little harder. Cyrus moaned and said, "That's no way to treat a left handed man." Winnie ignored his comment and continued to clean and dress the wound.

Cyrus was a man of his word. He ordered a new kitchen table and six chairs. Carpenter went to the General Store in Tappahannock and brought them home. The girls thought that Christmas had come again. The new table was made in Pennsylvania and delivered on the train.

Several months later, the April showers once again sparked the growth of saplings, grass, and wildflowers. On a cool April morning, Dr. Grunburg came to the farm before making his house calls. Winnie had sipped one cup of ginger tea and had just started another when the doctor stopped his wagon in the backyard. As he opened the kitchen door, Winnie placed his plate and coffee on the table. She picked up her cup of ginger tea and sat at the other end of the table.

The doctor came into the kitchen, spoke to Winnie and sat at the table. He placed his medical bag and hat on the table. Winnie thought that he seemed distracted. She asked, "Is everything alright?" He ate a fork full of food and said, "I thought I might ask you the same question. Cyrus told me that he might be having a baby. Do you know who might be having his baby? I don't recall going to his wedding." Winnie sipped more ginger tea and cleared her throat. She answered, "I thought Cyrus had discussed our relationship with you. Did he talk to you?" The doctor answered, "Well, yes he did. So, by the smell of your tea, I guess I need to do an examination?" Winnie replied, "Yes, I think you do."

After he finished his breakfast, the doctor said, "Alright, let's do the examination. If Cyrus keeps this up, I may have to find another nurse. You're going to end up as my patient more than my nurse." They both laughed as they walked into the bedroom. After the examination, the doctor said, "Winnie, you are with child. Congratulations." Winnie replied, "Thank you." The doctor said, "Well, you're probably my best patient. You already know what to do. Does Betty have an interest in being a nurse?" Winnie answered, "Oh no. She said she didn't have the stomach for nursing. She said she would rather do cooking and baking." The doctor looked at the ceiling and said, "Uh-huh, I wouldn't have predicted that she wouldn't want to work in the medical field." Winnie did not respond and asked the doctor about the patients he planned to visit.

Four months later, Winnie decided to go for an early morning walk. She hadn't been able to sleep well the night before. She walked past little Fannie's grave and walked behind the barn. She looked at the honey suckle growing at the edge of the yard. She was thankful that her children were able to grow up on a farm. They had always had a lot of room to run, play, and learn how to grow and harvest crops. They had also learned how to care for and manage farm animals. As she decided to walk back toward the house, a clear warm liquid gushed onto her legs and cotton shoes. The baby was finally on the way. This was the first baby whose water broke while she was outside. She walked around to the front of the barn and told Carpenter that the baby was on the way. He looked at William and William said, "I'll go get Martha." Winnie thanked them for always helping and she started walking toward the house. As she reached the corner of the barn, she felt a very strong contraction. She moaned, stopped walking and leaned against the barn. Carpenter came out of the barn and asked, "Are you alright? Do you need some help getting back to the house?" Winnie shook her head and told him, "No, I'll be alright. This one just dropped really fast. This baby is in a big hurry to get here. Just bring in some more firewood. I'll get Betty to bring in more water." Carpenter replied, "Alright, let me know if you need anything else." As she continued walking back to the house, the warm clear fluid continued to ooze down her legs. When she opened the door, she called, "Betty, I need you to boil two pots of water and get more water from the well. The baby is on the way." Winnie went to the pantry and picked up her medical bag and some clean rags. As she prepared the bedroom for this baby's birth, she felt more comfortable than any of the previous births. Even if Martha didn't make it to the house before the baby arrived, Betty would be able to take care of the younger children. She would also be able to follow Winnie's directives for delivery if needed. She sat on the bed and looked at the yellow baby clothes that she placed on the back right side of the mirrored dresser. Ever since she had lived in the house, she had placed the new baby's clothes on the back right side of the mirrored dresser.

Martha arrived before the baby was born. She helped Winnie deliver a healthy baby boy. His hair was sandy brown and his eyes were blue. He did not have the large forehead like Gruen. His cheeks were wide like his mother's cheeks. Martha cut the umbilical cord and handed the newborn to Winnie. She told her, "This baby looks just like you. He has blue eyes like his father, but he certainly doesn't look like him. Looks like you made this one all by yourself." Both women laughed as Winnie reached for her newborn son. She told Martha, "I certainly didn't make him by myself, but he does look like me." Martha asked, "What are you going to name him?" Winnie replied, "Bruce."

Bruce thrived through the winter of 1888. Winnie returned to nursing about one month later. Betty was fourteen years old and she could read and write. During one of her maternity visits, a patient mentioned that she would need a helper after the baby was born. Winnie discussed the matter with Dr. Grunburg and they decided that Betty would be able to take the job. She moved to a medium sized farm north of Urbanna. When she left in January 1889, Mary cared for Bruce and assumed Betty's household chores and responsibilities.

Cyrus continued to visit the farm once a week. He usually came on Wednesday mornings. He often shared information about how his Todd Steam engine had improved productivity and efficiency at the mill. Leonard Jennett Todd had patented a uniflow steam engine in 1885. The horizontal piston forced the steam in the poppet valve inlets. The steam flowed in one direction. He explained how the Todd engine allowed higher thermal efficiency than earlier engines. Winnie never imagined that she would learn about steam engines.

As a child, Winnie had imagined going on a picnic with the love of her life. Once she entered into the arrangement with Dr. Grunburg, she had resolved herself to not participating in such a romantic occasion. When Cyrus came to visit on Wednesday, he mentioned that many of the couples at the mill went on picnics. He asked Winnie if she liked picnics. Once she shared her childhood fantasy, Cyrus suggested a Saturday picnic. He told her that he would be working at the mill until 12:00 noon. Cyrus said that he would come and pick her up after he shut the mill down. Winnie agreed to make the food and bring a quilt. Cyrus told her that they would have the picnic even if it rained.

On Saturday, May 19, 1894, Cyrus arrived at the farm at 1:00 in the afternoon. Mary assured her mother that she would care for the younger children. She was visiting from her job as a domestic worker. Dr. Grunburg had gotten her a job at a medium sized farm north of Urbanna. She worked about two miles from the farm where Betty worked.

Cyrus and Winnie rode to the mill and set up the picnic behind the mill. A fresh water stream ran past the rear of the building. Once he showed Winnie the location, it was obvious that he had planned the outing for privacy. As Winnie straightened the quilt and placed the food on the linen table cloth, Cyrus went down to the edge of the stream. He pulled a twine that had a bottle tied at the end. As he walked up the hill, he broke off several vines of honey suckle. Winnie asked, "What do you have?" Cyrus replied, "A nice cool bottle of French white wine and flowers." He showed his classic cunning smile and said, "Only the best for my lady." Winnie replied, "Cyrus, you always say the nicest things to me." Cyrus answered, "You are the only woman that I have met who really listens to all of my steam engine stories, mill adventures, and ideas about improving existing machines. And you know, the boys are just perfect. One looks just like me and one looks just like you. You make my life complete." Winnie told him, "Oh Cyrus, stop trying to fill my head with a lot of sweet nothings. Come on and eat before the bugs take this food away."

Cyrus opened the back door of the mill. When he came back through the door, he held two crystal wine glasses. He told her that he had ordered the Waterford crystal glasses through the general store. Since his family was Irish, his mother always ordered Waterford crystal. Winnie admired the weight and lines of the heavy lead crystal.

After finishing one bottle of wine and starting the second, Cyrus began to caress Winnie's right arm. He moved closer and laid his head on her lap. She finished her glass of wine and lay down on the quilt. He asked her to take her hair pin out of her hair. As her bright red hair fell to her shoulders, he unbuttoned his shirt and placed it on the quilt. He unbuttoned the back of her cotton dress and pulled it down over her shoulders. As he continued to pull her dress down her body, she unbuckled his pants. He reached for the honeysuckle and systematically took the trumpet-shaped flowers from the vine. He tore open the petal, pulled the filament, and placed them over Winnie's bare pale body. He rubbed the nectar on her dark pink nipples, the center line of her stomach, and the inside of her navel. He placed the opened flowers on her pubic hair. As he leaned over to taste the sweet nectar on her chest and breasts, she reached for his penis. His erect manhood sprang through the front flap of his boxers. As he tasted down her body, the slow May breeze gently brushed across her nipples. Her nipples hardened and chill bumps covered her body. He tasted the open flowers that lined her navel. He moved down her abdomen to taste the seepage of sweet nectar that had coated her sticky clitoris. The sweet nectar caused him to salivate like a fountainhead. Cyrus placed his left knee between her legs and kissed a path up her body. He planted his lips on the soft ridge of her collar bone and tasted her sweet skin. He slowly slid his manhood through the layer of honeysuckle flowers and entered her vagina. She blissfully moaned as he kissed her neck and plunged in and out of her. The friction of their warm bodies projected a sweet, floral, aromatic fragrance. After he exhausted his desires, he gently lowered himself onto her flower covered body. Cyrus grabbed her waist and rolled onto his back. Her vibrant red hair fell onto his face. He parted her hair and grabbed both sides of her face. He gently kissed her lips as he whispered, "I love you." She rested on top of him as they relished the perfection of the moment. He slowly turned to his left and lowered her to the quilt. They fell asleep on the quilt as the sinking sun faded behind the mill and created a shadow on the quilt. They slept together by the light of the full moon.

Two months later, Winnie was rudely awakened by the facts of life. Mr. Tate, the plantation owner, died and his children eventually asked Winnie's father, Thornton Tate Sr., to leave the plantation. He was a proud man and he didn't want to ask his children for help. As he continued to age, his health began to decline. In his early eighties, Thornton Sr. could no longer function as a productive agricultural laborer. He moved to his son's farm and served as an advisor to the farm workers. His health continued to deteriorate and on Monday, August 13, 1894, Thornton Tate, Sr. died in the town of Occupacia, Essex County, Virginia.

Carpenter drove Winnie and her children (Nanny, Gruen, and Bruce) to Thornton Jr.'s farm. The farm house faced Occupacia Creek and Thornton Sr. was buried in the side yard under the black walnut tree. Winnie's daughter Mary could not get time off from her job to travel to Occupacia. Her eldest daughter, Betty, took time off from her work and informed Winnie at the funeral that she was moving to Philadelphia. Betty left the service and traveled to Tappahannock. She planned to take the ship to Baltimore and then travel by rail. The family managed to salvage some happiness from the sad occasion.

Thornton Jr. and his wife's last child was a boy. He was born on April 24,

1890 with light brown hair and blue eyes. Winnie was happy that she had an opportunity to meet Temple. Temple was four years old and Bruce was age six. The family joked about how they looked like twins.

After returning from Occupacia, Dr. Grunburg informed Winnie that Betty's employer needed another housekeeper. He told the family that he would find a replacement. When Betty learned of her grandfather's death, she packed her items and left after two days notice. She seized this event as an opportunity to experience life in the big city. Dr. Grunburg and Winnie discussed the situation and decided that Nanny would be able to handle the job. Nanny moved to the medium sized farm north of Urbanna at the end of August.

Several weeks later, Winnie began to feel lethargic. This was the first time since moving to the farm that all of the cooking, cleaning, and laundry were her responsibility. Dr. Grunburg was concerned that she may not have accepted all of the girls leaving home. When she started feeling nauseous, the doctor decided to give Winnie an examination. After the examination, the doctor announced, "Winnie, you are again, with child. I would say that you're about four months along." Winnie counted back four months and May would have been the month of conception. She smiled as she recalled the picnic behind the mill.

Five months later, Winnie gave birth to a third son. Martha helped deliver Roland on Saturday, February 23, 1895. Just like Gruen, he had a large forehead and deep set eyes. Cyrus was very proud of having three sons. He kept his promise and gave Gruen a job at the mill. Gruen cleaned the inside of the mill and cleared the weeds and grass on the grounds.

Chapter 18

Winnie's ability to quickly go on house calls was complicated by the girls leaving home. Once again, she relied on Martha to care for the boys. Martha's boys were grown and had left home, so she enjoyed having young children in the house again. She sometimes sent Winnie's boys to the fields with Tom, while she did housework.

Roland continued to thrive through the winter of 1895. As the boys grew older, Winnie sent them to the barn and fields. Carpenter and William taught them how to care for the animals, mend the fences, and tend the crops. After dinner, she taught the boys how to read and write. During dinner, Carpenter and William often talked about how Roland watched as they worked on farm equipment. He often bruised his fingers and hands because he attempted to connect attachments and lift equipment like the adults. Bruce liked to ride the animals, but he did not like handling the equipment. When Gruen made it home in time for dinner, he told his younger brothers about the steam engine at the mill. The boys tentatively listened to the details of its operation. Roland begged to visit the mill, and occasionally Gruen took him for visits. Even at five years old, he seemed to enjoy learning how engines worked. Roland was fascinated with how things worked and moved.

Cyrus did not want to travel a long distance to visit Winnie any longer. He decided that it was time for her to move closer. Cyrus came to visit Winnie on a cool May morning. Winnie had fed the boys and the men. She prepared her plate and poured a cup of coffee. As she turned to walk to the table, she heard the faint sound of a horse drawn carriage stop in the backyard. She looked out the window and recognized Cyrus walking toward the house. He stepped into the kitchen showing his cunning smile and announced, "Good morning. Could you fix one of those cups for me?" Winnie prepared a cup of coffee for him as he sat at the kitchen table. He continued, "Well, my big brother finally came around to my way of thinking. I had told him right after Roland was born that I wanted you and the boys closer to my house. It appears that a young couple made Lester a good offer on this place. Lester accepted the offer and finally agreed to getting you a place closer to me. You and the boys will be moving to a small place near Brill Farm. I have relatives who operate a fishing business at Burham's Wharf. The property leads to the Rappahannock River and it's located at Cooper, Virginia. You won't be on the water, but it will be close enough that the boys could fish and oyster. They could bring some extra food into the household and earn some money as well." He took a sip of his coffee and Winnie sat and listened inquisitively. She had assumed that she would die while living in Jamaica, Virginia. Cyrus interrupted, "I've been busy at the mill this week, so it took me until now to make my way here with the news. I wanted to tell you in person, so I intentionally didn't tell Gruen. Lester has arranged the transaction for Monday." Winnie interrupted, "Monday! Do you mean two days from now?" Cyrus answered, "Yes. I know it's short notice. I'm sorry. Lester needs you and Carpenter to meet him at the Middlesex County Courthouse at 10:00 a.m. He'll handle everything. It's a small place, but the boys will be moving on their own before long. You have been doing a good job managing things, but I'm assuming you won't be having any more babies?" They both laughed and Winnie replied, "Well, no thanks to you." Cyrus took another sip of coffee and said, "I can't help it if you are the most irresistible woman in the world." They both laughed and she replied, "You should have run for President rather than running the mill. You always come up with such flattering comments."

On Monday morning, Carpenter and Winnie left for the Middlesex County Courthouse just after sunrise. Bruce was twelve years old, so he had to take care of Roland until their return. Winnie had taught him how to make biscuits and cook meat. Winnie decided to ride in the back of the wagon. She lined the wagon with a couple of quilts and carried her umbrella.

Winnie walked in the front as Carpenter walked several feet behind. Lester met them at the front door and took them around to a side entrance. Lester explained that he was selling them seven and three eighths acres for twelve dollars. There was a $1.75 fee, but Lester waived the fee. Lester explained that the deed was dated May 14, 1900 and they could move in immediately.

Upon returning to the farm, Winnie explained to Bruce and Roland that they would be moving to a new house. She told them that there would be more children to play with in the neighborhood. She emphasized that they would be able to go swimming and fishing. Cyrus shared the news with Gruen about the move when he came to work at the mill. He also told Gruen that he wanted him to go to Baltimore for training. Gruen had observed and listened to the men who maintained the steam engine at the mill. He had learned the machine quickly and the men often asked for his advice on how to manage complex mechanical problems. At seventeen, Gruen was considered an accomplished steam engine maintenance worker.

William had been a wonderful helper for Carpenter. When Carpenter told him that they were moving, William decided not to move. He decided to move in with Bett. He wanted to spend more time showing his son how to manage a farm. Martha always told Winnie that God would work everything out. William's decision to stay in Jamaica proved her words to be true. One week after they moved, Bett became ill. William moved into the Sing Shack and cared for her. She continued to grow weaker and died two weeks later. William was forced to raise William Jr. alone.

Martha decided to take William Jr. to live at her house. She took him to church events and he worked in the fields with Tom and William. William slept at his parent's house and worked with Tom during the day. Martha convinced William to come to some of the church social events. He met one of the women at the church and they married after six months. She agreed to raise William Jr. as her own child. William married Amanda and the three of them moved to a small farm north of Urbanna. They lived about five miles from the farm where Nanny worked. Within the year, Amanda was pregnant. William asked Winnie to be Amanda's nurse. Amanda gave birth to a son. William and Amanda named him Sidney.

Winnie was very busy as a nurse in the new community. There were many young families and many new births. Staying busy helped Winnie cope with the loss of not seeing Martha once a week. Even though the new farm was smaller, Bruce had to help with chores. Roland was five years old so he was only able to help with light duty chores and run errands for Carpenter and Bruce.

Traveling with one wagon limited the number of items that were carried to the new farm. They packed their clothes, linen, and the new kitchen furniture that Cyrus ordered and made the three hour trip. Winnie decided that she would attend church occasionally in the new community. She cherished the few relationships that she built with the women at Martha's church. She also noticed that most of the young families in the new community were arrangements also. The pale complexioned women had dark complexioned husbands. Most or all of the children were fathered by White men. She felt more at ease about her arrangement and believed that the younger church women would be more tolerant of her.

The new house was a small two story white house with a centered front door. The back door was also centered at the rear of the house. A hallway lead to the dining room and the kitchen was at the rear of the house. The stairs were to the right of the front door and led to two bedrooms and a sleep area at the top of the stairs. Gruen slept in the sleep area at the top of the stairs when he came home. He often spent nights at the mill. Carpenter and the boys slept in the smaller bedroom to the right of the stairs. Winnie slept in the larger bedroom to the left of the stairs. The sitting room was below her bedroom to the left of the stairs.

Moving to the new house created changes for everyone. Gruen continued to learn about steam engines. He went to Baltimore for training and did not return. He decided to live as a young White male. Bruce was 12 years old and he was working in the fields with Carpenter all day. Winnie continued teaching Bruce and Roland reading, math, and writing after eating dinner.

The country also had some learning and growing to do. President William McKinley was one year away from the end of his first term. His administration was popular because they brokered the deal for The Treaty of Paris in 1898. They promoted American labor as well as investments in foreign markets. President McKinley was re-elected in 1900. In March 1901, the second term President began a tour of the western states. On September 6, 1901, President McKinley was shot twice in the chest and died eight days later from gangrene. His Vice President, Theodore Roosevelt, assumed office. In 1904 he was elected President. President Roosevelt supported The Meat Inspection Act of 1906. The country seemed to be moving forward in spite of the multiple intermittent recessions since the Civil War.

In 1909, Bruce decided to move out of the house. He rented a room and started dating a fashionable young woman named Elizabeth. He continued to work in the fields with Carpenter. Cyrus kept his promise and Roland was allowed to go to Burham's Wharf to fish. He often sold the excess supply to the neighbors. During the fall and winter, Roland was able to use one of the boats at the dock for oystering. In 1911, Bruce married Elizabeth Stanley of Fredericksburg, Virginia. The newlyweds decided to leave Middlesex County.

1912 proved to be the year Roland left boyhood and became a young man. His older brothers had left home to pursue their dreams and he was left alone to help a rapidly aging Carpenter. Climbing the stairs at bedtime became more and more challenging for the former slave. Roland began to take over the more strenuous farm chores. At 17, he could handle the demands of a small farm during the warmer months and oyster during the colder months. He also thought that he could handle a tall dark complexioned young lady with coal black waist length hair. Family folklore identified Sarah's grandfather as Cherokee Indian. Some Native Americans sought refuge in Middlesex County in order to escape the Trail of Tears ordeal.

Sarah lived about a half mile behind the small farm in a wooded community called King's Neck. The property did not have a wagon trail.

Everyone entered and exited the community via a narrow foot path. Sarah was 14 and liked to flirt with young men in the community. She often carried washed and ironed laundry back to the White homes. She walked about 6 miles round trip to the general store. It was during those trips that Roland noticed Sarah. She walked with one foot directly in front of the other foot when parading for the young men. She did not have a lot of opportunities to parade. Her mother was the pianist for the church and carried her Bible at all times. She carefully monitored Sarah's comings and goings.

The United States business community monitored trends and transactions, but it did not prevent the recession of January 1913. The recession lasted until December 1914. Winnie no longer had the financial support of Dr. Grunburg, but they lived close to the Rappahannock River. On the first day of October, Roland began oystering from Burham's Wharf. He was able to sell oysters, bring some home to eat, and sell excess oysters to neighbors. The season ended at the end of March. During March and April, Roland repaired and painted boats docked at Burham's Wharf. Cyrus' cousin Phil hired Roland as a fishing party boat helper. He helped the paying customers take the fish off the hook, drove the boat, lowered and raised the anchor, maintained the engine, and cleaned the boat at the end of each day. The lucrative income from the seafood industry lured Roland from agricultural work. Carpenter's inability to work several acres of land forced him to find another source of income. He travelled north of Urbanna and cut wood with his brother William. On Saturday, November 21, 1914, Carpenter went to cut wood with William north of Urbanna. They usually cut a lot of pine wood. Pine wood is considered a somewhat soft and relatively light weight wood. Oak on the other hand, is a dense, heavy, hardwood. One day the men needed to cut several oak trees for firewood. They started cutting just after sunrise. At 11:30 a.m., they took a lunch break. They laughed, talked, and drank water. As they walked back to the work area, Carpenter complained of a pain in his chest and sat on a stump. After several minutes, he told William that it was hard to breath. William told him to wait on the stump while he hitched the wagon. When William returned to the stump, Carpenter was too weak to speak. William helped him to the wagon and drove back to the general store near the farm house. The owner sent a telegraph to Dr. Grunburg's house. Dr. Grunburg drove his carriage to the general store and examined Carpenter. Dr. Grunburg spoke to and examined Carpenter before he pronounced his cause of death as a heart attack at 2:00 p.m. William carried the body to Clements Funeral Home in Saluda. Carpenter was buried at Calvary Baptist Church on Sunday, November 22, 1914.

Carpenter was not Roland's biological father, but he treated him like a son. He showed Roland how to care for animals, tend crops, cut wood, start a fire, shave, shoe a horse, mend a fence, build furniture, and the proper technique for lifting heavy items. When he learned of his death, Roland lost a part of his childhood security. Carpenter talked to him while working in the fields and encouraged him to do his best. As he grew older, Roland noticed the hurt and humiliation each time Cyrus or Dr. Grunburg came to the farm house. Whenever Roland pressed Carpenter about why he didn't stop the relationships, Carpenter explained that he was chosen to take care of the household and to keep quiet. He told Roland that it was the way a Negro man had to live. He explained to Roland that his life would be different because he was light complexioned like his mother. Roland pledged allegiance to Carpenter and darker complexioned men, but Carpenter insisted that he take care of himself and let the White men change things. Roland always used profanity as he condemned the unfair treatment of Negro men and the blatant disrespect that his mother's relationship with Dr. Grunburg and Cyrus cast upon their home. Roland had noticed the cautious relationships that he and his mother experienced throughout the neighborhood. The neighbors seemed extremely polite and generous. They acted as if they wanted to keep him and his mother content. Roland felt as if the community had been instructed to accommodate them. Carpenter's death ended any hope that Roland would be able to ease some of the pain Carpenter suffered.

Roland's pain continued to grow during March 1915. He scraped, caulked, and painted the boats at Burham's Wharf during the day and prepared the fields for the planting before sunset. He was 20 years old and he wanted to start his own family. He had decided that he wanted Sarah Duke to be his wife. She walked past his home to go to the general store and to carry laundry. He had heard her talking with her brothers and sisters and she seemed smart and sassy. March ended and April began. Sarah had not walked past the small farm.

On a sunny April afternoon, Roland waited for Sarah's younger brother Philip to walk past the farm. He had been running errands with his sister Ellen. Phillip told Roland that Sarah was sick and she stayed in the bed. After several weeks, Roland asked Winnie if she would make a house call to Sarah's house.

On a cool May morning, Winnie put on her sweater, picked up her medical bag, and walked the path at the rear of her property. About a half mile into the woods, she came upon a small village. Six to eight houses were constructed in a semi-circle facing a large oak tree stump. She inquired about Sarah's house and was directed to the third house from the right. When she entered the house, it was obvious that a single bed had been moved to a sitting room. Sarah was lying on the bed and her mother sat in a rocking chair next to her head.

Sarah's Mother, Mary Duke, told Winnie that Sarah had gotten sick with a cold in February. She kept getting weaker and finally she lost her appetite near the end of April. A couple of weeks earlier, Mary started spoon feeding Sarah. It had been five days since Mary was able to wake Sarah and spoon feed her. Winnie opened her medical bag and raised her eyebrows as she realized the progression of Sarah's illness was not promising. She carefully listened to Sarah's chest and abdomen. Her breathing was shallow and weak. Winnie determined that a doctor should examine Sarah. She told Mary that she would send the doctor to examine her.

Winnie picked up her medical bag and gently placed her hand on Mary's shoulder. Mary thanked her for coming and asked if there was any charge for the visit. Winnie told her that the visit was free. She told Mary that God has a way of taking care of things. Winnie never considered herself a religious woman, but she had grown to respect the unexplained medical events that had happened throughout her nursing career. Watching the worried painful look on Mary's face brought the vivid pain that Winnie experienced after Fannie's death to the forefront of her thoughts. As Winnie slowly walked out, Mary said, "Sarah will be alright. She'll be alright. God will see her through." Winnie stopped, turned and said, "Mary, if anyone knows, it would be you." Mary began humming and rocking in the chair.

Winnie stopped in front of the door and looked at the small cabins that outlined the center of the community. She slowly turned and walked the foot path that led to her small farm. She said a short prayer for Sarah and her family. The thought of a mother losing a child at any age was very disturbing.

A couple of days later, Dr. Grunburg drove to Winnie's small farm and walked to Sarah's house. Her mother explained that she had been unable to wake Sarah for seven days. The doctor examined Sarah and told Mary, "There's nothing I can do. She's gone." Mary steadfastly replied, "Thank you for coming doctor. Sarah will be alright. Send me the bill. She'll be alright." Dr. Grunburg looked at Mary without speaking. He realized that she could not face the reality and pain of losing her daughter. Sarah's three sisters began to cry. Dr. Grunburg turned and slowly walked down the foot path to Winnie's farm.

When he reached the house, he had difficulty breathing. Winnie told him to have a seat at the dining room table while she poured a cool glass of water from the water bucket. Winnie asked about Sarah's condition and the doctor explained that Sarah was dead. Dr. Grunburg finished his water and rode off in his carriage to finish the rest of his house calls.

When Roland returned from The Wharf, Winnie met him at the side yard and told him of Sarah's demise. He did not speak and proceeded to hitch the horse for plowing the field. Winnie watched in silence as he worked in a more agitated manner than usual. She understood the pain he was feeling and the loneliness that he would experience in the days, weeks, and months ahead. She returned to the house and prepared dinner.

The Duke family was experiencing pain also. Mary had not left Sarah's bedside since the doctor examined her three days prior. She sat in the rocking chair hugging her Bible on her chest. She rocked, prayed, and sang hymns from sunrise until she fell asleep in the chair. Her oldest child, Edna, cooked for the family. Ellen and Ethel cleaned and cared for the younger children.

After lunch, several neighbors came to the house to visit Mary. Sarah's body had begun to smell of death and decay. The neighbors asked Mary if she needed help burying Sarah. She told them that she didn't need help with Sarah. She walked into her bedroom and picked up her silver plated hand held mirror. After singing and praying, she held the mirror to Sarah's nose and mouth.

The neighbors instructed Sarah's younger brother John to go to the barn and prepare the ice for the body. Large blocks of ice were stored in the barn under 2 to 3 feet of sawdust. John moved the ice to the center of the barn floor and covered it with as much sawdust as he could find. He used wooden crates and boards to create a cold rectangular storage area. As he started to nail the boards to the crates, he heard his mother scream a high pitched squeal that caused him to freeze with fear. At that moment, he knew that his mother had internalized Sarah's death. John dropped the hammer and slowly walked to the house. He could hear his sisters wailing in discord with his mother's piercing squeals. When John reached the door, several neighbors had arrived as well. Mary yelled, "Sarah is alive! My baby is alive! God saved her! Thank you Jesus!" The neighbors walked over to Mary and tried to calm her. She was five feet ten inches tall and weighed about 350 pounds. When she walked down the church aisles in her heels, the windows and table lanterns shook.

Mary calmed herself enough to pick up the hand held mirror from the floor. She walked to the head of the bed and placed the mirror about one inch from Sarah's mouth and nose. The neighbors gathered near Sarah's head and watched the mirror. After several seconds, a small white mist formed on the mirror. Mary yelled, "My baby is alive! My baby is alive! Thank you Jesus! Thank you Jesus!" The neighbors mumbled amongst themselves as they walked through the door. John could not believe that Sarah was alive. He asked his mother, "What should I do about the ice?" Mary told him, "Put that ice away! We won't need that now. Sarah is alive! God has worked a miracle!"

John ran back to the barn and moved the blocks of ice back into storage.

As he covered the blocks with sawdust, he heard many people talking. He ran to the barn door and watched as people walked from the west.

The community located to the west was called Do Dittle. Each family averaged 7 to 10 children. Most of the children worked in the fields rather than attend school. New fields were plowed by Mr. Bill and his two oxen. Mr. Bill used verbal commands to direct two black and white oxen. He commanded the oxen, "Get up Bright, Whoa back Ben." He had a deep clear voice and he never yelled at the animals. If a farmer had difficulty clearing his land or starting a garden, Mr. Bill would plow the land with his oxen. As the oxen plowed across the land, the snapping, cracking, and popping of the grass, vines, and roots could be heard a half mile away.

As neighbors learned of Sarah's recovery, they came from miles away. They gathered outside the house, sang hymns, and prayed. When Sarah was strong enough to talk, she told of a tunnel that she witnessed under construction. She told of a tunnel that connected two large cities. Lights lined the top of the structure.

Sarah remained weak for about six months. Her wavy black waist length hair came out in patches when she brushed each day and her family jokingly called her Patches. The family felt that God had saved Sarah and Christmas of 1915 was a very special holiday for the Duke family.

Chapter 19

A special healing was celebrated at the Duke household as special circumstances were developing in Europe. World War I began on June 28, 1914 with the assassination of Archduke Franz Ferdinand of Austria. The European allies rallied against Germany. On April, 1917, the United States officially declared war on Germany. Congress passed the Selective Service Act on May 18, 1917. This law required all male citizens between the ages of 21 and 31 to register for the draft. Roland registered for the draft on Tuesday, June 5, 1917. He listed Winnie as a dependent relative. She received his military pension pay. Roland was bused to Newport News, Virginia before boarding a ship to Europe. While in Europe, Roland learned to forge metal, repair wagon wheels and other blacksmith skills.

While Roland was learning new skills in Europe, Cyrus was attempting new skills at the farm. He decided to move in with Winnie after Roland left for the war. He told the men at the hardware store that he was repairing the foundation of the house.

On Friday, August 3, 1917, Winnie prepared breakfast for Cyrus. His green Chevrolet Series D was parked under the oak tree. As Winnie brought the coffee cups into the dining room, she noticed a black automobile in the driveway. She did not recognize the vehicle as Dr. Grunburg's car. She asked Cyrus if he recognized the vehicle. He leaned forward, pulled the curtain back, and peered at the car. He sarcastically said, "Well, that Ford Model T looks familiar. Big brother Lester has decided to come calling." Winnie flopped in the chair at the end of the table. Her stomach muscles tightened as she recalled Lester's last visit to the house in Jamaica, Virginia. She had warned Cyrus that his residence at the farm would create dissension in the White community. Her thoughts were interrupted by a knock on the door.

Winnie took a deep breath and walked down the hallway to the front door. Her legs felt as if she were stepping in cold molasses. As she slowly opened the door, Lester asked, "Is Cyrus here?" Winnie pulled the door open and stepped back toward the sitting room. She cautiously said, "Come in. He's in the dining room." Lester quickly walked down the hallway as Winnie closed the door and followed.

Winnie continued walking through the dining room and walked into the kitchen. She began cleaning the dishes and listening to the men's conversation. Lester sternly asked, "Cyrus, what do you think you're doing? You can't stay here." Cyrus put down his fork, sipped his coffee and replied, "Lester, I have told you time and time again. I love Winnie. I have the right to live my life the way I want to. You can't...." Lester interrupted, "Cyrus, I c-a-n cut your money off. Momma and Daddy may be gone, but you will not tarnish this family's name any more than you already have. The men at the hardware store are making jokes about my little brother making Black babies like a mill. Cyrus, you ...." Cyrus interrupted, "Lester, now you know damn well that all of my boys are the same color as you and I! That's a bunch of horse shit!" Lester angrily yelled, "You should have never laid down with that black bitch!"

Cyrus jumped up from his chair and charged Lester. Lester's head banged the wall and his hat rolled toward the kitchen doorway. Winnie back stepped to the back door as Lester threw Cyrus to the floor. Cyrus rolled his feet into Lester's legs and tripped him. Lester fell forward and hit his head on the dining room table. As he tumbled to the floor, Cyrus kicked his brother's chest and swung down to hit his face. His left hand struck Lester in the nose. He continued to pound Lester's face in an angry rage. Winnie realized that Cyrus was in danger of seriously injuring his brother.

She screamed, "Stop it! Stop it! Cyrus, please stop it!" She ran into the dining room and grabbed Cyrus' arm as he brought his arm back. As he swung forward, the momentum caused her to stumble over Lester's legs. Cyrus yelled, "Cut this shit out Lester! I'm not giving her up!" Cyrus used Lester's chest to stand up. Winnie anxiously watched as Lester rolled from side to side on the floor.

As he slowly sat up, blood flowed down the right side of Lester's face. The collar of his white dress shirt slowly faded pink as the blood saturated the rim of his collar. Winnie could see upon closer examination that the soft tissue above his right eye had been cut. She quickly walked to the pantry at the rear of the kitchen and picked up a jar of watercress. Winnie canned jars of watercresses each fall. She took the vinegar bottle from the shelf and walked to the kitchen counter. She poured some vinegar in a bowl and placed some watercress in the bowl. While she crushed the watercress in the vinegar, Cyrus helped Lester sit in the dining chair. Cyrus affectionately asked, "Lester, why do you despise my happiness? Lester wearily answered, "Cyrus, it's against the law."

Cyrus replied, "Lester, Winnie's brother served in the Confederate Army. Our family served in the Confederate Army. She has never done anything except raise my boys and love me. Damn it Lester! She's Confederate like me. I don't give a damn what her mother and father looked like. She believes in our way of life. She is one of us."

Winnie picked up a clean rag from the counter and carried the bowl into the dining room. She announced, "I need to put this on your eye. It will sting, but this will stop the bleeding. Cyrus, get one of your shirts for your brother. He can't wear this shirt back home." Cyrus went down the hallway and climbed the stairs to Winnie's bedroom. Lester held the watercress rag to his right eye. Winnie gently wiped the blood from Lester's right cheek. Lester relaxed as he realized that Winnie was a competent nurse. As Cyrus returned, Lester softly said to Winnie, "Thank you. I've heard you were a good nurse and now I guess I know firsthand." Winnie smiled and said, "You're welcome. Cyrus bring the soiled shirt to the kitchen." Winnie picked up her coffee and plate from the table. She wanted to give the brothers an opportunity to mend hurt feelings before Lester left.

Winnie placed the plate in the oven and sat her coffee cup on top of the stove. She began to ponder Cyrus' claim of his love for her. This was the second fight that he engaged with his brother in defense of his desire to be with her. Cyrus never married and he had visited her home once a week for over thirty years.

Her thoughts were interrupted as Lester said, "Cyrus you can't just park your car under the tree and stay in the house. I have been thinking about your situation. I want you to build a blacksmith shop on the northwest field. You told me that Roland has learned how to forge metal. When he returns from the war, he can take it over. If he doesn't return, well, you can get one of the Negroes in the community to run it. And, do me a favor. Park your car over at the shop. I'll get some men to start the work next week. Cyrus, you can't rub this in every respectable White woman's face. You've got to work with me. Cyrus, I really need you to work with me. This thing could turn ugly, really ugly." Cyrus replied, "Alright Lester, alright. I'll park at the shop."

During the war, Roland spent a lot of time at the army shop overseas. The majority of the Colored troops worked in the Service of Supply (SOS). They loaded and unloaded critical supplies at the docks in France. These service units were later sent to the battlefield to carry supplies, dig trenches, clear debris, and bury decaying carcasses. The war officially ended on November 11, 1918. Roland returned home one week before Christmas 1918.

All of the neighbors were proud of the Colored soldiers' service. They greeted and praised the soldiers for defending the Country. Roland remained humble about his contribution to the war effort.

He was not humble about his intentions to marry Sarah Duke. On Christmas Day, Roland asked Mary Duke for permission to court her daughter, Sarah. She agreed and Roland began dating his future bride. After a day's work, he washed, dressed, and walked to the Duke residence in King's Neck. He and Sarah sat and talked on the porch until her mother dropped a large piece of firewood in the wood box. The thumping sound indicated that Sarah needed to come inside.

After an eleven month courtship, Sarah and Roland were married on Thursday, November 27, 1919. Sarah wanted to wed Roland on Thanksgiving Day as a symbolic gesture of her thankful perspective of God allowing her to live. Roland did not like fancy celebrations so he asked Sarah to have the wedding ceremony at the courthouse. The ceremony was performed by Robert Buckley at the Middlesex County Courthouse.

When Sarah moved into the farm house, Cyrus moved out. He moved into a two story house about a mile away. His house was visible from the Post Office. Cyrus built the blacksmith shop in the northwest field and Roland worked in the shop six days a week. Cyrus parked his car at the shop and walked to the farmhouse. Sarah primarily cleaned, did the laundry, and cooked for the household. She continued to do laundry for hire and Winnie continued working with Dr. Grunburg.

Winnie and Cyrus spent most of their time in the sitting room near the front door. The room had been converted to Winnie's bedroom and the newlyweds took Winnie's old bedroom. In February 1920, Sarah began feeling tired. She asked Winnie to examine her. Winnie completed the examination and informed her that she was expecting a baby.

Roland was a very good carpenter. He decided to build two cradles and a new dining room table for Sarah. Winnie convinced him to build a cradle for the bedroom and one for the first floor. Roland built them at the blacksmith shop and transported them to the house on the wagon.

Sarah continued to perform household chores until the late afternoon on Thursday, September 2. Sarah experienced pain on both sides of her back as she washed Roland's work clothes. She decided to empty the laundry tub in the back yard. She threw the soapy water in a tall patch of grass and walked back to the house. As she reached for the kitchen door, a warm clear fluid gushed onto the stone steps. Sarah dropped the laundry tub beside the steps. She entered the kitchen and moaned in discomfort. Winnie was preparing a cup of tea at the kitchen stove. She looked at Sarah's face and knew that the baby was on the way.

About two months prior, Roland started building another room adjacent to the dining room. He had completed the outside walls, windows and the floor. He and Sarah had been sleeping in the room because climbing the stairs grew more and more difficult for Sarah as her abdomen increased in size.

Winnie helped Sarah to the unfinished bedroom and positioned the pillows behind her back. She went to her bedroom, gathered her medical bag, clean rags, and a small blanket that she had hand sewn for her first grandchild. Winnie could not move as quickly as she liked because her joints often ached and slowed her movements. She placed the items on the foot of the bed and instructed Sarah to rest and try not to push. Winnie exited the kitchen door and walked toward the blacksmith shop. As she reached the edge of the yard, Cyrus drove up in his green Chevrolet sedan. He saw Winnie and continued driving through the yard to the side of the house. She informed him of the situation and he volunteered to walk to the shop and inform Roland of Sarah's condition.

Winnie went back into the kitchen and filled the cooking pots with water. She put more firewood in the stove and moved one dining room chair into the bedroom with Sarah. Winnie also heated the food that Sarah had previously prepared for dinner. Roland and Cyrus came in and ate dinner. As the sun began to set, Sarah's younger brother John walked through the side yard.

Roland came outside and told him that Sarah was having the baby. As John ran to tell his family the news, Roland lit a camel cigarette and walked to the wood pile in the back yard. After finishing his cigarette, he split firewood. He wondered whether his first born would be a boy or a girl. He subconsciously hoped the baby would be a boy. He wanted his son to work at the shop, help in the fields, and learn how to fish, oyster, and crab. Roland carried the firewood inside and gathered two oil lamps. He filled the lamps with kerosene and Cyrus kept the fire blazing.

As the night wore on, Winnie checked each hour to see how quickly Sarah's cervix was dilating. The men nodded while sitting and talking at the dining room table. Just before sunrise, Winnie announced, "I think she's ready to push. The baby is on the way."

As Winnie returned to the bedroom, Cyrus made coffee in the kitchen. Roland walked to the kitchen, picked up the water pail on the counter. He turned and lifted his coat from the hook to the right of the door. He walked out to the well and drew a bucket of water. As he walked back to the house, he heard Sarah moan and scream concurrently. When Roland stepped into the kitchen, Winnie announced, "The head is out!" Roland placed the pail on the counter and walked into the dining room. Cyrus brought two cups of coffee into the room and placed one in front of Roland. As the men anxiously sipped the coffee, Sarah moaned in the adjacent room. Winnie announced, "It's a girl!"

The smack on the baby's buttocks rang crisply from the room. Cyrus and Roland listened expectantly for the newborn's cry. As the glow of the rising sun seeped through the curtains, silence fell upon the house.

Suddenly, there was a knock on the kitchen door. Roland walked to the kitchen and opened the door. Sarah's mother, Mary, and younger sister Ellen exuberantly stepped into the kitchen and asked, "Is it here yet? What did she have?" Roland solemnly replied, "I don't know. Come on in." As they entered the dining room, Winnie slowly opened the bedroom door and announced, "The baby didn't make it." Mary immediately yelled, "Oh Jesus! Let me see Sarah!"

Winnie stepped aside as Mary and Ellen tearfully entered the bedroom. Sarah quickly held the tiny blue-gray baby girl as her mother and sister hugged both of them. Tears streamed down Sarah's cheeks as she handed her first born to her mother. Mary sat on the bed and hugged, cried and prayed while rocking her lifeless, little grandbaby.

Cyrus walked to Winnie and hugged her as she said, "She never had a chance." Roland turned and walked to the kitchen door. As he opened the door and stepped out, he could hear Mary tearfully praying for Sarah, the baby and the household. The son who would have helped him was not born. The baby his wife wanted did not live. The life that he had planned did not materialize. Roland lit a Camel cigarette and walked to the blacksmith shop.

Two days later, Mary arranged a burial for the baby. Sarah and Roland did not attend. Cyrus took Winnie to the church in his green Chevrolet sedan. Mary and her family walked home after the service. On the way back home, Cyrus decided to take Winnie to his new work site. He had taken the position as the Postmaster in Cooper, Virginia. As they walked to the small white building, the cool breeze from the Rappahannock River roared past their ear canals. The drone seemed to erase the immediate pain of losing another family newborn.

In the months that followed, the loss of the baby was not discussed. Sarah returned to work and Roland spent more and more time at the shop. During January, Sarah again felt tired and sluggish. She asked Winnie to examine her. After the examination, Winnie informed Sarah that she was expecting a baby. Six months later, Sarah gave birth to Roland, Jr. He was born on Monday, June 20, 1921 with pale complexioned skin, brown eyes, and black hair.

Mary was able to celebrate the birth of her first living grandchild, but her health was deteriorating. The daily routine resumed as father time was quickly approaching his next victim. Mary died three months later. Roland Jr.

continued to thrive and the anxiety of losing the baby drifted to the back of Winnie's thoughts.

By July 1922, Winnie was feeling physically and emotionally healthy. Sarah was expecting a second baby and the Recession of 1920 was ending. The July first sky displayed a first quarter moon, but by the fourth of July a bright gibbous moon was forming. The Post Office was closed for the Federal holiday. Cyrus decided to take Winnie on a July 4th boating excursion.

Early Tuesday morning, Winnie began preparing food immediately after breakfast. She prepared food for Sarah and Roland as well. Cyrus and Winnie left for Burham's Wharf around 6:00 p.m. Most of the paying customers were returning from a day of fishing. The high volume of customers prompted Cyrus' cousin Phil to hire Roland for the day. Roland was washing the charter fishing boat as Cyrus and Winnie boarded Phil's pleasure boat.

Phil always tied the vessel to the dock on the port side. The 44 foot wooden deadrise vessel was painted white with a copper water line. The straight stern and the outside cabin were stained cinnamon. The helm was on the starboard side of the cabin door. The four adult sleep cabin was encased with sliding rectangular windows. Each window had brown and white plaid curtains. The bathroom was port side and the removable wooden table was centered toward the bow. The engine housing near the center stern also served as a table. Cyrus carried the basket of food to the boat and Winnie carried a blanket. He helped Winnie step onto the rear port side of the gunwale.

Cyrus walked up the hill to the office. He unlocked the door and reached down to the left of the door. He picked up a wooden pail and locked the office door. The pail appeared unused. As Cyrus unlocked the ice house door, Roland drove his horse drawn carriage onto the road. Cyrus exited the ice house with a bucket full of ice.

Winnie sat on a cushioned bench on the port side of the boat as Cyrus untied the vessel from the dock. Cyrus stepped down into the boat from the starboard gunwale. He sat at the helm, started the boat, and slowly piloted the vessel into the Rappahannock River. Cyrus stopped the boat about one mile off shore and dropped the anchor.

Winnie spread a white linen tablecloth over the engine house and Cyrus placed the two French white wine bottles in the wooden pail. As he placed the pail on the cabin floor, the hot July breeze continued to melt the ice. As they laughed and ate dinner, the sun slowly sank at the horizon. Cyrus flipped the switch beside the helm and the combination bow light bathed the inside of the cabin with a soft red and green glow. Cyrus picked up a bottle of wine from the wooden pail and stepped down into the cabin. As he opened the bottle, he asked, "Winnie, would you bring the wine glasses in here?"

As Winnie stepped down into the cabin, the port side sky was illuminated in red, white, and blue. Cyrus was sitting starboard side and patted the cushioned seat to his left. Winnie placed the wine glasses on the center table and sat beside him. The chilled white wine swirled around the glasses as Cyrus asked, "Would you do me the honor of lowering your hair on this hot summer night?" He handed her a glass and continued, "I promise to make it worth your while." Winnie took the glass from Cyrus' hand as she removed the black hair pin from her gray streaked once vibrant red hair.

Cyrus flashed his cunning smile and proposed a toast, "Winnie, to the good times and special moments like this." Winnie smiled as the clinking sound of the Waterford crystal coincided with the green spray of pyrotechnic displays from the Urbanna Creek. The varied colorful displays filled the cooling night air as Winnie and Cyrus emptied the wine bottles.

The French white wine seemed to relax Winnie's body as it stimulated Cyrus' desires. As she leaned forward and placed her glass on the table, Cyrus leaned forward and kissed her right lower jaw. He gently sucked on the skin that rounded her jaw and tasted down the right side of her neck. He leaned forward, placed his glass on the table, and pushed her torso back as he gently sucked on her ear lobe.

As Winnie adjusted her body on the cushioned bench, Cyrus unbuttoned her sleeveless white blouse. As she rolled to one side and slowly took off the blouse, Cyrus stepped out of his cloth shoes and unbuttoned his pants. As his pants slid to his ankles, Cyrus pulled the short sleeve cotton shirt over his head and tossed it beside the helm. Winnie caressed Cyrus' right leg and raised her hips as he pulled her pink cotton skirt and panties down her legs. When Winnie lowered her hips, Cyrus pulled her clothing and cloth shoes to the end of the sleep area. He lowered his boxers to his ankles and reached inside the ice pail. As Cyrus placed his left knee to the left of Winnie's right thigh, he cradled a three inch slither of ice. His erect penis brushed across her abdomen as he dripped the cold water between her breasts. Winnie moaned in startling pleasure as the ice cold liquid ran toward her neck and down each side of her torso. The chilling movement of the fluid paralyzed her breathing and relieved the smothering humidity of the sultry cabin air.

Cyrus planted his right knee beside Winnie's left thigh. He rubbed the slither of ice over her lips, down her chin, and around the base of her neck. As he rubbed the ice on her right breast, he tasted her collar bone and licked down her right breast. Winnie moaned in pleasure as Cyrus slowly and gently alternated tasting and icing each breast. After several minutes, Cyrus clamped the ice between his lips and slid the ice between Winnie's breasts and continued down the center of her torso to her navel. He twirled the ice around the inside of her navel. Winnie squirmed in blissful cool excitement. Cyrus rubbed the ice down her lower abdomen and placed the ice inside the lips of her vagina. Winnie audibly moaned as Cyrus sucked her clitoris and moved the ice to the center of her vagina with his tongue. As the ice slid to the cushioned bench, Cyrus slid his manhood into her pleasure zone.

Cyrus thrust his hips in a gyrating motion as the melting ice allowed their bodies to slide along the leather cushioned sleep area. As Winnie reached for his hips, Cyrus reached for more ice. He dripped the cold water onto her neck and placed the small piece of ice in her navel. Cyrus continued to thrust himself in a rhythmic motion as the ice melted in her navel. The thrusting motion caused the cool liquid to drain to her pubic hair. As the gibbous moon, the pyrotechnics, and the combination bow light shone down on the cabin, Cyrus and Winnie climaxed in a rainbow ecstasy while anchored off the shores of the Rappahannock River. Cyrus lowered his sweaty body onto Winnie's wet body and gently kissed her chest, neck, and lips. As they held each other, the pyrotechnic displays seemed more colorful than a prismatic spotlight. They held each other under the illumination of the gibbous moon and watched the end of the show.

Chapter 20

The voters of the United States watched in anticipation as the 29th President took office. Warren G. Harding had promised the voters that he would return the country to a normal way of life if he were elected. The country was recovering from the battle wounds of World War I and they wanted emotional and financial stability. The Harding administration started with great confidence from the voters. President Woodrow Wilson's administration had initiated a financial budget for the federal government. The Harding administration officially established a budget system for the federal government. The Harding administration was able to convince the major military powers around the world to stop the competitive production of naval vessels. In September 1922, the Harding administration vetoed the Soldier's Bonus Bill. This bill would have given World War I soldiers monetary compensation for their military service. Veterans were given an "adjusted service certificate". Soldiers who served in the United States were compensated $1.00 per day. Soldiers who served overseas (predetermined limits) were compensated $1.25 per day. This compensation was in addition to the regular war salary and benefits paid during the war. All compensation earned interest and was payable to the veteran in 1945. If the soldier were deceased, the family received payment. History records President Harding as a poor judge of character. His decision to veto the Soldier's Bonus Bill was the beginning of trouble for the Harding administration.

A few weeks later, Sarah gave birth to a healthy baby girl. Mary Ellen was born on October 6, 1922. She had a rudy complexion, light brown eyes, and straight black hair. Mary was a very pleasant baby. If she had something to eat and a dry diaper, she seldom cried. When Winnie gave birth to a stillborn little Fannie, Betty provided angelic relief from the harsh reality of delivering a dead baby. Mary provided the same relief to her mother. Sarah did not talk about her painful feelings after delivering a stillborn baby. She was taught to pray and ask God for relief instead of discussing her sorrows, concerns, or problems with another person. Sarah's family had taught her that God would provide the appropriate relief in every situation. Sarah's mother taught her to wait for the appropriate relief even if it took a lifetime to develop. Sarah desperately needed little Mary's pleasant demeanor.

Roland was not an openly affectionate man. He seldom shared his feelings, good or bad. As a child, he did not talk often. He observed, listened, and attempted to learn new concepts. He enjoyed solving mechanical and procedural challenges. He did not enjoy hugs and kisses from his mother and sisters. After marrying Sarah, his ability to openly demonstrate affection did not improve.

When Sarah gave birth to a stillborn baby, he did not talk about the birth with Sarah or anyone else. He dealt with his sorrow by engaging in more physical labor. When Sarah gave birth to the son he so desperately wanted to help on the small farm, he dealt with his joy by engaging in more physical labor. Roland spoke in a very stern clear voice and he seldom smiled. If he were amused, he often displayed a quick smile and moved on to the next issue at hand. He rarely told jokes or laughed out loud. As a young boy, he was sent to work with the men and his older brothers. He did not develop a love of a frolicking lifestyle and the artistic beauty of the world. After he returned from the Army, Roland used a lot of profanity when he felt strongly about what he was sharing. The time spent with Carpenter and William on the farm prepared Roland for the Army. The Army prepared Roland to survive a racially divided United States and the Great Depression. Roland loved Sarah, but he was unable to express his love in a soft affectionate manner. He loved his children, but he did not hug, cradle, or kiss them.

Roland often sat quietly beside the woodstove and contemplated the challenges of the day. If he were welding an item and he had difficulty molding the final product into perfection, he would think through all procedures for improving the finish until he retired for the night. If Roland were working on an engine, he would mentally review the performance of the engine as well as any misfirings and/or inefficient performance. He often verbally outlined the plan of attack for the next day's challenges. As Sarah sat at the end of the dining room table and read her Bible, Roland often softly talked through the steps that he believed were the solutions to the day's challenges. If one of his children took the initiative to hug or sit on him, Roland would not respond and sit solemnly. He would not openly return hugs and kisses. After about 10 minutes, Roland would say, "Alright. That's enough. Get down now."

Roland provided food, clothing, and shelter for his wife and children. He accepted accountability and responsibility for his family. In many respects, Roland handled his family like a military unit. As soon as the boys were old enough, he taught them how to plant and harvest crops, maintain machinery, oyster, crab, and fish. Roland left the responsibility of the babies, girls, and household to Sarah. Sarah had two still births and nine live births that followed Mary's birth. Emma, Edward, Jacob and Esau (twins), Nannie, Arthur, Carriebell, Sarah Nancy, and Charles were born in the small farmhouse.

Winnie continued to work as a trained nurse and midwife. She delivered babies for White and Negro families. It was not uncommon for Winnie to deliver all of the babies in a household. She delivered all of the babies for the Sidney family. Mrs. Sidney credited Winnie with delivering, counseling, and helping to raise all seven of her children. The Sidney family was White, but they considered Winnie a member of the family. The children and Mrs. Sidney called her Aunt Winnie.

Winnie was aging, but her services were still in demand. She continued to work with Dr. Grunburg as well as conducting independent house visits in the Negro community. Winnie also worked with Dr. Toldway, the first Negro doctor in Middlesex County. Winnie had established a reputation of providing quality care for all of her patients. If patients could not afford to pay for her services, she often provided advice and services for no pay.

Winnie developed a decreased ability to carry light loads, bend, reach, and walk. Her ankles and knees pained her every day. She developed red rashes on various locations of her body. The red rashes often itched and created a burning sensation at the site of irritation. Small white pimples often developed near the center of the inflamed sites. Winnie cleaned the pimples with iodine. If she could not reach the locations on her back, Cyrus cleaned the pimples with iodine. Winnie took aspirin each day, but the pain continued to plague her daily activities. With Cyrus' assistance, Winnie continued to work as a nurse until January 1929. Eventually, she developed shortness of breath.

By January 1930, Winnie's movements were confined to her bedroom and the dining room of the farmhouse. Her bedroom was located to the right of the front door. This location was convenient when Winnie needed to go to work, but the convenient location served no benefit to the quickly aging nurse. The location became a convenient stop for her grandchildren as they journeyed to their upstairs bedrooms at night. They came into Winnie's bedroom for goodnight hugs and kisses. Each morning, they returned for morning hugs and kisses en route to the dining room table for breakfast.

As Winnie's health began to fail, Cyrus spent more time at the farmhouse. He helped Winnie with daily activities and provided emotional support. Sarah maintained the household, completed laundry for White families, and picked tomatoes when in season. Winnie's health continued to deteriorate. By March, she was bedridden.

On Tuesday, March 25, 1930, Winnie developed extreme shortness of breath around dinner time. Dr. Toldway had told Winnie that her condition would slowly deteriorate. It seemed as if her condition quickly deteriorated on this evening. Cyrus told Roland that he needed to go to Dr. Toldway's house and inform him of Winnie's weakened condition. Dr. Toldway lived close to the farmhouse and he had been Winnie's personal physician for about 18 months.

Roland drove Cyrus' car to Dr. Toldway's house and Cyrus remained at Winnie's bedside. Dr. Toldway was the only Negro doctor in Middlesex County. Winnie had helped Dr. Toldway with some of his maternity patients. He came to the farmhouse and examined Winnie. When Dr. Toldway arrived, Winnie had a fever and was too weak to speak. After several hours, she slid into a coma. Roland and Sarah waited in the dining room. Sarah read her Bible and prayed as Roland waited solemnly beside the woodstove. With Cyrus at her bedside, Winnie took her last breath at 11:45 p.m. Dr. Toldway listed the cause of death as cardiac valve inflammation and rheumatoid arthritis.

At midnight, Sarah awakened Roland Jr. and told him to run to Mrs. Holden's house. Sarah was a member of the Missionary Club at church. Mrs. Holden was a member who lived near Sarah and she agreed to help prepare Winnie's body for the undertaker. While waiting for Mrs. Holden, Sarah gathered soap, clean white sheets and clean rags. Roland thanked Dr. Toldway for coming to the farmhouse and signed Winnie's death certificate. The doctor shook Roland's hand and told him that his mother had provided a great service to the community. Dr. Toldway promised Roland that he would ensure that Winnie would be buried at the proper location at the church. Winnie did not attend church regularly, but her community service and Sarah's family history with the church ensured that she would be buried at the front of the church. At that time, important church and community members were buried at the front of the church. After Dr. Toldway left the farmhouse, Roland walked back into the living room in order to view his mother before Sarah and Mrs. Holden prepared the body. As a tearful Cyrus held Winnie's torso, Roland leaned over and kissed his mother on the forehead. Cyrus told Roland that he would stay with her.

Roland silently and slowly turned to leave the room. As he stepped into the hallway, Roland Jr. opened the front door. Roland Jr. told his father that Mrs. Holden was on her way. Roland told his oldest child, "Alright son. Go on up to bed." Roland opened the front door and stood on the front stoop. He surveyed the darkness of the night before stepping off the stoop. Roland realized that life without his mother would be like stepping off the front stoop into the darkness. Winnie had always helped him plan his future. When

Carpenter was alive, the household routine and/or location did not change unless Winnie agreed to the changes. After Carpenter died, Winnie made all final decisions about the household. Roland realized that Sarah and his children would expect that he would be leading their family to the future. The thought of taking on this responsibility without the assistance of his mother's watchful advice would be the ultimate test of his leadership abilities. As Roland stepped off the front stoop, he could hear Cyrus weeping as he walked to the blacksmith shop. Roland realized that the last person who maintained his emotional stability from his childhood was gone. Even though he did not share long conversations with his mother, they both understood that Roland would be her protector if needed. Roland was Winnie's youngest child and they had lived in the same house since his birth in Jamaica. He spent the night in the shop cleaning and preparing items for the next day's chores.

When Mrs. Holden arrived, she and Sarah prayed and waited for Cyrus to finish his final goodbye. He hugged and kissed Winnie's hands and face as he wiped tears of sorrow. Cyrus mourned the loss of his lifetime partner, his lover, and the mother of his children. For Cyrus, the half century that he had spent with Winnie seemed to pass too quickly. Cyrus refused to leave the room as Winnie's lifeless, petite body was cleaned and wrapped.

Just before sunrise, Roland opened the front door and stepped into the living room. Winnie's body was neatly wrapped and lying on the bed. Cyrus was sitting on the foot of the bed. Roland announced that he was going to get the undertaker. Cyrus told Roland to drive his car to the undertaker's house. Roland returned to the farmhouse with the undertaker. The undertaker picked up Winnie's body just after sunrise on Wednesday, March 26, 1930. Cyrus left the house as the undertaker carried Winnie's body to the vehicle. Cyrus told the undertaker that he would pay all of the costs for Winnie's service. Shortly after the undertaker left the property, Cyrus drove home.

A funeral service was held on Thursday, March 27, 1930 at Calvary Baptist Church. Dr. Toldway had secured a burial location at the front of the church. Winnie was buried on the front western side of Calvary Baptist Church. Mrs. Sidney and her children attended the funeral. They sat on the front pew with Sarah and Roland. Cyrus watched the ceremony from the parking lot of Christ Church which bordered the cemetery on the western side.

After Winnie's death, Roland decided that he wanted to work on the water. He needed to feel the river breeze on his face and see the blue horizon touching the waterline. He felt more relaxed when he was working in and around the salt water of the Rappahannock River. Roland closed the blacksmith shop in 1931. He began oystering and charter fishing from Burham's Wharf. In 1933, President Franklin Roosevelt's administration created the Works

Progress Administration. States were given 8.5 million dollars to rebuild the infrastructure.

Cyrus ensured that Roland was employed. Cyrus purchased a 1933 Combination Farm Truck. The removable and stackable side rails allowed Roland to carry cargo and men. After the county decided to offer jobs to the Colored men, Cyrus arranged for Roland to be the foreman. The White men negotiated and confirmed jobs exclusively with Roland. Roland drove the truck and waited until the men loaded the cargo. If Roland tried to help with the manual labor, the White men stopped him. They explained to Roland that the arrangement did not allow him to perform physical labor. He was to negotiate the jobs, hire the men, and drive the truck. He was instructed to transport the workers and act as a foreman. He was specifically told not to perform any physical labor. Cyrus had secured his position in the community.

Cyrus protected Roland's employment and he provided for his grandchildren. The White women in the community continued to provide Sarah with opportunities to earn money. She often prepared cakes, dinners, and completed laundry. All of Roland and Sarah's children were able to find employment at a very difficult time in American history. During the Great Depression (August 1929 until 1939), Sarah and Roland's farmhouse was one of a few houses in the entire community that provided food to anyone who was hungry. Roland had trained the boys to build traps for squirrels and rabbits. Traps could be used several times and were more economical than firearms. If a firearm was used, each bullet would cost 2 cents, while traps could be reset multiple times with leftover table scraps. Sarah was a very good cook and she was able to cook all meats in a manner that resulted in a tasty meal.

After Winnie's death, Cyrus brought freshly slaughtered turkeys to the farmhouse every two weeks. He left the birds on the front stoop of the farmhouse. Sarah would not retrieve the fowl from the stoop until Cyrus' shiny vehicle reached the end of the long sandy driveway. When her children inquired about the identity of the generous stranger, Sarah avoided disclosing Cyrus' identity.

During fair weather, the children often played in the side yard. They were taught to stay away from adult conversations and encounters. They often observed a White man in a shiny car who visited the farmhouse on a regular basis. Whenever he visited, he never initiated a conversation with the children. Cyrus also placed bushel baskets of in season fruit on the stoop, displayed his cunning smile, and slowly drove away from the house. He continued the visits until his death in 1935.

Epilogue

I had the Blessed opportunity to spend a week with Sarah Duke in the small farmhouse before her death on October 9, 1980. Her health was failing and my father and his siblings were debating alternative solutions to her living alone. All of her food was delicious, but her homemade rolls were the best rolls I have ever tasted. And yes, the rolls were baked in a wood stove. When the stove from her early marriage days broke, her children wanted to purchase a new electric or gas stove. She insisted upon another wood cook stove.

I cherish the one on one time that my grandmother and I shared. It gladdened my heart when she formed a joyous resolved smile and told me that I reminded her of her mother, Mary Duke.

My father never had the opportunity to spend time with his grandfather or any of his father's relatives. He may have participated in activities with them, but he did not know their identity. He was denied the experience of building his self-esteem and taking ownership/pride in his ancestors. He was denied the opportunity to spend a week with Roland's relatives and develop a sense of his place in the family history.

My father decided to build a strong God fearing family base when he married my mother. My mother's ancestors founded First Baptist Church Harmony Village. This Holy union nurtured an atmosphere of truth. My parents have always told and advised my sister, brother and myself with the truth. We may not have wanted to hear or follow their advice, but it was always based on the Bible and spoken very clearly.

During our developing years, our parents taught, monitored, and nurtured our development. This often led to limited social events, limited dating, and standing on religious principles. Standing for our beliefs is a principle that we share with our paternal lineage.

I was unable to find my paternal lineage until the summer of 2012. While doing some research about the migration of North American slaves to Canada, it occurred to me that I did not know parts of my own family history.

My friend had mentioned that although she was Black, she was related to Thomas Jefferson. She encouraged me to continue researching each lead. We discussed how the new science of DNA testing was used to prove that the descendants of Sally Hemmings were from Thomas Jefferson's paternal lineage. After reaching several dead leads, it occurred to me that perhaps the same technology could be used to find the identity of my paternal great grandfather. Without DNA testing, I would have never discovered that Cyrus was my great grandfather. I would have never discovered that my ancestors are related to William The Conqueror, that my ancestors were friends with King Charles II, that my ancestors served in the British Navy as Majors, that they first came to Virginia in 1655, that they helped Governor Berkeley distribute land in Virginia, and that their name appears on 150 pages of the Virginia Colonial Abstracts, Volumes I and II.

Roland's great grandfather was a tobacco plantation owner with fifty slaves. His lineage served in the Confederate Army during the Civil War. Confederate is defined as an ally, an accomplice, and to band together. The Confederates of the Nineteenth Century believed that the Bible justified Slavery.

Leviticus 25:44-46 states that an individual may buy male and female slaves from another nation, but over your brethren the children of Israel, ye shall not rule one over another with rigor. 1 Peter 2:18 states that servants should be subject to their master with all respect. These verses were adopted by Confederates even though Galatians 3:28 states that there is neither Jew nor Greek, slave nor free, male or female, for we are all one in Christ Jesus.

My ancestors stood for what they believed. Cyrus stood for what he believed. Roland stood for what he believed. My father stood for what he believed. I stand for what I believe. Do you stand for what you believe? If so, you may be Confederate Like Me.

Author's Note

Readers who want additional information may reference the resources listed below. All of these sources were used to write *Confederate Like Me*.

Breen, T. H. (1985). Tobacco culture the mentality of the great tidewater planters on the eve of revolution. Princeton University Press.

(n.d.). Bureau of labor statistics history. Retrieved from website: www.bls.gov/bls/history/timeline.htm

(1997). T. W. Cutrer & T. M. Parrish (Eds.), The Civil War Letters of The Pierson Family Brothers In Grey. Louisiana State University Press.

Goldberg, J. P., & Moye, W. T. (1918). The first hundred years of the bureau of labor statistics. Washington, D.C.: U.S. Government Printing Office.

Hanna-Cheruiyst, MPH, CHES, CCE, CBA, C. S. (n.d.). A brief history of midwifery. Retrieved from www.socalbirth.com/become-a-midwife/history-of-midwifery

Haynie, M. (1959). The stronghold a story of historic northern neck of virginia and its people. The Dietz Press, Incorporated.

Head, T. (n.d.). Interracial marriage laws a short timeline. Retrieved from www.civilliberty.about.com

(2011). T. A. Wolf (Ed.), Historic Sites in Virginia's Northern Neck and Essex County A Guide. University of Virginia Press.

Legal information institute. (n.d.). Retrieved from www.law.cornell.edu/constitution/amendmentxiv

Lowe, R. (1991). Republicans and reconstruction in virginia, 1856-70. Charlottesville and London: University Press of Virginia.

McPherson, J. M. (1992). Ordeal by fire the civil war and reconstruction. (2nd ed.). New York: McGraw-Hill.

K. M. Stamp (Ed.), Records of Ante-Bellum Southern Plantations from the Revolution through the Civil War Series M Part 3: Other Tidewater Virginia

Schleicher, J. (2011, January). Recreating a 19th century flour mill.

Retrieved from www.farmcollector.com/equipment/19-century-flour-mill-aspx

Sharrer, G. T. (2000). A kind of fate: agricultural change in virginia, 1861-1920. Iowa State University Press.

Stillbirth. (n.d.). Retrieved from www.Marchofdimes.com

Time and date. (n.d.). Retrieved from www.timeanddate.com

U.S. Department of Commerce, Bureau of the Census. (1960). U.S. bureau of the census, historical statistics of the united states, colonial times to 1957 (Library of Congress Card No. A 60-9150). Washington, D.C.: U.S. Government Printing Office.

Washington, B. T. (1986). Up from slavery. Penguin Books.

Wikipedia-industrial revolution. (n.d.). Retrieved from www.en.wikipedia.org/wiki/industrial_revolution

Wikipedia-steam mill. (n.d.). Retrieved from www.en.wikipedia.org/wiki/steam_mill

Wilson, J. C. (1984). Virginia's northern neck a pictorial history. Norfolk, Virginia: The Donning Company/Publishers.

Wilson, W. J. (1980). The declining significance of race blacks and changing american institutions. (2nd ed.). London: The University of Chicago Press, Ltd.

(1996). E. D. Campbell, Jr. & K. S. Rice (Eds.), A woman's war southern women, civil war, and the confederate legacy (1st ed.). Richmond, Charlottesville, Richmond: The Museum of the Confederacy; University Press of Virginia; Carter Printing Company.

Wunderlich, G. (n.d.). Myths about antiseptics and camp life. Retrieved from www.civilwarscholars.com

CPSIA information can be obtained at www.ICGtesting.com
Printed in the USA
LVOW10s1249230115

424054LV00005B/573/P

9 781595 945402